RACING WITH THE WIND

Book 1 in the Agents of the Crown Trilogy

by
Regan Walker

WHO MIGHT MANAGE MARY CAMPBELL?

Hugh studied the great black horse in front of him, concentrating now upon its rider. Each moment brought more amazement. A girl sat the stallion, dressed in men's riding clothes, long legs clinging to the beast's flanks and golden hair streaming out behind her, a pennon of liquid sunlight. She was like a goddess riding upon a mythical beast.

He held his breath as she raised her arms and tilted her face up to the sky. It was the most alluring sight he'd ever seen, like a bird flying.

"Who is she?"

Lord Baynes smiled. "Ah. That would be our Mary. Have you not met her?"

"I have not had the pleasure. Does she always ride like that—in men's breeches, astride, so fast and so…reckless?"

A look of amusement crossed his companion's face. "She does."

RACING WITH THE WIND

Book 1 in the Agents of the Crown Trilogy

by
Regan Walker

www.BOROUGHSPUBLISHINGGROUP.com

PUBLISHER'S NOTE: This is a work of fiction. Names, characters, places and incidents either are the product of the author's imagination or are used fictitiously. Any resemblance to actual events, locales, business establishments or persons, living or dead, is coincidental. Boroughs Publishing Group does not have any control over and does not assume responsibility for author or third-party websites, blogs or critiques or their content.

RACING WITH THE WIND
Copyright © 2012 Regan Walker

Digital edition created by Maureen Cutajar
www.gopublished.com

ISBN 978-1-941260-20-3

To my best friend, Judy, who inspired the character Elizabeth, and who encouraged me to write this story. With her "seeing heart," before I'd even written the first word she assured me I would one day be a published author of historical romance. I wish that each of you could be blessed with such a wonderful friend.

ACKNOWLEDGMENTS

No book comes into being without the help of many people. Among those I must thank would be my mother who taught me to read when I was four and convinced me I could travel the world through books. Then, there were the authors who inspired me: Kathleen Givens, Virginia Henley, Marsha Canham, Cynthia Wright, Shirl Henke and so many others. (Virginia and Cindy were kind enough to read my manuscript and make suggestions.) Those masters of historical romance were my unofficial mentors. I must also thank my critique partners and fellow authors, Jackie, Mary and Susan—and Jill—from the San Diego Chapter of the Romance Writers of America, each of whom helped me make the manuscript better. The last of those who made the book what it is today was my editor, Chris Keeslar, who with his professionalism and patience coached me through the final changes. I could not have done it without you!

CONTENTS

"When one does not love too much, one does not love enough."

—Blaise Pascal

Prologue

A tall figure stood among the trees, another shadow in the gloomy night. Swirling mist covered the ground around him like a soft gray carpet. A chateau loomed ahead, a dim monument in the light of a pale half moon that revealed only shades of gray.

He waited for a drifting cloud to obscure the moon's faint glow before daring to steal across the wide expanse of lawn. His boots made no sound as he crossed the stone terrace and became one with the wall of the elegant mansion. There he paused and listened. All was quiet save the rustle of the leaves stirred by the gentle breeze.

Looking up, he peered though the mask that covered his face and fixed his eyes on his goal, a window high above. Barely disturbing the mist, he reached for a thick vine and climbed.

His dark hair was loose at his nape and he was clad all in black, moving like a wraith. The clouds continued to drift in the night sky, uncovering the half moon. A glimmer of silver reflected from his chest where he wore a brace of pistol daggers; the weapons were unique and of a French design, and he had used them before to great effect. A smile came to his lips as he considered the legend that had spread about him—a larger than life figure who successfully stole secrets from places believed safe from intrusion. They called him *L'Engoulevent*, the Nighthawk. He came only at night, swooping down and disappearing before anyone roused. An occasional glimpse by a servant or a guard had provided only partial descriptions. Some said he flew with a cape. Others said he wasn't human at all but rather a dark and ghostly apparition. But the Nighthawk was very real. Tonight his target was the home of a French general believed to be the author of Napoleon's plans to invade Russia.

Perched above the ground, clinging to the vine, he reached for the edge of the leaded window. The latch gave way with a quiet click. He slipped through the opening and dropped into a low crouch on the thick rug. Surveying the bedroom before him, he could see the sleeping form of a young woman in a white poster bed, her dark hair spread upon the pillow. She did not stir as he moved past her and toward his destination.

At the end of the hall he located the study reported to hide the secret documents he sought. Cautiously he entered the spacious room lined with traditional dark wood cabinets and tall book-filled shelves, and stealthily moved to the carved wood desk facing a marble fireplace. Reaching into his shirt he pulled out a small black velvet case. Inside were the delicate tools that had opened the most secure locks in France.

Working with only the pale light from the windows behind him, he opened the locked drawers and captured his prize. Placing the correspondence and map inside his shirt, he surveyed the room. He knew there would be more.

His gaze came to rest on an old painting of a French military officer in dress uniform hanging over the fireplace. The officer's white breeches reflected the room's meager light, but he cared not for the painting, only for the secrets it might guard. Silently he crossed the room and lifted the gilded frame. The cast-iron safe set behind it made him smile as if encountering an old friend.

He set the painting on the floor to once again work his magic with the lock. Again he was successful. Ignoring the velvet jewelry cases and money, he reached instead for the letters and papers. Not bothering to decipher the words in the dim light, he added these documents to those in his shirt, closed the safe, and returned the painting to its original position. His mission complete, he crept down the hall to the bedroom where he had first entered the house.

The young woman stirred in her sleep, restless in her dreams. He should have departed without disturbing her, but something made him pause. Perhaps it was her beauty. Her face, with its delicate features and well-shaped lips, was turned slightly to the side. Upon closer inspection, she looked to be about eighteen.

He bent to hover for a moment, breathing in the fragrance of lavender. Her lips were warm as he bestowed his kiss. He knew he was keeping alive the legend, and there was no benefit to a legend when one's purpose was to remain unknown. Yet, he could not resist. There were few enough pleasures in the life of duty that he'd chosen for himself.

Her pale eyes opened slowly, heavy with sleep. Placing his finger on her lips to quiet any words, he whispered to her in the perfect speech of the French aristocracy, "I leave you my kiss and a wish for a good life, beautiful mademoiselle."

She gasped as she took in his masked appearance, but then a faint smile came to her lips. "The Nighthawk," she whispered, and reached for him, entwining her fingers in the hair at his nape.

Without saying a word, he gently pulled her hands from his neck and moved to the window and back into the night. He had accomplished his mission. The Nighthawk might be a thief, but he was not a despoiler of innocents.

More's the pity.

Chapter 1

London, 1816

Standing at the edge of the ballroom, Lady Mary Campbell smiled to herself, thinking it was a bit like standing on the edge of a cliff. Stepping forward would bring a drop into the unknown. It was a step she had no desire to take.

But, then, she had no choice. She'd postponed her dreaded debut as long as possible, and at nineteen she was well past the age most ingénues greeted their first season. Dressed in ivory satin she was, but she could hardly wait for the day she could wear red. And though she would have preferred her long hair down and flowing free, tonight it was drawn up into a pile of curls.

Gazing into the immense room with its crystal chandeliers, hundreds of candles, and men and women in elegant finery, Mary let out a deep sigh. It was all very glorious, of course, but it wasn't the Tuileries Palace where she had waltzed last December. It wasn't the world she loved, the world in which she thrived, the world of books and ideas. It wasn't the countryside, where she could ride her horse and forget everything. It wasn't even her uncle's world of statesmen. Those men, she was certain, would not give a thought to the gowns or balls for young women entering London society, and she wished she could follow their example. No, Mary was not at all at home in this place where young men mingled with their future wives—wives they would dominate and keep from truly seeing or enjoying the world.

That was one reason she was not anxious to wed, and she had several. But at the request of her mother, the dowager countess of Argyll, she had come to this ball and would dance with the young men. And when her sweet mother insisted her only daughter go to court and curtsey before George, Prince of Wales, the Prince Regent, Mary had bowed to the gracious request and sweetly obeyed.

Her best friend, Elizabeth St. Clair, bubbled on at her side about the grand decorations and the pretty gowns, but Mary's mind was on the *Times* article she'd read at breakfast describing Napoleon's exile on the island of St. Helena. There was a small note at the bottom of the article saying recent information suggested Napoleon's defeat in Russia was, in part, due to the legendary Nighthawk. She longed to meet the mysterious man, that stealer of secrets, if indeed he existed. But if he did, she was certain he would not be wasting his time at some tedious London ball. The world did not revolve around a dance, not even the waltz.

Elizabeth tugged on her glove. "I say, Mary, do you agree?"

Mary realized she had missed what her friend was saying and tried to recall the original question. She wanted to show support for Elizabeth, whose blue eyes were wide with wonder at the beautiful gowns and the handsome young men; her older sisters had already taken their place in London society, and Mary knew Lizzy was anxious to join them.

"Well, it is *rather* as I expected, Lizzy. It's like being offered up to the highest bidder, is it not? 'Tis strange so many go so willingly to the auction block."

Elizabeth's side-glance stopped Mary's reflection. "Oh, do try and enjoy yourself, Mary. It's not so bad. Besides, you're gathering many admiring looks!"

"I think you are imagining that. Recall the conversation of the Baroness Johnson in the retiring room we overheard. She could barely wait to tell her friends that the Campbell hoyden who reads philosophy and rides horses like a man is here."

"Actually, you were most gracious to her, Mary; more the lady than she. I rather think she's just a jealous old biddy. Besides, I wasn't talking about the women. It is the men who cannot take their eyes off you."

Mary's cheeks warmed. Her friend was exaggerating again out of kindness and loyalty. Her mother, too, remarked in a caring way about her appearance, and her uncle complimented her gowns, but Mary knew their words were merely encouragement to wear the female frippery she disdained. Her heart seized with a pang of regret as she wondered if her father would have thought her pretty. He had not lived to see her blossom into womanhood.

"Lizzy, I am not seeing what you are, but since *you* asked, I will do my best to be happy. After all, you are here, and I do love to dance."

As if summoned, two young men approached and asked for the first quadrille. Mary resolved to be nice.

So it begins, she thought to herself.

One young man offered an arm. Green eyes met blue. His kind face was framed by light brown hair, and he smiled, leading her smoothly out into the room. They were soon gliding across the polished wood floor. To her surprise, Mary's spirits lifted.

As the dance took a turn, Mary's gaze drifted over her partner's shoulder, drawn unbidden to two men standing in front of a pillar. She did not recognize them, but the dark stare of the taller man pierced her gown, corset and chemise and touched her very skin. Feeling exposed in a way she never had, she shivered, and she was glad when her partner whirled her away.

And yet, she continued to surreptitiously watch the man, drawn to his overwhelming presence. He wore black, his white shirt and cravat the only contrast to the dark brown hair that fell in waves to his nape. He exuded a kind of power unlike any other male in the room. There was nothing the dandy about him.

Taking a long draw on his brandy and gazing around him, Hugh Redgrave, Marquess of Ormond and only son of the Duke of Albany, drew a breath and held it as his eyes came to rest on a girl gliding across the dance floor like a swan over a lake. The tall young woman with hair the color of spun gold and fine features set in an oval face was striking, but it was more than her beauty that drew him; she moved with a grace beyond her years and had a fire in her eyes that set her apart from the other debutantes.

He had found the evening tiring until now. The ball served only to remind him he was nearing the age of thirty, and as his father's heir, the pressure to select a wife from among the young ladies presented increased with each passing year. Comforting himself with an occasional mistress to warm his bed was serving his needs just fine; he was in no hurry to take a wife. When he did, it simply would be an arrangement among peers. Far better to see marriage as a matter of business, as so many others did. That would have one advantage: He could never lose someone he loved.

Yet, he wanted to delay the inevitable for a while longer. He had a good excuse. His work had kept him away from England, and if he were fortunate, it still might. Perhaps the Prince Regent had a new assignment for him.

As was his usual practice, Hugh had made this appearance in the ballroom before retiring for a game of cards. Leaning over to his friend, the second son of the Earl of Lindsey, he chuckled. "I feel a bit like a fox watching baby chicks. Do you think we make their mothers nervous?"

"They do watch us with skeptical eyes," Griffen Lambeth replied. "No doubt they are worried any minute we will pounce."

Hugh nodded. "Indeed. And how little we've done to deserve the reputations we have."

"I'm not sure I agree with that, since you have cultivated yours as a cover for your other…activities, have you not? And by cultivation I'm not just speaking of your latest indulgence, Lady Hearnshaw. Before her there was the countess of—"

"I confess I have done. It seemed necessary at the time. Just like my sneaking back to England every year or so to put in an appearance at a ball and leave the impression I was still in London, ready to pounce at any moment. All is part of the show."

His reputation as a rake, a man of the world who would seduce any woman who took his fancy, would unsettle the mamas, he knew, but better the mamas think them rakes than know them as spies. Not that he intended to dance with anyone. No matter there were some real beauties at the ball tonight; his previous encounters had taught him young noblewomen were silly and too talkative, prattling on about town gossip and matters of the home. Insipid. A night with one would precipitate a quick marriage. No, it was best to stay with women who posed no threat to his bachelor status. Older, more experienced women, women who willingly offered their bodies while not asking for his heart.

Still, he was curious about the blonde girl. There was something special about her. "Who's that dancing with Arthur Bywood?"

Griffen's eyes scanned the couples. "Ah. I wondered if you'd noticed her. That would be Lady Mary Campbell, daughter of William Campbell, the late Earl of Argyll. You remember, the one killed in that horrible riding accident."

Hugh's mind seized at the memory of another riding accident, one that had forever changed his life. But that was not what Griffen referenced. "She couldn't have been very old at the time."

"No, she was quite young. An only child. I understand it was heart-rending. Now some young cousin or other will inherit the title."

Hugh's eyes followed the girl as she moved gracefully away from and back to her partner. She was laughing at something her partner was saying, her head thrown back in unusual abandon. It was a sensual display, and to his surprise his body responded; his trousers were suddenly too tight.

"All the *ton* has been anticipating her," Griffen offered. "This is her first season."

Hugh was puzzled. "Anticipating her? Why is that?"

"Surely you have heard, my friend. The fiercely independent—and some say rebellious—Mary Campbell? While our young fops here will dote on the girl, I expect the young men's fathers hope she does not choose them. She has a reputation."

"What kind of a reputation?"

"Well, a diamond of the first water she may be, but still a diamond in the rough. Too intelligent for a young woman, and both headstrong and outspoken with a tongue that cuts like a blade."

"A bluestocking hellion?"

"Just so. Of course, it all can be explained, her having been raised without a father. The dowager countess, her mother, is a gentle woman, and she was clearly not up to the challenge. Lady Mary will be…difficult to manage."

"Hmm."

"Have you really never met her, not even when you were younger?"

"No." Even as Hugh said the word, he wondered why that was. The Campbell estate lay only a short ride from his family's country home. Then again, he'd been on the Continent for several years. "Have you?"

Griffen chuckled. "Oh, aye, and it was most disconcerting. A rare bit of baggage, that one."

Hugh turned to his friend, suddenly curious. "Don't be obscure. Tell me."

"Well, she stared at me with such a bold look I'll not soon forget… There's no fear in those piercing green eyes, I can assure you. It's a bit off-putting in a female that young. Nor is she shy with her opinions."

Hugh's gaze returned to the young woman. He sensed again that she was different, but perhaps it was simply as Griffen suggested and she would be difficult to manage. While he loved a challenge, he did not need a difficult and marriageable young woman. Not now. Not ever.

As he and Griffen turned toward the card room, Hugh silently pitied the man who ended up with her.

Chapter 2

Mary stared out the large mullioned windows of the study in Campbell Manor, a beautiful stone mansion set against groves of trees and well manicured sloping lawns and gardens in Ruislip, twelve miles outside of London. It was her home and she loved it, especially on such a rare spring day. The morning sun pierced the leaves of the trees, leaving a dappled pattern of light on the grass beneath. Through the window she heard a bird loudly chirping.

A shuffling noise caused her to turn. Her uncle Adrian, Lord Baynes, sat in one of the tapestry wing chairs flanking the stone fireplace, a pile of papers in his lap. The scene made her smile. With thick silver hair and blue eyes, he was a man of great presence, wisdom and quiet authority. Respected by kings, he'd become a diplomat preferred by the Crown for its most difficult tasks.

Mary's heart filled with gratitude. It was at his table in London where she'd first been introduced to the world beyond England, where she'd learned of war and its effects, of leaders whose pride and ambition had rent the countries of Europe. In the last few years, she had persuaded him to take her along on a few of his trips to the Continent. They had traveled to Vienna and Paris, and her life had become exciting. She had every intention of going with him on his next venture, if only she could be certain he would take her.

"Those must be interesting papers you're studying so intently, Uncle."

He didn't look up. "It's that lingering business in Paris. I would not bring work to a visit with you and your mother, but I need to study the issues I will soon be facing. It's a chessboard, and the pieces seem to be moving all at once."

"Sounds fascinating," Mary said.

He peered up at her, concern lining his face. "Too fascinating, I fear."

She did not want him to dwell on his worries; he might change his mind and leave her behind. So she reached for a different subject. "The crocuses have come up, Uncle, and the first roses will soon be in bloom."

"Yes, your mother is a wonder with flowers," her uncle murmured, returning his attention to his papers.

Mary smiled, gazing at several purple blooms just outside the window. Her mother did love gardens, and those around Campbell Manor were well tended. Mary loved them, too, but her father's passion—and hers—had always been books. They spilled off the shelves lining the study and the library. With them, she could travel the world without ever leaving home, and she had done so many times.

Though unusual for a young woman, Mary read nearly every day. Now she reached for the book she had been reading the evening before, the philosophical writings of a Frenchman who encouraged men to "Think well."

"I thought you were reading *Waverley*, that novel by Walter Scott, the author the Prince Regent so admires," her uncle said, amusement in his voice. "I see you are back to Pascal."

"Cannot I read both at once?"

"I suppose you can, but why ever would you want to?"

"Variety, Uncle." She sighed. "I like books that make me think, but I also like romantic tales. *Waverley* has opened my eyes to what happened to the Scots in the uprising in 1745. I know the Campbells sided with the Crown, but I cannot help but sympathize with the Highlanders. They only wanted their independence. It's a melancholy story."

"You're just like your father. Unafraid to question the actions of the British government. I always respected him for it, though it got him into trouble more than once. I fear it will be so for you."

"But you have told me more than once that Father was a loyal subject of the Crown. And so am I. And the Prince Regent loves the book! Why, he even asked the author to dine with him."

"Hmm," her uncle murmured without looking up, and then asked, "Are you keeping up your French?"

One of Mary's tutors had seen to her initial learning of the language. Philippe Dumont had taught one of the aristocratic families of France before the Revolution and his escape to England. As an only child living in the country outside of London, Mary had had a lot of time on her hands. She had been so enthusiastic about all things French, she'd even spent every dreary afternoon for a full stormy winter learning to make delicacies with her mother's new French pastry chef.

"*Mais, oui!*" she enthused. "And my German to a lesser extent. I want to be ready for our next trip."

"If I can arrange for you to see more of Paris this time, you will need to speak French very well indeed." Her uncle raised his head from his papers. "I forgot to ask you, Mary. How was your first ball?"

"Are you certain you want to know?" It still wearied her to think on what had begun her season.

"Of course I want to know! Did you enjoy yourself?"

"So many trivial conversations, so many formal greetings, so many awkward introductions. It was not at *all* like the dinners I attended with you on the Continent. Were it not for Lizzy, I think I should have left early." Then she recalled the tall man with the piercing dark eyes who had drawn her gaze all evening. She had not been able to stop thinking of him since.

Her uncle shook his head. "A young woman needs to be able to converse about more than politics, my dear. More than wars and governments. Proper young ladies concern themselves with other things. Surely the dancing was pleasant?"

"Oh, I do love to dance, so yes, I enjoyed that part. But I have no illusion that the ton welcomed me."

She shook off thoughts of the ball and returned to her contemplation of the morning. The sun struck the desk in front of the window, and sitting in its warmth, she was cheered. It was a lovely day to ride Midnight; the long green carpet of grass framed by boxwood hedges beckoned from outside.

Mary walked across the room to where her uncle sat, leaned down and kissed him on the cheek. "I thought I'd ride Midnight for awhile. Do you mind if I am gone for an hour?"

"No, not at all," her uncle said. "But do return for luncheon—dressed in *ladies'* apparel."

She just smiled at him, winking a yes as she left the room.

A few minutes later, she was dressed in her riding clothes and headed for the stables, her maid Milly shaking her head in despair. Long ago Mary had decided not to ride a horse as other women did; the only way to ride was fast and hard, and only a man's clothes and a man's way of riding would allow her the freedom for which she longed. With her mother's grudging approval, she had riding clothes designed: a cut-down man's white shirt, close-fitting tan riding breeches, a black velvet vest and black Hessian boots. She especially loved her boots and the feel of the smooth black leather clinging to her calves.

Today was warm enough she wouldn't need a jacket, and Mary's long legs rapidly covered the ground leading to the stables. Her heels hit the stone walk with a determined click. That sound, the stable boy had told her, always signaled her approach. She tossed her head, causing her long hair to fall in loose waves down her back.

The ton would have found her outfit shocking, but only her family, the servants and a few friends had ever seen it. There were rumors about her riding, of course. But even if others *had* seen her, Mary didn't care. She'd pay any price for the freedom and exhilaration of riding Midnight. She had fallen in love with the great black stallion, a gift to her uncle from a foreign dignitary, and it seemed the stallion reciprocated. No one else could master him—just as no one would ever master her.

* * *

Sitting in his wing chair, Mary's uncle pondered the work ahead. He half wished he could talk Mary into spending the entire season in London, but that was a losing battle, for she had no love of the social whirl of the *haut ton*. They had compromised with her agreeing to attend several balls and social events, which would have to be enough. Perhaps she would find a man she could care for, a man who would love her strength. If not, he was prepared to arrange a good match.

Then again… Adrian's thoughts returned to Paris, and to the great help she had been on his last trip. Her beauty had disarmed the French dignitaries and their allies; her quips had been well placed in the few conversations she'd been allowed to join, and her strong opinions, coming from such a young woman, had amused the leaders. But what he valued most were her judgments regarding the men he met with. And her ability to do things he himself could not.

On his last trip to Paris, due to an unusual turn of events, he'd kept her with him when the preliminary business began. Discussions eventually commenced in earnest, and while the men turned their attention to pressing issues Mary faded into the background, moving to the other side of the large meeting room with a book. The others were turned away when Adrian next glanced up and saw his niece sitting next to the minister's desk.

He'd watched surreptitiously as Mary lifted a paper. She had clearly seen something she thought was important, for she carefully reviewed the note before putting it back. And she had been right about its importance he had been pleased to later discover, for she recalled the note *that she had memorized word-for-word*. Oh yes, he wanted to take her with him on his next trip. When he was back in London, he would speak to the Prince Regent about including her.

His visit had brought him other matters to attend, however. Here in Ruislip, he was close to the Duke of Albany's country estate, so he had sent a note to the duke's son and been delighted to learn Lord Ormond could see him. Adrian had liked the young man when they'd first met, following a session in the House of Lords when Ormond had come to see his father, the duke. Adrian's new mission was to strengthen the ties between England and the restored Bourbon monarchy, and the Prince Regent himself had suggested Ormond might prove useful. The continuing turmoil in France and the occupying allied armies were making the resolution of issues more difficult.

Thinking again about his past days in Vienna, Adrian almost laughed. The Congress of Vienna! The word *congress* amused him greatly, given the group's methods. The European diplomats convened to decide upon issues arising from France's Revolution and the war with Napoleon, but they never met in session. Most of their discussions took place in informal meetings, often ending in heated debates. It seemed to Adrian that men forever argued over land and boundaries. He doubted they would ever stop.

* * *

It was nearly eleven in the morning when Hugh arrived at his destination astride his chestnut Thoroughbred. The man with whom he was to meet, now reclining on the terrace with his newspaper, rose to greet him.

"Welcome to Campbell Manor, Lord Ormond."

"I'm grateful for the invitation, Lord Baynes. You picked an amazing day for it. It isn't often I am asked to attend a meeting with a diplomat on a sunny day in the country."

"I was thinking we might enjoy our conversation even more if we were to discuss our business while taking a stroll around the grounds. Would that be acceptable?"

Hugh nodded. "It would please me a great deal. I need to stretch my legs."

The two proceeded to enjoy a lively discussion as they walked the path winding down toward the river. Hugh was more than relieved to hear the statesman shared his belief that France's leader, Louis XVIII, needed to show clear reform if he was to hold the esteem of his people. He hastened to tell the older man, "You'll find Louis warm to your desire to bond the two countries just now. In fact he may be delighted, Lord Baynes. He prefers the English to the other allies swarming—"

Hugh stopped mid sentence, his attention drawn to the black stallion that thundered across the wide green lawn. The horse's muscles rippled along its huge flanks, and its long mane and tail trailed out behind like great black flags as it galloped in front of him. The scene reminded him of another day, another black stallion. That stallion had lost its rider.

It was not often he allowed himself to think of it, to think about Henry. Just like always, the guilt and pain below the surface of Hugh's cool composure welled up inside him. In his mind he saw again the crumpled body of his younger brother. A cold sweat broke out across his face.

"Is something wrong?" his companion asked.

"No…*no*. Just a passing memory."

Shrugging off the vision, Hugh studied the great black horse racing toward a copse of trees, concentrating now upon its rider. Each moment brought more amazement. A girl sat astride the stallion, dressed in men's riding clothes, her long legs clinging to the beast's flanks and her golden hair streaming out behind her, a pennon of liquid sunlight. She was like a goddess riding upon a mythical beast.

He held his breath as she raised her arms and tilted her face up to the sky. It was the most alluring sight he'd ever seen, like a bird flying. He stood mesmerized.

"Who is she?"

Lord Baynes smiled. "Ah. That would be our Mary."

Mary Campbell…the ingénue I watched at the ball?

"Have you not met her?" Lord Baynes inquired.

"I have not had the pleasure." Hugh's eyes continued to follow the girl in wonder as she dropped her hands, took hold of her reins and leaned forward to stroke the stallion's neck while the beast slowed to a trot as she neared the trees. "Does she always ride like that—in men's breeches, astride, so fast and so…reckless?"

A look of amusement crossed the statesman's face. "She does, though not many have observed it. And she would take exception to your description of her as reckless. She is not your typical young lady."

"So I've heard." Griffen's description of Mary Campbell returned to Hugh. And this was the second time in only a few weeks that another man was surprised they had not met.

"Would it surprise you to know I once forbade her to ride that way?" Lord Baynes asked.

"No," Hugh said, reminded again of what Griffen had said. "It wouldn't surprise me at all."

"It was a few years ago," Lord Baynes continued. "Of course it did no good. She persisted, as is her wont, and thus you see her here."

Hugh couldn't miss a pleased note in the older man's voice. He was *proud* of the girl. "She is stubborn?"

"Oh, no," Lord Baynes corrected. "I wouldn't call her stubborn. More…determined. When she sets her mind to something, there is little that can stop her. She can indeed be persuaded against taking a path, but the argument had best be sound. In this case, she believed propriety less important than the accomplishment of mastering a horse no one else could. Now she races with the wind."

"It still seems foolish to me to be riding like that." Hugh watched as the girl and stallion disappeared behind the grove of trees. Turning to the diplomat he said, "Perhaps you might introduce me?"

His voice remained calm, imparting nothing of his desperate interest. Duke's son or no, Lord Baynes was likely also aware of his reputation as a rake. Still, they'd be working together and at some point he'd likely encounter the girl, so perhaps the older man would relent.

Lord Baynes's face was a mask of reserve, but then it softened as if he had made a decision. "I'm joining the ladies for their luncheon today, so if you stay I'll be happy to do that."

Hugh smiled. "If that's an invitation, Lord Baynes, it would be my pleasure to accept."

* * *

Mary loved the power of the horse beneath her, the blur of the landscape as she gained speed and the wind on her face as she rode. There was a fierce wildness inside her, a restless energy that craved action. Midnight was a worthy companion, for the horse shared her wild nature.

She clenched Midnight's flanks with her thighs and raised her arms to embrace the sun. It had taken her a long time to be able to ride this way without fear—and conquering that fear had given her even more satisfaction. The victory had not come without a few falls, and her uncle had soundly scolded her for each; the bridge of her nose still bore a faint scar. But she'd refused to give up and finally had been rewarded.

She returned Midnight to the stables. As she left the horse with the groom, Mary remembered her uncle's words and considered what to wear for luncheon. Dressing as a young lady was now necessary. It was her uncle's wish she be at ease among the nobility where she would one day take her place, and that meant dressing as one of them; though Mary wondered if she could ever be happy in a society where women were so often confined to the home. But she loved her uncle, so she would dress to please him. After all, he had given her great freedoms.

The gown she chose was appropriately unusual. Though the ball had seen her in the ivory that labeled her a debutante, she preferred jewel tones for her attire and disdained the pastels preferred by most women her age. For that reason she chose a deep amber traveling gown. The bodice dipped in a crescent across her full breasts, and tiny white lace edged the neckline and cuffs of the long fitted sleeves. Her maid told Mary the color of the gown highlighted her hair, which she tied back with a slender black ribbon since she was at home. Only one piece of jewelry graced her body, a small gold signet ring on her right hand, a family heirloom her mother had given her when she turned seventeen. Mary's initials were engraved in flowing script in place of the great aunt's that once it had borne.

Reminded of the lateness of the hour, she hurried. Lunch and her uncle waited. Milly wanted to fix her hair but there wasn't time.

"Milady, I can put it up in but a minute!"

"No, Milly, leave it as it is. You can put it up before we leave for London. I am already late and I must hurry lest Uncle be upset."

Milly sighed and shook her head, a frequent reaction.

Racing down the stairs, skirts flowing out behind her, Mary might have been fleeing a fire. Her cheeks felt flushed from the ride, and wisps of loose hair fell about her temples as she stepped onto the terrace—where she came to an abrupt halt. The round table was set with several dishes, and a man was seated with her uncle and her mother.

Even from a distance, the man was sensual beyond her experience. The power of his body, the casual way he leaned back in his chair... And there was so *much* of him. With one black-booted leg stretched out and dark hair waving down to his nape, he seemed a pirate relaxing on the deck of his ship. There was something familiar about him, too.

Oh, God. It was the man who had watched her at the ball.

Slowly Mary walked to the table. As she drew near, the man looked up and smiled then rose from his chair. Her stomach tightened. That dark stare and handsome face... Men did not usually disturb her, at least not their looks. This one did. He was a force, so much masculinity in one man.

His eyes followed hers as she appraised him, amusement evident in his wry smile. *How arrogant! How annoying! How embarrassing.*

Her uncle and the man both rose, the dark-haired visitor towering above her, well over six feet.

"Mary, allow me to introduce Hugh Redgrave, Marquess of Ormond, the Duke of Albany's son," her uncle said. "Lord Ormond's family estate is not far from here. You've not met him before because, as we were just discussing, he's been away. He resides mostly in London."

Mary remembered her mother speaking of the Duke and Duchess of Albany, but she had no memory of meeting them. She considered the tall man as his eyes followed a path from her face down her body and back to her lips. His eyes drew her into their depths, so dark and intense at first she thought they were black. Soon she saw they were the darkest brown, the color of aged brandy. But if eyes were windows to the soul, as the French liked to say, his soul was too dark to see clearly.

The man was arrogant and too sure of himself, so she determined to boldly meet his stare. Few men held her penetrating gaze when she bestowed it, a fact she took pride in; but he did. A wave of heat passed between them. Her heart raced in her chest.

The visitor bent over her offered hand, warm lips brushing her knuckles, and Mary felt the touch all the way to her toes. Forcing herself to regain control, she said, "It's an honor to make your acquaintance, my lord."

He chuckled in response. Damn the man's smugness.

Mary sat down, and her mother smiled at her. "Have you been riding this morning, dear?"

"I have." Mary felt a wave of pleasure wash over her. She forgot all about the smug Lord Ormond and said, "'Tis a lovely day, and Midnight is in fine form."

Mary picked up a bite of fish with her fork but instantly put it down; her appetite had deserted her when she saw Ormond's continuing regard. How odd. Her appetite never left her unless she was ill, and that was a rare occurrence. A servant brought a plate of cheeses, bread and fruit to complement the lunch, and she considered the fruit, thinking she might have a piece, but at last she decided against it. A rich claret was also brought, and this she sampled. At the very least she could manage a glass of wine.

* * *

Hugh contemplated the girl briefly and could not resist asking, "Midnight?"

"My horse. Have you seen him?"

"I have." Hugh shot the girl's uncle a glance. "He's magnificent."

The girl's eyes lit up and she flashed white teeth at him. "Yes, he is a beauty."

Clearly she loved the great stallion. Her smile dazzled Hugh, and the image of her long legs wrapped around the flanks of that big black beast was still fresh in his mind. Suddenly he saw those long legs wrapped around him. The image surprised him, as he'd come here on business and not to ruin the daughter of a peer. But her beauty had beguiled him. And having seen her in breeches, he recalled well the curves that were hidden beneath her skirts. Slightly unnerved, Hugh made an effort to engage in lighter conversation.

"Did you hear about Prinny's latest escapade?"

He'd thought the ladies would enjoy the gossip, but Lady Mary's reply was terse. "He is *always* having some escapade." Abruptly she turned to her uncle. "What do you think about the sad state of affairs on the Continent? Have any of your dispatches said whether the political climate is improving?"

The chit had dismissed him! Hugh's throat tightened, but he quickly damped the anger that flared within him by taking a sip of wine. "Surely you do not bother with matters of a political nature on the Continent, Lady Mary?"

"Why, of course I bother," she said sharply. "And having been to the Continent, having met some of their leaders, it's a wonder to me we are not still at war even now."

Hugh regarded Mary's uncle, well aware of the work the man had been doing before returning to England. "Has she accompanied you to Paris, Lord Baynes?"

"Yes. She has," the elder statesman said. "And quite to the advantage of the Crown."

As the girl glanced at Lord Baynes, a smile in her eyes, Hugh wondered just what it was that had she done in Paris. It became obvious to Hugh that the older man was all too comfortable with his unusual niece, no doubt indulging her every whim.

The countess had not participated much in the conversation, and Hugh now found himself noting how very unlike Mary she was. Petite in stature, with auburn hair, blue eyes, and a quiet, gentle spirit, it seemed his friend Lambeth had been right; the woman would have difficulty controlling her daughter's rebellious tendencies.

Talk continued as Mary and her uncle exchanged observations about the situation in Europe and the way ahead for France now that Napoleon was exiled and the aging Bourbon king had been restored to the throne. Hugh was surprised at the frank exchange between the two, more like two diplomats considering options than an uncle with his young niece. But before he could think to comment, the conversation took a turn.

"Mother, shouldn't we be off soon?" Mary asked.

The countess paused as if remembering. "Oh, yes dear, you are right." Acknowledging her guests she added graciously, "Gentlemen, it's been delightful. However, since my daughter has agreed to join me in some shopping and we have friends to see in London, I am afraid we must be away."

The two women said their goodbyes and departed, leaving Hugh to ponder the effect Mary Campbell had on him. She was indeed outspoken, and yet he grudgingly admitted her comments accurately reflected the situation in France. Obviously the girl possessed an active mind and was well informed. A strong woman with a sharp mind? He knew another like that; a woman in France who had made such an impact Napoleon had even thrown her out of the country.

Of course, there was something disturbing about Lady Mary that he'd never considered with Germaine. He could not stop thinking about those long legs he had seen wrapped around her black stallion. Nor could he prevent himself from drinking in recollections of her beautiful face, her unusual green eyes and her full lips. He had wanted to kiss those lips even as she provoked him to anger.

No, he reminded himself. That would never happen. She was a young, *marriageable* woman. Not his type at all.

Chapter 3

"Mother, can we stop at Hatchard's bookshop?"

Traveling the streets of London with her mother a few hours later, searching for items to purchase, Mary relished the activity swirling around her. The noise of the passing carriages and the shouts of their coachmen cracking their whips only increased that excitement.

The strange sound of the cockney calls from vendors selling their wares entertained her. One could buy fish and bread and all manner of food if one had the coin to do so. Mingled together were men dressed in fine coats, trousers and hats, and ladies in flowing skirts, pelisses and bonnets. Ragged street children brushed by, teasing each other while playing their games, adding to the cacophony of sound.

"Of course, dear. Did you have something in mind? We've not much time to browse."

"I want to pick up a new novel by the author of *Pride and Prejudice*. Ever since I learned the author was a woman, I've been anxious to see what more she might write. Word has it this new novel is dedicated to the Prince Regent."

"Who can imagine the Prince of Wales reading stories of love?"

Mary smiled. "Oh, I can imagine most anything of Prinny, Mother. And he and I seem to share a love of certain novels, which amuses me greatly."

The stop at Hatchard's did not take long, and with a copy of a book titled *Emma* tucked under her arm Mary decided with her mother to have tea before going on to Lord Baynes's town house.

They were just seated at a table looking out onto the street when her mother pulled off her gloves and leaned in close to whisper.

"This is the perfect time to pick up a few things you will need for Lady Huntingdon's house party. She and her husband the earl will make for wonderful hosts. Perhaps a new gown and a warm cloak would be nice. The evenings are still quite cool."

"If you think so," Mary said. A long sigh escaped her as her attention shifted to the people strolling by outside. She didn't mind participating in some of the season's events, but she had no desire for a whirlwind of parties and gentlemen callers. While she often took joy in shopping, she wasn't sure the purpose behind a new gown was to her liking. This house party was intended to bring eligible young people together, and Mary despaired of the matchmaking, of having to carry on meaningless conversations with men looking for wives to tend their homes but not do anything really interesting with their lives. She would not have Midnight to ride there, either.

Her mother took a sip of tea and joined her in gazing out the window. A wistful expression crossed her face.

"You're thinking about Father, aren't you?" Mary could see the sadness in her mother's eyes, and that made her feel sad, too.

"Yes, I am," her mother admitted. "I was thinking of that time many years ago when your father joined me in this same teashop just after a session in the House of Lords. France was our topic of discussion that day, too. I think your conversation at lunch must have reminded me…and then, being here again always stirs my memories. It might surprise you to know how much of his life he shared with me. Even the politics."

"I am glad to know he shared all he was with you," Mary hastened to say. "The memories seem to please you."

"They do," her mother admitted. "And the memory of how I loved him. How I *still* love him." Her mother's eyes filled with tears, but turning to Mary she smiled. "Just now I was remembering when I first realized he was the one."

"How did it happen?" Mary could not recall her mother ever talking about this before.

"It was the evening we were both invited to dinner at the Earl of Danville's home. When I saw William across the table, my appetite deserted me. I rather had to pretend my way through that meal."

Mary's heart stopped. No appetite? Was that a sign? Surely not. It had just been the ride. Yes, her vanished hunger had been a simple lingering effect of her ride.

"I eventually got my appetite back," her mother continued, "but by that time I was quite smitten. Later, William told me it was the same for him." She smiled. "He told me he fell in love at first glance. He was such a handsome man, with that winsome smile and those bright green eyes. And a quick wit, too. I shouldn't wonder he captured my heart so easily."

Mary hastily took another sip of tea. In her mind she saw the lazy smile of Lord Ormond, and a sudden shiver rippled through her.

"I just remembered," her mother suddenly interjected, "that Lady Huntingdon—then Lady Emily—was at that dinner where I met your father."

"She was? Was she married to the earl then?"

"No, we were both unmarried at the time. Emily and I were quite like you and Elizabeth, very good friends."

That made Mary think about her good friend. What would Elizabeth say about her meeting Lord Ormond? Mary and her mother had been invited to Lizzy's family home for dinner that night, so she would have a chance to ask her. Perhaps that was a good thing. Lizzy had a keen understanding of people. She would surely have something useful to say about Lord Ormond.

* * *

As the eldest son of the Duke of Albany, Hugh had always known he would one day inherit his father's title. Nonetheless, he did not wish that day to come soon. A duke's life was all about social responsibility, his father would remind him, which left little room for adventure; and though Hugh did not shy from the path for which he'd been groomed, his life had taken a turn many years ago that led him far from the quiet life of an ordinary nobleman. His father had been aghast when Hugh first told him he was going to France. He was the only heir, the man pointed out; it was out of the question, not to be done. But after Henry's death Hugh had been so plagued by guilt that he could not stay. Everything reminded him of the boy.

Now he'd returned. Though he'd been in the field for a number of years, the restoration of King Louis to the throne of France allowed Hugh to spend most of his time in London, a change that pleased his father. And because the family's investments and properties were well managed, Hugh hoped he could continue the pursuits he found most interesting, his secret work, the business of the Crown.

Before taking the fourteen-mile ride back to London that afternoon, he stopped to say goodbye to his mother. His father wasn't at home, having left the day before to visit one of their estates in Scotland. The duchess was a woman of strong character, tall, gracious and handsome, with dark brown hair and blue-gray eyes. A decade younger than his father, she had only a few gray strands suggesting her age. Their conversation went well enough to start, but as Hugh gathered his things to leave, he anticipated the subject that always produced silence on his part.

She stood at the arched window in the parlor, looking into their extensive gardens, and spoke without turning. Bluntly. "Since you're going to be spending more time in England, Hugh, perhaps you can turn your attention to finding a wife. It is time you marry."

Silence hung in the air so thick it was tangible. He knew he was being rude, which he hated, but this was an old conversation; she was ever anxious for him to wed and father an heir. He supposed it wasn't unreasonable on her part. He was the only remaining son.

When he finally spoke, his voice was barely above a whisper. "Not yet."

"Son, do not wait too long. There are many wonderful young women out this season. Surely there must be *one* who suits. Your father has been making inquiries."

Alarmed at his father taking a more active interest in his personal life, Hugh decided to hurry his leave-taking. He repeated his answer but this time in a stronger voice. "Not yet. I find my work for the Prince Regent most interesting, Mother, and I think a few years more will not matter."

And thus the conversation ended as it so often did; she turned to face him and he saw the disappointment etched in that lovely face. Hugh hated to argue with her, but this was a subject he tried to avoid.

"All right, Hugh. We can discuss it again when your father returns."

On the ride back to London, he eagerly turned his mind to France. It was there he'd found the work he had come to love, the work that allowed him to forget, at least for a time, the sadness surrounding Henry's death. But there was more to consider now, so many unanswered questions. Could Louis be persuaded to make the changes that would be needed? Would the allies agree to remove their troops from Paris? And what role for England in this new world the Congress of Vienna had carved for them?

* * *

Several hours later, Hugh sat staring into his fireplace. Having taken refuge in the library of his town house in Mayfair, he stretched his long legs out in front of him, crossing his boots at the ankle and dangling a brandy snifter from his fingertips.

Only the flames from the fire and a few candles lit the room; his faithful valet always remembered his desire for the warmth of a cozy nest and had drawn the burgundy velvet curtains over the tall windows facing the street. The shelves on either side of the fireplace contained his favorite books, many of them beloved old friends.

In the leather chair next to him, Griffen Lambeth crossed one foot over his knee and nursed his own drink. It was customary for the two to meet in Hugh's London home to consider the business of the day before they went to a club for dinner, which tonight would be Brooks's. The pair was supremely comfortable together and had been since they met at Eton. Though both did well at university, and both had been anxious to leave their days of formal education behind, Lambeth was the scholar.

As a second son, Griffen Lambeth had more freedom in his pursuits, and he had taken up writing historical accounts of European wars some years ago, but he'd found the effort disappointing. Since his return from France, Hugh had taken advantage of Lambeth's boredom and urged him to join work of a different sort. His gift for strategy soon made him indispensible.

"I finally met Mary Campbell," Hugh remarked, rising to add another log to the fire.

Lambeth raised an eyebrow. "You don't say. When?"

"At Campbell Manor, near our country estate. Her uncle is Lord Baynes—Prinny's favorite diplomat at the moment. He invited me there to discuss the current business in France, and she joined us for lunch."

"What did you think of her?"

"She is…quite an interesting young woman." Hugh conjured a picture in his mind of the smiling girl with golden hair and unusual green eyes talking about the black horse she loved.

Lambeth laughed. He switched his attention from the fire to his friend, his drink forgotten. "Define 'interesting.'"

Hugh thought back to the big black stallion and Mary's long legs wrapped around it. "Have you seen her ride?"

"No, but I've heard rumors she is a fierce horsewoman. And that her style is…well…unconventional."

"Yes," Hugh readily agreed. "I would say that it is. She is quite the free spirit on a horse, and she rides a magnificent black stallion, a Friesian. Few women could handle it."

"A stallion?" Lambeth looked surprised. "That's an odd choice for a lady's mount, isn't it? Even for her."

"Because young women don't ride stallions? This one does—and quite well." Hugh pictured her once more, galloping free, raising her face to the sky, hair streaming behind her like golden fire. It was an image he would never forget. Then he frowned when he thought of the luncheon. "She is rather intelligent, but she has a strong will and a sharp tongue to go with it."

Lambeth chuckled. "Well, old friend, I did warn you."

Hugh nodded. Turning, he held up his brandy in mock toast, a wry smile on his face. "Yes, you did. And I intend to heed your warning and keep my distance."

Chapter 4

Mary had been looking forward to the dinner at Elizabeth's that evening; it would be an easy affair, one of the easiest engagements of her upcoming time in London. Viscount Rossington and his wife had been good friends of her parents and remained close to her mother after her father's death. Mary had often spent time in their home visiting with Elizabeth and her three sisters, Caroline, Charlotte and Emma. Elizabeth was the youngest of the four girls, a petite beauty with copper-colored hair that reminded Mary of fall leaves. Mary teased Elizabeth that her blue-gray eyes always betrayed her emotions, but Mary valued Elizabeth's rare gift of understanding people's hearts, and it meant a great deal to her that Elizabeth in return admired her strength.

After dinner the two retired alone to the library, as was their custom. Neither of their mothers seemed to mind. In front of a warm fire, the girls shared their favorite drink, a ruby port. Though most young women found tea more appropriate, Mary and Elizabeth liked the taste of the rich red liquid, and a glass of port had a way of making their conversation more interesting.

Elizabeth spoke up suddenly. "Mary, remember the trees you used to climb at Campbell Manor?"

Mary sat indolently before the fire. "How can I forget? That was where the stable boys spent their time. I could not resist joining them."

"I suppose it's not surprising, then, that you eventually started dressing like them."

"Now, Lizzy, even *you* must recognize how much easier it is to ride astride in breeches."

Her friend set down her glass, a look of incredulity on her face. "Assuming you want to do that. You won't find me on one of those beasts. I prefer the comforts of a carriage."

"To me a carriage is merely a way of getting from one place to another when dressed up in finery. I prefer the freedom of riding astride. The feeling of being one with the horse, of racing with the w—"

"You are ever the adventurer, Mary, taking risks for the sheer joy of it. You were always getting us into one kind of trouble or another. I still shudder at the memory of that summer you led me on a tour through the bedchambers at Hatchland. I don't think my parents ever got over it."

Mary smiled. "Well, there wasn't much else to do that summer if you'll recall. I can only tolerate so many music lessons and so much embroidery. I can do the handwork, but it leaves my brain wanting. I didn't even have Midnight then."

"You were in your element with those tours," Lizzy said. "I'll not deny it."

Mary thought back to that day so long ago when they were both still young girls. Mary, her mother and uncle and Elizabeth's family had been invited for the day to Hatchland, the country home of Lord and Lady Chester. That afternoon, when the adults were viewing the sculptures in the great hall, Mary had stolen away with Elizabeth to the parts of the estate she found more interesting. She had led her friend into the master bedchamber, and there the two of them discovered, in a carved wooden armoire, furs and lace and a thin gossamer chemise. She'd been scandalized, for she had never considered the old countess would wear such attire.

Even more scandalous had been the sudden appearance of the earl's valet striding into the bedchamber to discover them, the chemise dangling from Mary's hand. Even though she maintained complete decorum, Mary had quickly been labeled as the instigator of the incident. What followed had been supremely unpleasant.

She shrugged. "Don't remind me of that day, Lizzy. I might have been good at stealthy maneuvers, but not good enough."

"I remember. I was mortified. You were punished for the episode."

"I was," Mary agreed. "An apology to Lord and Lady Chester, and I was confined to my bedchamber for a week. There were only so many books I could read! You were lucky they saw you as a mere follower. Of course, the sentence didn't last as long as they'd hoped. I soon discovered I could climb out my window and down a tree next to the manor, a skill that has served me well on many later occasions."

Lizzy shook her head. "You're incorrigible, Mary. No wonder your mother gave up."

"You're making me feel guilty, Lizzy. But you're right. I suppose she did give up trying to change me. It was easier to let me go my own way. And at least we are friends today."

Mary took another sip of port and thought about the past. She'd been often in trouble as a young girl, but nothing ever came of it. She could never resist searching out new challenges, rules notwithstanding.

"I am thankful," she announced to her friend, "that you were always willing to be dragged into my adventures."

"Reluctantly," Lizzy admitted. "I always worried where they might lead. Speaking of which, are you looking forward to Lady Huntingdon's house party? That shall be an adventure."

"I don't know." Mary hesitated. "I mean, I've never been to one, so this will be new and therefore possibly the adventure you envision, but it will also mean being with the same people for several days. What if I don't like them? Worse, what if they don't like me? Remember when—"

"Of course you will like them. And they will love you!"

Mary, who knew the rumors about her, just rolled her eyes; Baroness Johnson's comment they'd overheard in the retiring room at the ball was not the only one made about her. She impersonated for Lizzy several stuffy old women sipping tea and acting haughty, talking about that hellion in a gown.

Elizabeth stifled a laugh. "Do you know who is invited to the weekend?"

"Actually, no. I just assume it will be some of the earl's friends—and an even number of marriageable men and women. That is the part I look forward to the least. I dislike being constantly on parade. I really wish you were going to be there."

"I do as well," Lizzy replied. "And it was kind of Lady Huntingdon to invite me, but as you know it is the same weekend as the christening for Charlotte's little one. I simply have to attend! I will be anxious to hear about the weekend when you return, though. You must tell me everything. And don't let that ancient incident with Ian McAllister set you off the young men of the ton who might want to be your suitors!"

"I'll try, Lizzy, but even if I wanted to join in the ritual of the ton's parties, how could any man truly find me attractive once he learns how little I care for the mores of the society I'd be asked to join?"

"Oh, they find you attractive," Lizzy promised, "even with your independent reputation. Still, one day you will have to decide if you want a home and a family that a husband would bring. Not every day can be an adventure."

Mary rose to stoke the fire, thinking about that. "Lizzy, have you ever met Hugh Redgrave, the Marquess of Ormond?"

Her friend pondered the question for a moment. "Lord Ormond? No, I haven't met him, but I know the name. My sisters used to speak of him and his friend. I believe the friend's name was…Lambeth? Yes. Griffen Lambeth. According to Caroline, they were among the most dashing men at her coming out. But they did not marry, and now they have reputations as rakes—which I assume does not bother them in the least. I recently heard my sisters saying Lord Ormond has taken up with the beautiful widow Lady Amanda Hearnshaw."

"Isn't she a horsewoman?" Mary thought she'd heard the name, as she always listened when anyone talked of women equestrians.

"I would not be the one to ask, Mary, but I cannot imagine any woman in England riding as well as you."

"'Taken up with,'" Mary repeated with a frown. "I presume she is his mistress. Men have so much more freedom than we do. Although, I wager Lady Hearnshaw is hoping for more."

"That seems a risky way to catch a husband, if that's what you're implying."

"Perhaps you have the right of it," Mary allowed. "Still, I cannot imagine she would enter into such a relationship without hoping for marriage, for children, for more…."

"*You* would hope for more, Mary," Lizzy said.

"Certainly I would." Then, thinking about her own lonely childhood, she added, "I could love a man who didn't stifle me. And I'd want a family…*children* with him. I'd want to care for them and—"

"Not all women want that. Besides, my sisters tell me some men of the peerage treat their mistresses better than their wives."

Mary shook her head. "I'm in no hurry to have a man tell me what to do, married or not." *Unless I truly loved him and trusted him, for such a man would know my heart.* "It seems we must endure so many rules while they must observe only a few. If a woman were to live her life as a rake does, she would be called something quite different, and it would not be flattering."

"Nevertheless," said Elizabeth, "being a rake has its consequences. Even now, I am sure the family of every girl coming out this season is wary of Ormond and his friend."

Mary wondered if that were true. It did not seem to her that such men suffered overmuch. "Lord Ormond is a most handsome man, though he is also presumptuous and arrogant." She found the latter unforgiveable, no matter that he would one day be a duke. Titles meant little compared to the man.

Elizabeth regarded her suspiciously from where she sat. "*You* met him, Mary?"

"Did I forget to say? He was visiting my uncle on business this morning and stayed for luncheon."

"And? What did you think? You must tell me!"

"He has a presence about him," she allowed. "And he's very tall, with broad shoulders, long legs and dark wavy hair, the kind you want to run your fingers through. His eyes…it was as if they could see right through me. He was at the ball, too—the tall one dressed all in black, save for his shirt and neck cloth. Did you not see him?"

Elizabeth's eyebrows rose. "I did see such a man. Wasn't he the one next to the handsome blond?"

"I think he was standing next to a man with lighter hair. Do you think that was his friend, Lambeth?"

"It could have been. A very dashing man in a midnight blue coat," Elizabeth went on. "I don't remember much about the other except that he was tall. What else can you tell me about Lord Ormond?"

"He's confident. Actually," Mary admitted, "his confidence is rather overwhelming."

Elizabeth raised a brow. "And what, pray tell, is that blush for?"

Mary shook her head. "I was remembering his smile. It was both annoying and rakishly charming. Of course, that was just before he took the conversation down a rabbit trail with some gossip about the Prince Regent he probably thought ladies should find interesting. I couldn't have cared less. Still, I cannot forget him. I've never been both angry and intrigued at the same time."

"I don't suppose you are seeing him as yet another adventure?"

"Heavens no!" Mary protested, though she thought perhaps she should change the subject. "Tell me about his friend. Lambeth, you say? It must have been him in the blue coat."

Elizabeth's face lit up. "He is one of the Earl of Lindsey's sons. I think you may have met him once. You mentioned it, I am certain."

"Did I?" Mary said. "I do not recall the name, and I did not recognize him at the ball." Of course, she was not too surprised. She often failed to remember men when introduced to them in a large group. Lizzy remembered everyone.

Her friend continued, "I know only what my sisters have said about him. Caroline danced with Lambeth several times in her first season, I think. Or perhaps it was Charlotte. Anyway, he was younger then and did not have the reputation he does today, but as I recall they spoke of him as kind and charming. Thoughtful as well."

Mary considered. "We might see him at the next ball."

A wide smile spread across Elizabeth's face. "Well, then. That settles it. You must introduce me to Lord Ormond—and his friend, Mr. Lambeth."

Mary's gaze returned to the fire, and she took another sip of port. "Perhaps I could. But first there is the Huntingdon house party, and at some point I'm hoping to go to France again with my uncle."

"Do you think he will take you?"

"I think he will, after what happened the last time. I believe he found me…useful. And he feels guilty for being away so much."

Lizzy sighed. "You have a wonderful ally in Lord Baynes, Mary. I hope you do not take him for granted."

Warmth flooded Mary when she thought of her uncle. "He's a dear. I'm hoping to always be a part of his work, at least in some small way. Life can be so dull without adventures, and I want to do something important. Something significant."

"But, Mary," Lizzy realized suddenly, "if you go to France soon you'll miss weeks of the season!"

Mary shrugged. "You know I really don't care about that. The young men here are not interesting to me, and the older ones are more like my uncle: interesting but not attractive. At least, not attractive enough to make me want to marry one. Besides, I'm not ready to give up my freedom. I have begun to wonder if there ever could be a man for someone like me."

"Of course there is, Mary. You just have to find him, no matter how long it takes."

Lizzy was so understanding, so hopeful. Wanting to bring a smile to her friend's face, Mary stood and raised her chin; then, in a voice of mock snobbery she announced, "Time and Mary Campbell wait for no man!"

The two girls broke into peals of laughter.

Once their mirth had run its course, Mary returned their conversation to her favorite subject. "In truth, I am *so* looking forward to seeing Paris again."

Her friend's countenance turned serious. "I have an odd feeling about you going this time, Mary. Some of your uncle's work seems mysterious and…perhaps not for someone with your tendencies. I worry about you."

Mary scoffed. This was yet another reason—besides discretion—she'd not told her friend all she had done in Paris to help her uncle on the last trip. She would not have Lizzy worry more. "You worry too much! About everything!"

"But sometimes I am right," Elizabeth answered.

Chapter 5

The house party was an inevitable rite of passage for a young woman's first season, Mary knew. If only Lizzy were joining her, she might have looked forward to the weekend, but as it was she traveled alone in her carriage, without even Milly, since the Huntingdon country estate lacked rooms for all the guests' servants. Mary's mother had offered one bright spot by revealing that Lady Huntingdon had acquired a French cook recently immigrated to London. It was gratifying to know the food would be good. French cooks were one of the benefits England had reaped from the tumultuous times in France.

It was a cold, gray afternoon as the carriage pulled up in front of the Huntingdon estate, but Mary was pleased she had arrived in time to change for the dinner that would be the first event in the weekend's activities. Having spent much time in the damp carriage, she longed for a hot bath, a warm fire and some tea before she had to brave the other guests.

The front door opened as if the butler had anticipated her knock, and she entered the stately country mansion to find the earl and his wife waiting to greet her.

"I am so delighted you could come, Mary," said Lady Huntingdon, a woman possessed of great elegance and of an age with her mother. She had soft brown hair and kind gray eyes, ageless in their appeal.

"Thank you for inviting me," Mary replied as the butler took her cloak. "My mother sends her regards."

Peter Hastings, Earl of Huntingdon, enthused heartily to his wife, "The weekend has become a livelier event now that Lady Mary is with us."

Mary knew the earl to be a man of letters and fond of debates, and though he had raised only sons, he was not afraid of an animated discussion with a woman. Seeing him again, she recalled their last conversation about the classics, how she'd hated having to learn Latin but loved the antiquated volumes. A servant was summoned to show her to her room, and Mary followed the young maid upstairs, content she had accepted the invitation to the house party. It might be a good weekend after all.

* * *

As the Duke of Albany's son, Hugh had social obligations, including the house party to which he now headed. Rather than take a carriage he had ridden his favorite Thoroughbred, for there would be a hunt on Sunday, but as he dismounted at Lord Huntingdon's very comfortable country estate he considered the thick gray clouds above him and hoped that they would be favored with sun by then.

His prior business had taken more time than he allowed, leaving him hurried and in a foul mood as he handed the reins to the stable boy. Shaking off the road dust from his greatcoat, Hugh gave the young man instructions for his horse. His things had been brought ahead by his valet earlier that day, and he was grateful to think he would soon have fresh clothes.

The earl's longtime butler, Harris, a very proper older manservant, greeted him. "I'll ask Francis to show you to your room, my lord. The earl and the countess are indisposed at the moment. Dinner won't be served until eight, so there is time for a bath and a brandy."

Ah, the man knew his tastes. "Wonderful, Harris. I have been thinking of nothing else for the last few miles."

If he were to admit it, that wasn't quite true. He had been thinking about the lovely Mary Campbell and her luscious lips and long legs. But he shoved those thoughts aside and followed the footman.

The room assigned to him was reminiscent of his library in London, apart from its heavy four-poster bed. Decorated in dark burgundy and browns, it had a stone fireplace and dark wood furniture. A man's room. A fire was already burning nicely as Hugh sank into the comfortable chair.

"Do you need help with your boots, my lord?"

"No, Francis, this I can do." He pulled them off, dropping them to the side of the chair.

"I'll have some brandy brought, my lord."

"Thank you, Francis. That would be most appreciated."

The footman was a good sort, he decided amiably as he stood and began to peel off his clothes, already feeling the day's tensions draining from his body.

* * *

Mary fidgeted as the young maid struggled with the long line of small, covered buttons on the back of her green velvet gown. The girl had been eager to assist but was not as swift at dealing with the frippery of female attire as Milly.

Twisting around, Mary could see the frustrated look on the girl's face as she worked. The servants would have a difficult time attending to the added burden of weekend guests, and she wanted to cause no one hardship. "I'm sorry this gown is being so difficult," she said.

"I'll soon have them done, milady."

"What's your name?" Mary asked.

"Amie, milady."

Mary held still to allow the young girl to secure the last button. "Well, you have been a great help to me, Amie."

"Thank ye, milady."

Mary stepped back to see the effect in the oval mirror. The gown was the same color as her eyes, a warm jade. That had been her mother's idea, and she was pleased with her appearance. The low neckline fitted well just below the upper swell of her breasts, but the long row of buttons had set back her determination to be on time for dinner. When her unruly locks were finally tamed into a simple chignon at the back of her head, Mary descended the stairs to the lower level, smiling to herself at the conversation she'd just had.

She was still smiling when she entered the large parlor already crowded with the guests. Brandy, sherry and hot spiced wine were being served, and the conversations were boisterous. Mary breathed in the inviting aroma of spices mingled with the scent of the logs flaming brightly in the great stone fireplace. The surrounding draperies were rich fabrics in shades of green, brown and yellow—the colors of the countryside—and they blended well with the dark oak paneling. A huge pair of stag antlers hung over the fireplace to complement the paintings of hunting dogs and horses. Mary appreciated the countess's efforts to make the room warming to her guests.

She recognized several people immediately, including the young man she had danced with at the ball: Arthur?—yes, that was right—Arthur Bywood. A nice young man, if perhaps a bit too enthusiastic. Though he was a few years older than Mary, her time with her uncle and her uncle's colleagues made him seem very young. She would have to be careful not to unduly encourage him.

Scanning the room, she saw several young women she knew, including Lady Harriet Wilby, though they did not have much in common. Lady Harriet and her friends were among those girls who seemed silly to Mary, those giggling females who tittered at every handsome male. Their presence only reminded her how much she missed Elizabeth.

Mary's eyes came to rest on the fireplace and the familiar face of the Earl of Huntingdon. Leaning one shoulder against the mantel, dressed in a brown velvet coat and a gray waistcoat, the earl blended well with the room. Sipping from his drink, he had fixed his attention on a tall, broad-shouldered man with dark hair in a coat the color of coal, and he did not see her. The second man had his back to Mary.

The earl raised his head as he spotted her, and the warm smile on his face told Mary he was happy to see her arrive. The man talking to him turned, and Mary's knees suddenly sagged.

Lord Ormond.

Her knees. How could that happen at the mere sight of him? More importantly, how was she going to get through the weekend if this sort of thing kept happening? Ormond had a way of unnerving her. Instantly, though, she resolved she would not be undone by a man, and especially not this one.

Squaring her shoulders, she smiled as the earl strode to her side.

"Lady Mary, how lovely you are this evening!" He bowed over her hand.

Ormond was just behind. Dropping his head in a graceful gesture, almost a bow, the man straightened and gave her an amused smile. "It's good to see you again."

The earl's eyes shifted. "Have you two met?"

"Yes," Mary offered. "At Campbell Manor last week. It seems Lord Ormond knows my uncle."

"Why, yes, that would make sense," Lord Huntingdon was quick to reply. Mary could not say what the older man was thinking, but it seemed he had some knowledge to which she was not privy.

Lady Huntingdon appeared. "Mary," she announced, "you're just in time to walk with us. Shall we, husband?"

"By all means, dear." The earl then offered his arm to his wife and looking back into the room announced to his guests, "We are being summoned to dinner!"

Everyone began moving toward the dining room, and the aroma of the evening's meal drifted into the hall to entice them.

Lord Ormond offered Mary his arm, which she took.

"You do look fetching tonight, Lady Mary. Green becomes you."

"Thank you, my lord." Mary tried not to be unnerved by the wink he gave her, or by the warmth of his arm beneath her hand, but his very presence made her shiver.

They followed the Earl of Huntingdon and the countess into the dining room. A long mahogany table was set with crystal and Spode china painted with birds and flowers; and the center of the table held an attractive arrangement of greenery from the garden. Though the room was elegant and the smell of the waiting meal inviting, Lord Ormond's scent of brandy and the woodlands was more inviting still. Mary's stomach would not be calm.

She hoped for relief with the seating arrangements, but no, she was directed to a seat that put Ormond on her left. Arthur Bywood was on her right, however. Though she would not have sought him out, the talkative young man from the ball now held her full attention—or tried to. There wasn't much opportunity to interact with Ormond, whose every moment was taken up with Lady Harriet on his left. The girl, who had a sweet round face with brown eyes and curly hair, was all smiles and gazed adoringly at Hugh Redgrave. Well, that was just fine with Mary. She had better things to do than giggle at the rake.

Much to Mary's chagrin, once the food was served, despite her anticipation of the sumptuous meal prepared by Lady Huntingdon's new cook, her appetite disappeared again. The beef roast with a dark rich sauce and fowl accompanied by roasted vegetables smelled marvelous, but Mary managed only a few bites. She did move her food around her plate in what she thought was a rather convincing imitation of eating, however, and by the time dessert was finished and the men rose to retire to the library for port and cigars she had consumed more wine than food and more than enough of Mr. Bywood's charm. Her only thought was to escape for some fresh air.

Familiar with the estate after visiting with her mother the year before, Mary was anxious to be on her way. She bade Arthur Bywood good evening, and avoiding Lord Ormond, who was still the subject of Lady Harriet's adoration, hurried down the hall, past the game room and library to the French doors leading to the terrace.

She was glad her velvet gown was heavier than the ones she usually wore, for she was confronted by cold air as she stepped outside. Moving across the terrace in the dim light, she descended the steps into the gardens before becoming aware of the sound of boots on the stone terrace behind her. Glancing over her shoulder, she saw Ormond striding after her.

"Are you intending to walk in the gardens, Lady Mary?"

"Yes," she said. "I wanted some air."

"May I join you?" he asked.

"Yes, of course, my lord," she said as he caught up with her on the stairs, but she was thinking *oh, no*.

"We didn't get much of a chance to talk at dinner."

Mary detected no smirk on his face from the corner of her eye. "No, but we were both pleasantly occupied, were we not?"

"You might say so," he allowed.

They walked side by side down the stone path, without saying anything, and at the end entered a small hedge-framed alcove nestled deep in the gardens where the first roses of spring had begun to bloom. Mary was glad there was a full moon; otherwise the gardens would have been quite dark.

Ormond broke the silence. "I've been wanting to speak with you about your last trip to France with your uncle."

"Yes?" She wasn't about to discuss France in detail with this man, not even if he did work for the Crown. But he did not push for details. Instead, he sighed.

"It's dangerous for you to be in France just now, Lady Mary."

"Really?" His attitude was most irritating. She had done just fine in France, which was why her uncle was going to take her with him when he returned. Why was it that men who did not even know her felt obliged to warn her against things she wanted to do? "And what concern would that be of yours, my lord?"

"I'm simply concerned about any possible impediment to the Crown's work. A young woman would require protection—and of course I wouldn't want you subjected to unnecessary danger."

Impede her uncle's work? The man was insufferable! She had been helpful before and could be again. Certainly she would not allow Lord Ormond to hold her back, not when life was finally offering both excitement and purpose. She had no intention of staying behind in England if her uncle would take her with him.

"You know little of me, my lord, even less of my ability to confront danger. And I am certainly not under your protection."

"Nevertheless, perhaps you should consider not going with Lord Baynes on his next trip."

Mary stared at Ormond, feeling her anger rise up into her throat. "Surely you realize, my lord, that you have no say in the matter."

She went to step around him then, but his broad shoulder blocked her way. Trapped in the alcove by that powerful body, she felt his coat press into her gown, and though Mary was tall, she was forced to look up to see Ormond's face. As she did, prepared to give him more of her thoughts, she made the mistake of gazing into his eyes. They were dark pools in the dim light. She stared, her lips parted. As if that were invitation, he bent his head to hers.

He hesitated. She could not move, fascinated as she was by his eyes, his mouth. Apparently that was all the approval he needed. Before Mary could object, the man's lips descended on hers.

Too startled to voice the objection her mind was screaming, Mary was caught up in the kiss. Lord Ormond's soft warm lips teased hers. Quickly he deepened the kiss. The intensity of the heat between them rolled over her, and she gasped as his tongue plunged into her mouth, unintentionally parting her lips farther.

He slid one hand around her waist, and the other moved to the nape of her neck as he pulled her to him, crushing her breasts against his chest. She had intended to push him away, but when she raised her hands to his chest they involuntarily moved to his shoulders and from there to the waves of his dark hair. A soft moan sounded from her throat. The scent of his masculinity intoxicated her, and she melted into his heat. Instinct replaced all, guiding her tongue to duel with his.

Her hunger for him was shocking, her driving need to draw him closer. Her mind protested, but her body succumbed. Mary's mind raced as she returned his kiss. *Not this man!* she told herself. *He is dangerous and much too experienced.* But still she was unable to tear herself away.

It was Lord Ormond who ended the kiss, resting his forehead on hers, giving her time to draw breath. Her hands dropped to his chest as she tried to still her pounding heart, and he brought his hands up to cradle her face, tilting her head so that she was forced to look at him.

"Lady Mary," he whispered, his lips close to hers.

Mary released a ragged breath. "You should not have done that. Someone might have seen. And it was most ungentlemanly."

She could see his wry smile, even in the dim light. "No one has seen us. And I never said I was a gentleman. Given the way you just responded, I would not think you want one."

Fury consumed Mary, its sudden heat making her cheeks burn. She was angry with herself for still craving his arms around her; she should have steeled herself against his seductive charms. How could she have allowed herself to forget her resolve? "You are most presumptuous, my lord, to believe you could know what I might want!"

She pulled away, and they stood for a long moment looking at each other. Then a self-satisfied smirk appeared on his face, causing Mary's anger to shift.

With an abruptness that suited her resolve to escape, Mary simply said, "Good night," and left him.

She walked briskly back to the terrace.

* * *

Watching Lady Mary retreat, Hugh was at a loss for words. He had not meant to kiss the blonde minx, but he had been drawn to her, to the low cut of her gown, to that creamy golden skin and those full breasts—and to those parted lips. Her gown was the same soft green as her eyes—eyes he could get lost in. All during dinner he had smelled her scent of gardenias, a smell that was to him more potent than the best brandy. A heat had flowed unbidden between them. By the glazed look in her eyes and her slight shiver when he took her hand, he knew she had felt it, too.

Yet, nothing had prepared him for how he had responded to the feel of her lips. How could anything as simple as an intention to warn her turn into something threatening to upset his world? *Damn.* He was an experienced man, a man usually of great self-control, yet this headstrong young debutante had just undone him. Her innocent passion had ignited a fire that still smoldered within him. One impetuous kiss had nearly driven him to cross a very clear boundary he had set for himself long ago.

"Good night, Lady Mary," he said under his breath, aware she could not hear him.

He did not follow. It was best to let her return without him so that no one would suspect they had been alone together.

So much for keeping his distance.

* * *

Mary flew up the steps to the terrace, her mind and heart racing, her only thought escape. She had been kissed before; there were always boys around Campbell Manor, and a few had stolen kisses. Then there was her sixteenth summer and Ian McAllister. The memory was still painful.

Ian had been the most handsome man she'd ever seen, tall and lean with sandy blond hair, flashing blue eyes and a smile that stirred her heart each time he looked in her direction. She had become instantly infatuated with him, and in her young mind it seemed he felt the same. One afternoon he kissed her as they walked along the river. She had maintained her virtue, but she'd thought she might be losing her heart. The more she saw him, the more she believed it.

One cool morning Ian was to join her for a ride. After waiting for more than an hour, impatience had taken over and Mary informed Hudson, their butler, that she would be riding near the river and asked him to send Ian to join her whenever he arrived. She had gone to the stables knowing her horse would be saddled and ready.

Upon entering the building, her eyes searched the gloom for the stable boy who was nowhere in sight. Pausing only briefly, she headed for the reins of her dark bay gelding but froze when she heard a moan coming from the last stall; a stall she knew held no horse. There came a rustling in the hay, followed by a man's groan. A female voice responded.

"Oh, Ian. Oh, yes!"

The voice was familiar, too. She recognized it as that of the daughter of one of the neighbor's servants, a girl whom Mary had seen around Campbell Manor a great deal that summer.

Another moan followed. Already fearing what she would find, Mary trod silently forward. The wooden door to the stall was ajar, allowing her to see the servant girl lying on the hay, her camisole drawn down to her waist and her skirts drawn up to reveal bare legs wrapped around Ian McAllister's thighs, his shirt still on and his breeches pulled down to his knees. He was perched above the girl, kissing her, as his movements became more rhythmic. Mary did not have to imagine what they were doing.

Fool! her mind had screamed. Tears welled in her eyes and a deep ache settled in her chest as she turned from the entwined pair and strode back to her horse, not caring if they heard her boots on the hard ground. Grabbing the reins, she galloped away from the stable and did not look back. Ian had not come to Campbell Manor again and Mary was glad of it.

Until now, Ian's kiss had been her only real experience. It had not prepared her for the kiss of Hugh Redgrave. In truth, nothing could have—nor for the man himself. Despite his reputation, she had allowed him to erode the guard she had placed about her heart. He was like a gale force wind blowing through her life and body, a force she seemed unable to resist.

As she reentered the house, her lips were still pulsing. She could feel the flush in her cheeks, and her body was tingling in ways she had never felt before. In a hurry to get to her room, she looked down as she passed the library, where the sounds of the men's conversations filtered into the hall, but Lady Huntingdon unfortunately picked that same time to leave the chamber where the women had settled into card games.

"Oh, please excuse me!" Mary said with a start, bringing her palm to her heart as she almost crashed into the countess.

Lady Huntingdon eyed her with concern. "Mary, are you all right?"

"Yes, of course. I'm fine." Mary fumbled for an explanation. She didn't favor card games, so she would not likely have joined the other women in any event, but she had absolutely no desire to do so now. "It was a lovely dinner. I just thought I'd retire early to be ready for a full day tomorrow."

"Of course, my dear," the countess replied. "Let me know if I can do anything for you. Remember me as your mother's good friend—and yours—while you are here."

"I will, and thank you," Mary said. A moment later she was hurrying on toward the stairs and safety.

* * *

Emily Huntingdon watched her young guest flee and wondered which young man had captured her interest. She obviously had been kissed, and Mary was not a silly girl. In fact, Emily and her husband had always thought the young woman exceptional. Whoever it was, he was surely a very special man.

Before she could move, Hugh Redgrave entered the hall from the terrace. Lost in his thoughts, eyes on the floor, he did not see Emily as he strode down the corridor while muttering under his breath. He soon reached the door of the library, where the men were smoking their cigars, and disappeared inside.

A slight smile teased Emily Huntingdon's lips. *Ah, yes. A very special man indeed.*

Chapter 6

Hugh stood at the window looking out of his room and dragged his hand through his hair. The morning sun was already falling on the gardens below, and memories of kissing Mary Campbell the night before flooded his mind. He hadn't set out to follow her, and he certainly had harbored no intention of kissing the minx. But in her fury she'd been irresistible.

He hadn't slept well. What man would after the events of the night before? He had tossed in his all too comfortable bed, and when he had finally succumbed to Morpheus, he had been plagued by dreams of a golden-haired girl with liquid green eyes and full lips soft and warm beneath his.

Shaking off the dream, he considered the activities planned for the day. As the men parted last night, the earl had mentioned archery in the morning and a picnic in the afternoon. Perhaps some time with a bow and arrows would improve his mood, he decided, having enjoyed the sport as a younger man. It wasn't easy for him to fall into the pastimes of the idle peerage; he was used to the challenge of more interesting pursuits, but he supposed for the weekend he could throw himself into them.

With that in mind, he strolled late into breakfast when most of the guests were already gone. After hastily devouring some bread and fruit, and swilling some tea, he hurried to catch up with those already on the archery field.

Arthur Bywood saw him coming and hurriedly brought him a bow and a quiver of arrows as he walked onto the lawn. "Ormond! Come join me in trying to save the reputation of the men as fierce competitors."

"Are we standing that badly?" Hugh inquired.

"We started well, but since Lady Mary began to shoot, the women have racked up the points. She is holding down the women's side of the match rather splendidly. Doing *too* awfully well, actually."

Hugh took the bow and arrows from the younger man and brought his hand over his eyes to shield them from the sun. Mary Campbell was nocking an arrow and preparing to shoot. She let the arrow fly, and from what Hugh could see, struck very near the target's center. Obviously she hadn't had any problem sleeping last night.

The next contender was a young man Hugh had been introduced to last evening, James Fairchild, a friend of the earl's son. Trying to show off his prowess with the sweeping hand movements of a court jester, Fairchild missed the target by a wide margin, which sent everyone into gales of spontaneous laughter. Hugh's eyes were on Mary, who was laughing as she tucked loose wisps of golden hair behind her ear.

With Hugh's arrival the men rallied, and it was a draw by the time the noon meal arrived. The pleasure of dining on freshly roasted chicken, bread still warm from the morning oven, ripe fruit and the earl's special wine beckoned. Lady Huntingdon had arranged the picnic on one of the lawn's green slopes with ground cloths spread out for guests to sit on. Hugh was suddenly starved, and he seated himself where he had a good view of Lady Mary. Arthur Bywood was sitting next to her, regaling her with stories of his recent travels.

Next to Hugh was Lord McGinnes, an avid horseman who wanted to know about the horses Hugh was breeding at the Albany country estate, a new line of Thoroughbreds raised for strength and speed. It seemed to Hugh the man was more horse mad than even he was.

"Will I get to see these fine animals you speak of, Ormond?" asked the dark-haired lord.

"You will. I brought my chestnut for the hunt tomorrow."

"I look forward to it," McGinnes announced, with a gleam in his eye and a twitch of his dark moustache. "For I intend to ride with you all. Never tire of the sport. Love a good romp."

Hugh noticed Mary glance his way. Though he was fascinated by the way the sun glinted on her hair, he also found himself wondering if she could have been listening as he spoke of his new venture. He was amused to see she had just missed something in her ongoing conversation.

"I'm sorry, Mr. Bywood, might you say that again?"

"I just wondered if you wanted some grapes, Lady Mary."

The woman accepted Arthur Bywood's offer, and she had him put the grapes not into her hand but into her mouth. The visual, with her tongue reaching out to collect the grapes, stirred Hugh immensely. At the same time, he experienced profound irritation with the young Bywood, who reminded Hugh of an eager puppy given a new toy.

Conversation abounded as the meal was consumed and the group relaxed on the lawn. Mary expressed her opinions on books she was reading, discussed a few of her favorite poems and also the ones she found wanting. Hugh listened to her comments, as did many others, and to his surprise he found he did not mind her views so much. At least she wasn't giggling mindlessly like Lady Harriet, who had plopped down next to him. Once he even *agreed* with Mary. He'd read the poem she was deriding, and it really wasn't very good.

It was truly a shame that he wasn't looking to marry at present. The more he discovered about the young woman, the more she captivated him.

* * *

Dinner that night was to be another grand affair. Mary chose a sapphire silk gown embellished with jet beadwork at the neckline. A shocking garment for her age, she supposed. The gown revealed her curves more subtly than the last one, too, but once again she found the color striking. Even the young maid Amie commented how the garment made Mary's eyes appear blue.

As she entered the dining room, Mary saw that Lord Ormond's dark indigo velvet jacket complemented her attire. *Thank God I'm not sitting next to him. We'd look a matched pair.* She felt her cheeks warm at the thought and fought the smile that threatened to appear on her face. Hugh Redgrave was not a man to be trifled with. It was bad enough she had melted into him when he kissed her. The things she had heard marked him as a man who, even when married, might take other women to his bed. Many did in the peerage, and he would be no different. Not to be trusted.

Instead, she was seated next to Lord McGinnes, who was anxious to learn about her horse. He'd heard rumors of her riding a huge black stallion and wanted to know if they were true, for he knew of no woman who would ride such a beast. A friend of her uncle, McGinnes had been widowed two years earlier. Lady Huntingdon had told Mary he was yet to sire an heir and was in the market for a new wife. He seemed very pleased to learn Mary had some talent as a horsewoman.

She managed to get through dinner without looking at Ormond. McGinnes dominated her attention talking horseflesh. Afterwards, however, Lady Huntingdon took her aside.

"Mary, Lord Ormond could not take his eyes off of you the whole evening!"

"Surely not," Mary said, trying to sound indifferent.

"Surely so," said Emily, smiling.

"But…he's quite a man of the world, isn't he?"

Lady Huntingdon gave her an understanding smile. "You can't believe all the stories, Mary. I know Lord Ormond and his reputation, but he is more discreet than you would guess, and his idea of honor does not include taking the virtue of young innocents."

"Thank heaven for that," Mary said, feigning relief. In truth, it meant little to her that he might be discreet with his mistresses, and she was surprised her mother's friend would suggest as much. She wanted no part of that scene.

Lady Huntingdon encouraged the guests to enter the parlour and asked some to contribute to the evening's entertainment, imploring one or another to play the piano while brandy, port and tea were served. Lady Harriet obliged. The young woman played a soft tune as background for their conversations. Much was made of Mary's success with the bow. She was not as good with a piano, however, and was content to sit and listen.

To Mary's surprise, Lady Huntingdon asked Ormond to go next. Never would Mary have guessed he played well enough to entertain. It was her experience that few men did, though she was familiar with great performing artists such as Mozart, Haydn and Beethoven. All of those were men, but she could not name any among the peerage who played.

Though reluctant at first, Hugh acquiesced after a chorus of pleas for him to display his talent. Settling himself on the bench he took command of the piano, filling the room with a beautiful sonata.

Mary was enthralled, watching the grace and ease with which he commanded the instrument, his long fingers powerfully stroking the keys. The guests stopped talking and listened, enraptured, as if Pan were playing his pipes. Mary's resolve to ignore the man began to weaken.

He played with such artistry, with such abandon. She already knew he could make her knees wobble with his kiss. What other hidden talents did the man possess? And how dangerous would it be for a young woman of no experience to be curious about them?

* * *

Sunday dawned as beautiful as it was cool. Church claimed some of the guests who rose early, including Mary—and Ormond. She loved to sing the hymns, having grown up with them as a child. Watching Ormond in the pew ahead of her, from what she could see he did not look at the hymnbook but knew the words. As the service ended, they left the church, each seeming to avoid the other.

Due to church and the scheduled hunt, breakfast was served late. A special air of excitement circulated among the men, as this would be the last hunt of the fox hunting season. Some women would ride to the starting point and return just for the exercise, but none would actually take part in the sport. And none rode astride like Mary, improper as that was deemed. For that reason, she expected to stay behind.

Mary planned to read. She'd already decided that at least for the rest of the morning she would begin the new novel she'd bought while shopping with her mother. Yes, some time in the library away from the men and Lord Ormond would be just what she needed. She could continue to avoid him until the time came for her to return home.

In anticipation of the quiet day, she chose a simple topaz-colored gown and pulled her hair back into a chignon at her nape. Her mother would have considered the outfit the picture of understated elegance. Mary thought it plain.

As she descended the stairs and entered the breakfast room, Mary experienced the high level of excitement among the men anticipating the hunt. She joined the guests piling their plates with food from the handsome carved sideboard. The offerings included eggs and ham, some mixed egg dishes, fresh-baked bread and fruit. It was a good country breakfast, and the air was filled with enticing smells. The hot tea was welcome, since Mary had another restless night.

Arthur Bywood was the first to greet her when she carried her plate to the table, his blue eyes sparkling as he asked her to join him. She slid into the chair next to him as he unleashed a long dialog about the events of the season ahead and the ball where they'd first met. Although Mary held little awe for that evening, she tried to be polite.

He smiled at her often as they ate. It was clear he saw her as a love interest, which Mary regretted. There was, however, little she could do about it.

Lord Ormond strode into the room a few minutes later, already dressed for the hunt, handsome in his black coat, white breeches and black boots. Mary's heartbeat accelerated. Her eyes fixed on a lock of dark hair that had fallen onto his forehead, making him look more the rake than ever and so unlike Arthur Bywood whose every hair was smoothed into place. Like a great thundercloud, he dominated the room, and she found herself wondering why it had to be him who stirred her blood.

* * *

Hugh's eyes were immediately drawn to Mary. He did not like the way young Bywood was drooling over her and felt a disturbing wave of jealousy course through him.

Jealousy was not an emotion he allowed himself. As a man with no lack of women willing to come to his bed, it was ridiculous to be jealous over attentions paid to one of the season's young innocents. But that kiss in the garden had drastically altered his classification of Mary Campbell as a typical ingénue. That reality and another sleepless night had him nearly snarling at Lord McGinnes, who had merely inquired if Hugh was looking forward to the hunt.

"Yes, of course," he replied, too curtly. "So glad the weather will be good."

Gathering his plate and asking for tea from the servants, Hugh joined McGinnes and some of the other men at one end of the long table, briefly nodding to Lady Mary and young Bywood as he passed. Engrossed in his emotional turmoil, he barely noticed Lady Harriet and one of the other young women move their plates to sit closer to him.

Fortunately, breakfast was a short endeavor. When it ended, the earl rose and reminded all the riders that the time for the hunt was approaching. Mary stood, wished Arthur Bywood good luck on his ride and left the room.

Hugh observed Mary's departure, aware that she would not be coming along on the hunt. For some reason he could not fathom, he wanted to see her before he left, so he exited the dining room to seek her out.

In his hasty departure, he nearly collided with Lady Huntingdon. Apologizing, he asked if she'd happened to see Lady Mary, since the empty hallway provided no clue. The countess gave him a knowing smile and directed him to the library. Hugh thanked her and strode off in that direction.

Opening the door to the library, he found Mary reading alone. Her head popped up from her book as he closed them inside, but she offered no greeting, waiting for him to speak instead.

"Lady Mary, the hunt is about to begin and I wanted to speak with you if you have a moment."

"Of course, my lord," she said. "What is it?" She set her book aside.

"I did not get to talk to you yesterday, and…I wanted to apologize for my behavior that first night." What he really wanted was to be with her again, but he was not about to say that.

Mary stared straight into his eyes, seemingly unmoved. "Think nothing of it, my lord. It's forgotten."

He paused, taken aback. He hadn't been sorry for their kiss and he'd hoped for a different reaction. "Right, then." He waited to see if she would say more. She just picked up her book as if to dismiss him. Miffed, he frowned and left.

He was not in a pleasant mood as he hurried after the men gathering for the hunt.

* * *

Mary read for most of the morning, trying not to dwell on Ormond's kiss, and was returning from a walk in the gardens with Lady Huntingdon when they heard shouts from the carriage lane in front of the manor. Exchanging a frantic look, the two hurried without a word toward the source of the voices. At the front of the estate they encountered a great commotion.

Several returning hunters reined in their horses, the animals' coats white with sweat and prancing in an agitated state. The men's faces showed their anxiety as one of them shouted, "A carriage! We must have a carriage!"

Women poured from the house, everyone curious to know what had happened.

"Ormond tried to save Arborn as he was falling from his horse," the man shouted upon seeing Lady Huntingdon. "It was on the treacherous jump near the river, my lady. 'Twas lucky Ormond was able to slow Arborn's fall, but in the process both ended up on the ground. They are lying there now, injured."

Lady Huntingdon's hand went to her throat, and Mary was similarly horrified. Experience had taught her how bad riding accidents could be, and fox hunting held some of the worst dangers. Only the best riders could make the jumps and quick turns. As a young child she'd been standing near the stables when they brought back her father's broken body. That memory had not faded with time.

She had learned to bind broken ribs and patch up damaged bodies, and so she spoke up to Lady Huntingdon. "I want to go. I may be able to help." She would not be left behind on this rescue effort.

"Oh, Mary," said her hostess. "Are you sure you wish to be a part of this?"

"Yes," she insisted. "I want to go with them."

A carriage was brought, and she began to climb in. One of the earl's men saw her and took umbrage. "See here, young lady. What are you about?"

She paused in her effort to reach the carriage seat. "I'm coming along. I might be able to help."

"You would only get in the way," the man scoffed. "We intend to bring Ormond and Arborn back here for the doctor."

"It is best if we first try to tend them where they are, good sir. I am coming."

Surprisingly, her confidence convinced him. "All right then, I'll not fight you if you are determined, but hurry!"

Mary had barely closed the door before the carriage raced off after the men on horseback.

When they arrived in the clearing, Mary saw Ormond on the ground leaning against a tree. Although conscious, he was holding his right side, obviously in pain. Lord Arborn, an older man with thinning gray hair, was stretched out on the ground next to him. His eyes were closed.

Mary ran to Arborn's side to check for a heartbeat and broken bones. His pulse was slow but steady, and his only injury appeared to be a deep gash on his forehead and the bump rising beneath it. The gash was bleeding profusely.

Ormond answered her unspoken question. "He hit his head as we fell."

Mary spoke urgently. "We need to get something cold on this. Is there a creek nearby where I can get some water?"

One of the young men tending the horses spoke up before Ormond could reply. "Aye, m'lady, just yonder is the river."

"Can you find a cloth to soak and bring to me?"

"Aye, m'lady, I'll see to it."

Mary hastily searched her surroundings for any plants that might be of use and found some chickweed near the edge of the clearing. Quickly she went to pick some, returned and dropped down next to Lord Arborn.

She glanced at Hugh and had to tear her eyes away from his sensual mouth, a mouth she very much wanted to kiss her again. "How are you doing?"

"I'm all right, Lady Mary. I think just my pride and ribs are injured."

"I can help with that," she said, crushing the chickweed in her hands.

"My pride or my ribs?"

"Your ribs, sir." Her mouth twitched as she tried not to laugh.

His dark eyes never left her. "I look forward to your efforts, Lady Mary."

Damn the man. He even had the temerity to stir her when he was injured. Her cheeks flushed with heat. The truth was she looked forward to touching him.

The hunt having ended with Lord Arborn's fall, the men who'd not yet returned to the estate milled about, waiting to assist them. One of them walked by and called out, "Good show, Ormond. Gallant of you."

"It was nothing," Ormond called back. "I was just there at the right time. And it will be worth it just to have my Lady Mary here tend my injuries."

Mary saw the other man wink at Ormond as he walked away. She decided to ignore that and concentrate on her more critical patient, since Ormond didn't appear to be suffering overmuch. Not if he could make jokes like that.

Having cleaned Lord Arborn's wound and staunched the bleeding, she applied the juice from the chickweed plant, took the cold cloths her young helper brought her and placed one atop the bump, which was quickly approaching the size of a goose egg. Then, satisfied she had done all that was possible, she motioned to the men standing nearby to take Lord Arborn to the carriage. Two of them lifted the unconscious older man and carried him to the waiting vehicle.

They returned for Ormond. After being helped to his feet, he slowly walked to the carriage and climbed in with their assistance. Mary went last.

Back at the estate, Mary followed the men into the house and gave instructions to the servants who hurried to make the injured men comfortable. Someone had already sent for a doctor. Since there was nothing much she could do for Lord Arborn, except to ask that they keep cold compresses on his head until the physician arrived, Mary went to check on Ormond.

He was lying in his bed, his shoulders propped up with pillows. Lord McGinnes stood near him, speaking in a low voice. A manservant near the door awaited instructions.

She knew it was not exactly proper for a young woman to be entering a man's bedchamber, but Mary had no intention of letting propriety get in the way of any help she could provide. She addressed her desire to Lord McGinnes: "I'd like to verify his ribs are not broken and bind them for support." To the manservant she said, "For that, I will need you to remove his shirt."

Lord McGinnes seemed disturbed by her words. "Lady Mary, perhaps you should wait for the doctor. Harris has called for him. Surely a young lady like yourself should not be attending this."

"It is not the first time I've seen an injured man's chest, Lord McGinnes," she replied, brushing off his concern. "Waiting for the doctor will only leave Ormond longer in pain."

The manservant helped Ormond doff his shirt, and then Mary leaned over him to carefully probe his ribs for any breaks. Lord McGinnes dropped into a chair before the fireplace to watch.

Mary moved her fingers gently over his skin, and as she did she saw Ormond wince.

"I'm sorry. I know it must hurt," she said as she tried to keep a medical mind. Touching his warm skin was turning out nothing like her other experiences helping injured men. His skin was like satin stretched over rock. Those muscles flexed each time her fingers moved across a rib, and the dark hair on his chest was fascinating, calling out for her to explore its texture. Suppressing her errant thoughts, she continued feeling for damage.

But her mind would not leave the thought of his naked chest. He bore several scars that dark chest hair did not hide. There was a short scar over his left nipple and a longer one down his right side just above his injured ribs. They appeared to Mary like healed wounds from a sword or a dagger. This was the muscled chest of a warrior, not that of a member of the nobility. Where had he been that he sustained such injuries?

She wondered but she did not ask. Continuing to probe his injured side she concluded, "I think you only have a few cracked ribs, Lord Ormond. They will be painful and you will be bruised, of course, but you were lucky. There are no full breaks that I can detect."

"That is good news indeed," he said, smiling.

Mary asked the manservant to find something to bind Ormond's ribs. The man left and returned shortly with a long sheet of linen, which at her direction he began tearing into strips.

"That will do nicely. We need only provide a brace," Mary offered by way of explanation.

She took a long strip, rolled it up and then began to unwind the cloth around Ormond's chest. The manservant held him away from the pillows, and each time Mary moved closer her heartbeat accelerated. The heat coming off his chest mingled with the smell of horse, sweat and man, and her mind began to reel. Forcing herself not to think about that masculine scent, the swells of that muscular chest or the dusting of dark hair tapering down toward his breeches, she willed herself to continue the process. The manservant stepped back.

Ormond's face reflected pain at the continued movement, though he smiled each time her head came close to his. Pretending not to notice, she wrapped the makeshift bandages around him several more times until she was certain his ribs were well supported. On the last wrap, her face passed very near to his.

Their eyes met. For a moment, neither moved. His proximity along with the warmth of his skin beneath her fingertips sent unexpected chills coursing through Mary, and for a moment it was as if they were back in the garden.

Lord McGinnes twisted in the chair behind her and shattered the spell. Mary lowered her gaze and returned to her work, tying off the bandage. She stood and backed away from the bed, gathering up the unused torn strips. The thought of her fingers stroking Ormond's naked chest would not leave her, however. She feared she could not look at him without blushing.

"Lady Mary, I can see you have this well in hand," said Lord McGinnes with admiration. He turned to Ormond and said, "I expect you'll be having dinner in your room."

"I think I might just do that," he replied to McGinnes, but his eyes were on Mary.

* * *

Hugh had experience with broken ribs and knew his were only bruised or cracked, but he would not have denied Mary the opportunity to touch him for the world. Hugh had tried to keep his lap covered with the remnants of his shirt so that she would not notice his arousal. In spite of the pain from his ribs, his body had responded the moment her cool fingers touched him. Added to this sweet torture, her gardenia scent set off tremors throughout his body. He could not seem to take his eyes off her face.

The urge to pull her onto the bed was nearly overwhelming. Watching her now, he thought she might be as affected as he, and that was pleasing.

"I think I could benefit from a brandy about now," he said to no one in particular.

McGinnes chuckled. "A most reasonable request, Ormond. Could use one myself."

Without being asked, the manservant hurried off to retrieve the drinks.

Mary glanced at Hugh, not commenting on his request for alcohol. "I'll see you get some willow bark tea with your dinner. It will help with the pain and the swelling."

"Thank you, Lady Mary. And thank you for tending my ribs. They feel better."

Lady Huntingdon entered. "Good afternoon, Lord McGinnes, Lady Mary. How's our hero?"

"Ah, Lady Huntingdon," McGinnes said. "You've missed a grand display of medical talent."

Lady Huntingdon raised her brow and shifted her gaze to Hugh and to the bandages covering his ribs. "You do seem to know what you're doing, Lady Mary. Where did you learn this?"

Mary stood quietly for a moment before she explained, "I have spent a great deal of time around horses and their riders. Given my father's accident, I took a particular interest in learning what might be helpful."

"Remarkable," Lady Huntingdon said. "Well done. Well done, indeed. Can I be of any assistance?"

Mary shook her head. "No, it is done—at least all I can do for him. Anything more will have to await the doctor."

Lady Huntingdon glanced at Hugh. "I'm thinking you are not minding this, Lord Ormond."

"There are compensations," he agreed with a wink. He saw color rise in Mary's cheeks.

The butler appeared, offering McGinnes and Ormond each a brandy from a small silver tray. "I understand you asked for this, my lords."

"Ah, Harris." Hugh sighed. "Efficient as ever. You have my gratitude. The pain is less for Lady Mary's ministrations, but this will certainly help." He accepted the offered glass.

* * *

Mary watched as, following on the heels of the butler, there came a group of men to congratulate Ormond on his efforts to rescue Lord Arborn, each recounting what they'd personally seen of the deed. Many accolades were tossed his way, and Mary could see true respect in the men's eyes. In response to Lord McGinnis's exclamation of "'Twas an amazing save!" came shouts of "Hear, hear!"

At last the men departed, and Mary gathered her things to follow Lady Huntingdon out as well. As the two neared the door, Mary paused and looked back. "Are you a hero then, Lord Ormond?"

Amusement crossed his face and in a soft voice he said, "No, but I don't mind if *you* think so."

Mary ignored the comment, especially as he grinned at Lady Huntingdon, who'd looked back when he made the remark. Then the earl's wife leaned back into the room and said, "I believe it's the only conclusion one can come to after all those men raved about your courageous dive, shielding Lord Arborn at great risk to yourself. It seems a miracle to me the old lord isn't dead, taking a fall like that."

Hugh said nothing. A faraway look crossed his face, one that Mary was hard pressed to decipher.

Lady Huntingdon wished Ormond well, thanked Mary and left. Mary followed, but just as she stepped through the open door, he said in a more serious voice, "Thank you, Lady Mary. Truly. It means much that you saw fit to tend me."

Not trusting herself to speak, Mary glanced back over her shoulder, nodded once and hurried away.

* * *

Doctor Everard arrived a short while later. He first examined Lord Arborn, who by this time was awake, before coming to see Hugh. The physician predicted a full recovery for Arborn but cautioned it would take some time to know for certain, as the man still exhibited signs of confusion. When the doctor finally assessed Hugh's ribs, he agreed they were likely only cracked and complimented the job Lady Mary had done.

"It seems I'm not as needed here as I would have been without the young lady."

"And glad I am of that," Hugh said, still reclining on the bed. "It's a bit unusual to find a young woman like that who is willing to minister to the injured. How many debutantes do *you* know can tend wounds?"

"I've not seen any," agreed the doctor, "but I understand this young woman is most unusual in many ways."

Hugh couldn't possibly agree more.

* * *

Mary did not return to visit Ormond as he took dinner in his room. Instead, she endured the attentions of Lord McGinnes and Arthur Bywood at the evening meal. Bywood retold the story of the hunt and the accident repeatedly, while the older man talked about his horses. Fortunately, Mary and the earl eventually found an issue to debate.

"You must see the value in all young women knowing more than a few herbal remedies, Lord Huntingdon."

"Certainly you were proof of that today, Lady Mary," her host replied. "But do you really think many young women would want to add those skills to the list of talents they must already acquire to hope for a husband?"

"No, I don't expect they would. But my point is they should have the choice."

The earl smiled, fondly shaking his head. "I daresay, Lady Mary, you are one of the most interesting young women my wife and I know. I don't think I need tell you that you are a lot like your father. He always had a cause, and that cause was usually ahead of its time. I do so miss the man." Huntingdon stared off into the distance. "He was one of my closest friends."

Unbidden to Mary's mind came her earliest memory, a tall man with sandy hair and green eyes, smiling at her as he lifted her onto her first horse. She had grown up without knowing the man she was told she so resembled, and without the painting of him hanging in the library at Campbell Manor she would never have been able to recall his features. Looking at it always brought tears to her eyes. She could not remember her father's voice any longer, though, and that saddened her.

"I miss him, too." *I miss the family I never had.*

When dinner was finished and the men rose to take their brandy in the library, Mary thought of Ormond and was tempted to look in on him. In her mind she saw him bare-chested again, lying against the pillows, and decided it would be best if she didn't. But, unscrupulous rake or not, when she went to bed it was with some regret she had not stopped in to see him.

* * *

The next morning saw an exodus. Mary watched the guests depart as she stood chatting with Lady Huntingdon in front of the estate. Ormond came out slowly, a servant carrying his luggage, which was loaded onto a carriage provided by the earl since Ormond could not ride his horse. It was tied on behind.

"Are you returning to London, Lord Ormond?" Lady Huntingdon asked cheerfully.

"Yes," he replied. "I have some pressing business. Thank you for a…most eventful weekend."

"You're teasing me, Lord Ormond," his hostess answered with a smile. "You were the one who provided the entertainment."

He chuckled good-naturedly. "I suppose I did."

Mary couldn't help but admire his roguish smile and easy manner, for she believed they masked the pain he must still be feeling from his injured ribs. His dark eyes glimmered with amusement as he bantered with Lord Huntingdon's wife, then at last he carefully climbed into the waiting carriage. Once inside, he popped his head out through the window.

Mary smiled. "I wish you a quick recovery, my lord."

"Thank you," he replied, "for your kind attention to an injured man. And for the good conversation. I enjoyed it." He said the last with a wolfish smile, grinning like a boy who'd just stolen a fresh baked tart from the kitchen. Then he was gone, leaving Mary alone with her thoughts.

Almost immediately, she experienced a hollow feeling that displeased her. She did not want to miss the man. She *would* not miss the man. He was a dissolute and a rake, and she reminded herself, dangerous.

While waiting for her carriage, she walked alone in the garden…and found herself drawn to the alcove where he'd kissed her. The feel of his lips, his scent—that rich, masculine smell that was his alone—returned to haunt her. Visions of his smile and his long fingers upon the piano keys flitted through her mind. Though the man aggravated her, she wanted to be wrapped in his arms again.

This has to stop! She was thinking about him overmuch. If she didn't distance herself, she really would be in danger of joining the list of women who found the Marquess of Ormond irresistible. That would never do.

Mary walked idly back to the mansion, her thoughts drifting toward what she hoped lay ahead. *Paris.* During her last trip to France, she had memorized the letter on the minister's desk because it contained a name she'd once heard her uncle mention to an associate. He did not know she'd overheard him when he said, "This is the work of the Nighthawk, and we can be glad of it."

Who was the Nighthawk? She had wondered at the time. Seeing the same word in French in the note open on the desk next to her, the coincidence was too great. She'd memorized what she'd read and provided the exact language to her uncle, certain it must be important. He had thanked her. And although he'd scolded her for getting involved, she could see he was pleased. And that was before she'd seen the article in the *Times*.

Her uncle had been a special ambassador for the Prince Regent for many years, but after Paris she'd wondered if he was involved in more than she realized. Clearly the name Nighthawk was a code for someone, someone the *Times* thought had helped defeat Napoleon. Mary was curious and intrigued, which gave her all the more reason to return to Paris. About that she must soon have a conversation with her uncle.

As it turned out, she did not have to wait long.

Chapter 7

It happened that very afternoon; her uncle called for Mary. To her delight, instead of returning to Campbell Manor, she was to return with him to London. That would allow them time to discuss Paris, and she could visit with Elizabeth, two things she very much wanted to do.

After saying her goodbyes to the earl and his wife, Mary climbed into the carriage and soon she and her uncle were bumping along over the country roads.

"How was your first house party, Mary?"

She gazed fixedly out the carriage window at the passing countryside and settled on, "It was certainly not dull."

"While you were saying goodbye to Lady Huntingdon, the earl told me of your ministrations to Lord Arborn and Lord Ormond after the fox hunting accident. The consensus was that you were quite brilliant."

Mary smiled, amused. "Is that what they think? Because a woman can treat a few injuries she is suddenly brilliant? I only did what I have done many times before. Men fall from horses. Bumps on heads and damaged bones are the usual consequences, are they not? Any one of them could have done what I did."

"You say that as if any woman your age *would* have. You are quite resourceful and calm in times of crisis, my girl. You must realize how unusual that is."

Mary sighed. "They probably thought me odd."

He grinned and shook his head. "Unusual yes, but odd? I think not. I saw respect in their eyes. There are worse things in life than caring about more than pretty dresses and dances."

That night, after a quiet dinner at his town house, Lord Baynes and his niece retired to the library for a glass of port. It was here that Adrian raised the subject of his next trip.

"Mary, I will be returning to Paris in a few weeks."

"I assumed you would," she remarked. "And I was hoping you might take me with you."

"I've been considering it, but I hate for you to miss so much of your first season."

Mary made a face, which almost made him laugh. "Uncle, you know how little I would mind."

"Yes, I am aware of your feelings on the matter, but it is important for your future."

"Possibly Paris could be *more* important."

Adrian could see the season held little interest for his niece. "I'll agree you were most helpful on my last trip, but there is now greater danger." He still wasn't convinced it was a wise idea to bring her along.

"What is it, Uncle?"

"If I tell you, Mary, we must keep this between us. It is a matter of the Crown's secrets."

"Yes, of course," she said, her eyes imploring him to trust her. He could think of few people he trusted more.

His gaze fixed on the fire crackling before them. At last he made up his mind.

"Our government has a French agent in Paris who is close to the new Bourbon government. The note from the French minister's desk you so well remembered has given us cause to wonder about that agent. Whoever wrote the note has provided the French with information concerning Britain's activities. I am telling you this so that you are aware our business in Paris is now more dangerous. We do not know which direction this will take. I cannot tell you more, either. If you come, I would ask only that you listen with your excellent French, watch with your eyes open, and stay out of harm's way. Even the streets have become more dangerous in the past few months."

"Of course I will listen and I will stay out of danger," she said at once. Then: "You never told me who the Nighthawk is, though all London has been gossiping since that article."

"No," he agreed. "I have not. I thought it best you did not know."

She looked puzzled then hurt. "You can trust me, Uncle. Is this agent you speak of the Nighthawk?"

"No. He is not."

When he said nothing more, Mary persisted in her pleas. "Can you at least tell me *something* about the Nighthawk? It's unkind to leave me wholly in the dark when I've been so helpful to you and the cause."

Adrian considered what might appease her. At last he said, "Well, he's the subject of legend—a French legend, actually. He is a wraithlike figure who supposedly robbed Napoleon of his most guarded secrets but was never caught. Then again, perhaps he is just the deposed emperor's excuse. A figment of the imagination."

"I cannot believe that. He must be real," Mary replied. "And if he is real, I would very much like to meet such a courageous figure. The very idea he could sneak under Boney's defenses in order to help bring him down? A masked creature of the night, a thief of secrets… How wild, how daring, how *romantic!*"

Seeing his niece's eyes light up, Adrian was anxious to change the subject. "Enough. It is best not to speak of him, especially not in France. Which brings me back to the important question: Would you feel comfortable with the role I described for you while I am in Paris?"

She grinned. "Of course, Uncle. I said I could do that. I just want to help, and I find the idea of being involved in the Crown's business exciting."

"Good," said Adrian. He was pleased she was accepting a limited and well-defined role.

"Uncle," she said after a moment. "Thank you for letting me go with you."

He sighed. "I'm not entirely comfortable with the idea, Mary, but do I know you want to be useful. You never shy from danger. In fact, that is my fear."

His niece got a strange look on her face. "Uncle? You should know Lord Ormond tried to talk me into staying home, though I cannot imagine what business it is of his."

Adrian let out another breath. "Actually, Ormond will be working with me in this next matter. He is aware of my past work for the Crown and it is not unreasonable he would wish you to stay behind—for your safety. However, if the Prince Regent agrees you should go, you will come with me. I will talk to him."

He could see the relief on her face as she stretched to kiss his cheek. "Thank you, Uncle."

His niece stood to leave. As she walked to the door, Adrian reminded himself of another matter he wanted her agreement on; he had promised her mother he would make this attempt. "Oh, and Mary? You *will* have time to attend the next ball before we go."

She let out a gasp and with pleading eyes asked, "Must I endure another of those so soon?"

"Yes, you must," he said, his voice firm. "The Countess Claremont's ball is the height of the season. Even those who avoid balls will attend. Think of it as an education, practice in dealing with members of society in a *normal* way. That's something you still need to learn, no matter how you decide to act in the future. And it'll give you something to talk about in Paris."

"You might be right," Mary agreed with a sigh. "Of course I will go if you ask, Uncle."

* * *

She spent the next few days in London at her uncle's town house, and during that time, several gentlemen callers, all young men who had attended her first ball, sought Mary out. Arthur Bywood was one of them.

Mary enjoyed seeing him, actually. His smiling face and blue eyes were now quite familiar, and his conversation was less objectionable than most, but she could not imagine him as a husband. He was more like a brother.

She thought about Hugh Redgrave, but she was also unsurprised he did not call. Rakes didn't pay visits on young debutantes. At least, not through the front door. They preferred stalking women through gardens. Each time she thought of their encounter in the Huntingdon garden and remembered their kiss, she found she could still taste him, still feel his lips on hers. Sighing, she vowed to let him go. He would never call. Nor should he.

The callers came and went in a blur of activity that left Mary feeling exhausted and Lord Baynes's parlor smelling like a flower shop as each young man brought a new arrangement of blooms. Though she loved their scent, Mary discovered the strong odor of lilies gave her a headache and requested they be moved to another room.

Fatiguing or not, the whirl of suitors was a small price to pay for some time in London with Elizabeth. Finally, one afternoon as they took tea in the parlor, Mary told her friend about the unexpected events that had taken place at the house party.

Lizzy listened attentively as she captured a stray lock of copper-colored hair with a pin. "You were quite brave to have played nurse to those injured men. I could not have done it. And to think Lord Ormond was sitting before you with nothing on! It was scandalous. Only you would have taken on such a task and known what to do."

"He only had a bare chest, Lizzy," Mary clarified. "But still, he wasn't like the others I've tended. It was different with him. I had trouble keeping my mind on the matter at hand. His body is hard and powerful, and his chest bears scars from cuts with a blade like one who has been wounded in battle. My own thoughts *were* scandalous. I wanted to touch him, to run my hands over that hair on his chest, over his scars. It was all I could do to concentrate on his damaged ribs. I think I'm losing my mind."

"You are blushing, Mary!" Lizzy said with a laugh. "And talking about all you felt…well, it makes my skin tingle, too. There is definitely something between you. It's too bad it couldn't be Arthur Bywood instead, though. He may only be a younger son of an earl but he's in love with you, I am sure of it. Didn't he bring you that enormous bouquet of flowers staring me in the face?"

Mary casually surveyed the flowers dominating the room. They were beautiful, and she did love the shades of purple and pink. "Yes, he did."

Lizzy looked smug. "I said you would be a success, Mary. And he is charming, you must agree."

She nodded. "I suppose he is. Very likeable and all, but I keep seeing him as the brother I never had."

"Oh, dear," Lizzy said. "He would be quite disappointed to hear you say that. But it's nice to have admirers."

"I suppose it is, though I feel badly he is wasting his time with me."

"Surely he does not see it that way. He likes your company. And, he is getting much practice in courting. That, too, is part of the season."

It was so like Elizabeth to find something good in every circumstance, and Mary appreciated her friend more and more. But when Mary told her about Lord Ormond's garden kiss, Lizzy looked more thoughtful than ever.

"Mary, this attraction to Lord Ormond…do you think it is serious? He is, after all, a decade older than you, and experienced. Remember his reputation?"

"No. I mean, yes. Oh, I don't know. I have no desire to be one of his many women, of course. At times he frightens me, but I think that's because when he is near me I lose my convictions. All of them. I know it sounds awful, but it's true."

"Are you worried about losing your heart?" Lizzy asked.

Mary chewed on her lower lip. "I might be."

Lizzy's eyes were wide. "What is it about him that attracts you so?"

"He is not the man I first imagined him to be, Lizzy. He's domineering, yes, and sometimes overwhelming. But he is also brave and kind. And he seems all right with my…ideas. When he touches me, he is…tender, almost protective. And I find I desire his touch more and more. His kiss…well, it was wonderful. I know it sounds wicked, but there it is. And did you know he plays music? Beautiful music."

"He does?"

"Yes, on the piano. He played for us one evening and it was extraordinary. He has a charming laugh, too. And there is something mysterious about him that draws me. It is as if he has depths that need exploring. He is anything but boring."

"He certainly seems to stir your passion," Lizzy laughed.

"Oh, yes, he does that. But despite his kiss, he's been honorable. And Lady Huntingdon made me think he may not be the rake that people believe. At least, not always."

"I have heard the same about his friend Mr. Lambeth."

Mary fought surprise. "You've been asking about him?"

Elizabeth blushed. "Well, yes. I asked my sister Caroline. She confirmed what I remembered, that he was kind and thoughtful when she knew him in her first season. Of course, it was years ago. Since then he has built a reputation along with his friend Ormond, one that quite contradicts the rest. Still, Caroline thought he might be reformable. If only I could attract his attention the way you attracted Lord Ormond's."

"Lizzy, you may not want the kind of attention I'm getting. You see, I don't seem to be able to resist the rogue. Still, you are beautiful and have so much to offer. How could this Mr. Lambeth not notice you?"

"You have a point about the attention, and that does worry me. About you, I mean. Lord Ormond could be dangerous, Mary, even if he's not what people think. Particularly if you are seen alone with him. It could ruin you. You must be careful. And then of course he might be exactly what people think. A rake might trifle with a young woman such as you."

"I will…try to be careful," Mary agreed. "Thankfully, his own behavior has put me off on occasion. His arrogance has helped a number of times to dampen my enthusiasm for him."

"So you are safe?"

Mary was not at all sure she was safe when it came to this man with cavern-deep eyes and strong arms that wrapped around her like a vise, arms she did not want to leave. She rolled her eyes. "Yes, I would say I was safe, Lizzy. Like a rabbit staring into the eyes of a wolf."

* * *

The next day Elizabeth talked Mary into attending a morning garden party featuring a breakfast out of doors in the fresh air with several young men and women from the first ball and from the

Huntingdon house party. Mary actually enjoyed herself, though Lord Ormond did not attend. His absence was disappointing if predictable. She reminded herself that it wasn't as if such a man would participate in the usual escapades of men seeking mates, especially if he was nursing wounded ribs. She supposed rakes had their own parties, too, and she was not at all certain she wanted to know anything about them.

Being with Elizabeth was great fun, and Mary enjoyed the tasty food on which they dined. Afterward, she accompanied Elizabeth and her oldest sister Caroline on a shopping excursion. Caroline had a special shop she wanted to show the younger women, though she saved it till last.

A redhead like Elizabeth's other sisters, Caroline was grinning by the time they reached their destination, which made Mary wonder just what was sold here. The sign hanging over the door told them it was a place offering ladies' undergarments, but she couldn't see much through the bow window. It was one of many new shops springing up on Brook Street close to the well-traveled Bond Street.

As they entered through a paned glass door, a bell chimed announcing their arrival. Mary and Elizabeth stepped onto the dark wood floor and surveyed piles of sheer fabric and lace laid out on long wooden trestle tables. There were many bolts of fabric, but also silk undergarments on display. Mary's eyes grew wide when she realized how little they would cover. The transparent underthings captivated her.

"These are certainly different than the plain shifts I wear," Lizzy whispered into her ear.

Mary ran her fingers under a diaphanous cream-colored chemise with small bows at the top. "I can see my fingers through this one. It would leave little to the imagination."

"I believe that is the idea, Mary," said Caroline.

Lizzy picked up one of the chemises, fingering the fabric. "The flower embroidery on this is unusual, and the detail very fine."

Caroline joined her sister to look. "They are from France and so terribly exciting for a husband. French women certainly know how to entice a man. I'm sure one day you both will want to have several of the lacy things."

Mary picked up a chemise with delicate lace at the top. Her breasts tightened in anticipation as she considered how the sheer silk would feel against her skin and wondered what a man like Lord Ormond would think if he could see her in it.

Of course, that would never happen. So why wait for the approval of such a man? "I like them very much and think I will not wait for such a day."

Surprisingly, Elizabeth agreed. When the proprietress told them she had several samples for sale, they decided to buy those and also order more. Elizabeth was fondest of a pale blue garment Mary thought beautifully complemented her friend's eyes. Mary's favorite was the chemise she first fondled.

"It will make me feel positively wicked!" Lizzy exclaimed, coming close to giggling.

"I suppose it's all right you have some, but best not let Mother see them for a while," said her older sister.

With their outrageous purchases tucked under their arms, the three young women went in search of a teashop. Finally they were seated, and with cups of the steaming liquid in their hands Caroline recalled for them stories of her early marriage demonstrating the value of see-through chemises. Breaking off the corner of her scone, she said, "No man can resist seeing his wife through one of them. As hard as my George labors over his Parliamentary journals, I have found it easy to distract him when I'm wearing one of these. There is no doubt they have been responsible for the quick arrival of our three children."

While Mary was not the type to giggle, she did smile broadly at the thought of how Lord Ormond's face might look upon seeing her in her new purchase. The idea made her tingle in many different places. At the same time, however, it shocked her. She decided to keep the thought to herself.

* * *

It had been several days since Hugh arrived back at his family's country estate to convalesce. Sitting around was anathema to him, and so finally he decided a short ride would be just the thing to confirm, as he suspected, that his ribs had not been badly cracked and were healing well. He set off quickly, before his mother could object.

When his horse wandered off course, he did not redirect its path and soon found himself near Campbell Manor. It was a greater distance than he had planned to ride, he admitted to himself, though in the back of his head was a fear that it had been his destination all along. The thought only got stronger when he came upon the object of his reconnaissance. She was galloping along the river on her imposing black stallion.

Hidden by the grove of oak trees, he watched. Mary had never seemed more beautiful to him, her golden hair streaming out behind her, and she laughed wildly with the apparent joy of simply riding her horse. It was a sight he'd never tire of. Her zest for life captivated him, and he realized he wanted her not just in his bed but in his life.

Good God. He was losing a battle to keep himself unmoved by the girl. What was he going to do with her in Paris? It was not a good idea for a young innocent to be there, not now. Not with all the dangers that might arise. He would have to work harder to persuade her uncle to see reason.

And, perhaps he would attend the next ball to speak to Lady Mary himself.

Chapter 8

Rain pelted the windows of Adrian's study. It had been pouring in London all day, and now the drops sounded like hailstones hitting the glass, making him exceedingly glad to be sitting by the fire in the comfort of his overstuffed chair. He set down his glass of brandy just as Withers came to the door.

"My lord, Lord Ormond has just arrived. He apologizes for not having an appointment but was hoping you might have a few minutes for him."

"Of course, Withers. Please show him in."

"Very good, my lord." The butler dipped his head and departed.

It was not an unexpected visit. Adrian had been to see the Prince Regent a few days before, and since Mary had told him the young lord was opposed to her going to Paris, he had expected the man to seek an audience. "Good afternoon, Lord Ormond. Come in and warm yourself by the fire."

His guest raked rain from his hair as Adrian handed him a glass. "Thank you, Lord Baynes, a brandy is most welcome. It's dreadful out there today. And, please...call me Ormond. Since we will be working closely together, I fear 'Lord Ormond' an unnecessary lot of words."

"Of course, Ormond. Please sit down."

The two men retired to the wing chairs in front of the crackling fire with their drinks, and after a moment Adrian inquired, "How are the ribs?"

"Much better, thank you. I suspect they were only a bit damaged. I can even ride again."

"My niece told me about your heroic act. Is Arborn recovered?"

A look of surprise crossed the young lord's face. "Your niece is too generous. It wasn't really bravery. I was merely in the right place as he started to fall. And, yes, Arborn seems to have recovered."

"Perhaps he should leave the foxes to younger men," Adrian suggested. "I myself gave up the hunt years ago."

"I'll let you tell him that." Ormond said with a chuckle. "I think he expects to ride the hunt forever."

The two men were silent again, each nursing his drink, until at last Adrian's visitor appeared to take a deep breath as if gathering his strength. His face became serious and his tone grim. "Lord Baynes, I want to talk to you about our troubling issues in France and about your upcoming trip."

"Of course," Adrian replied. But he wasn't going to make this easy. "What concerns you?"

Ormond began by sharing with him some further information he'd received concerning their French agent and the general suspicion that he might be passing England's intelligence to France.

"One of those that you folks call a double agent…." Adrian sighed, displeased.

"Possibly," Ormond said soberly. "The information you brought back from your last trip is truly damning. The descriptions of the British troop placements are something he would have access to in his work for France, though the detail is rather surprising. Our reports also suggest certain factions are looking for the Nighthawk."

"I wondered about that," replied Adrian. "I suppose it will make this next trip to Paris more than a little interesting. Will you still be joining me?"

The young lord set down his drink and ran his fingers through his hair. Letting out a long, slow breath he said, "Yes, I think I must. To sort this out, and to be available to you should the need arise. I also have some other business there that demands my attention. But I will come later, after you arrive. I've sent a message to our chief agent in Paris, Sir Martin Powell, to expect me. He's a good friend and can be counted on. Besides, I have a feeling we're going to need his help."

"I am glad you will be coming," Adrian conceded. "Your advice is welcome. I know Louis well, but some of the intrigues in his court and the men coming to meet with him are more in your realm of experience. Does our French agent in Paris know who you are?"

Ormond seemed to consider before he said, "No, not as far as I know. At least, we've never met. And I intend to tread carefully with him."

Adrian couldn't agree more. "Yes, it is certainly a time for caution. I imagine there are things it is better we keep unknown, in particular your past work for the Crown."

Ormond nodded. "But there is another matter I was hoping to discuss with you. I believe your niece desires to go with you. Since there are now added risks, I was thinking perhaps you might consider leaving her in London."

Adrian thought he detected more than just solicitude for Mary's safety in the other man's voice, which he found most interesting. "Yes, I'm aware of your thoughts on that subject. Mary has told me of your…conversations. But it's been decided. She will go."

Hugh frowned. "Does the Prince Regent know?"

"He does. In fact, it was Prinny who approved Mary's participation. I guess I never told you, but it was Mary who retrieved the information from the French minister's desk. The

Prince Regent knows, which is one reason he believed it a good idea to include her. He thought she might be helpful again. He remembered her and called her 'the Swan.' That was the picture in his mind when she was first presented at court."

* * *

Listening to Lord Baynes, Hugh felt his heart sink. *Of course a swan.* A vision of Mary gliding across the dance floor in white satin came to mind, though he preferred to picture her galloping across a green field like a fierce Valkyrie. Regardless, he was not surprised Prinny had been taken by her.

"Is Lady Mary truly aware of the danger? After all, she's not been trained, and Paris is somewhat unstable just now. If she's been told all that—"

"No," Lord Baynes interrupted, "she doesn't know all we're engaged in. She's only aware there is an issue regarding an agent. Nothing more."

Hugh loathed the danger Paris might present for Mary. He had an unexpected desire to protect her. She should be safe at Campbell Manor, not roaming the streets of Paris. And he did not need the distraction.

"Does she know of *my* work?"

"No," Lord Baynes said, his countenance serious. "I didn't think she needed to be burdened with those details, not even the few I know. But she does know you will be working with me at some point. Oh, and she has recently been asking about the Nighthawk." With an amused look he added, "It seems she admires him—as does much of London thanks to the *Times.* I told her what everyone believes they know about the French legend."

"I can only hope she does not learn more." Hugh was reluctant to accept the fact that he could not persuade Lord Baynes to keep

Mary in England, but with the Regent giving sanction, he gave up trying.

Lord Baynes seemed to sense his hesitation and said, "I agree we will have to try and limit her involvement, Ormond, and hope her fondness for adventure does not become a problem."

They could hope.

The older man's intense perusal made Hugh uncomfortable, and eventually Lord Baynes spoke. His question was entirely unexpected. "Ormond, do you care for Mary?"

Hugh was not prepared to answer, not even to himself. He took a moment to breathe before saying, "I'm just concerned that an untrained young woman is involved. We have to assume they are alerted to our suspicions. If they track the information back to that letter, that day with Mary in the minister's office—"

"Yes, it is a concern," Lord Baynes agreed. "Mary's wellbeing and safety are paramount. But we both have orders."

"Indeed." Hugh wasn't sure what else there was to say.

Lord Baynes suddenly shook his head, as if remembering something unpleasant. After a moment he leaned forward and said conspiratorially, "There is another matter concerning the Prince Regent and his approval of my niece."

"Oh?" asked Hugh, frowning. What could be worse than the danger they were putting her in?

Mary's uncle sat back and gazed into the fire. "As I said before, when I reminded him of her and that day she was presented at court, he smiled and said he remembered the Swan quite well. But the look in his eyes told me he might have more interest in her than just as a help to my work. I am a bit worried that he may call for her when he returns from seeing about plans for that Pavilion he so adores. Mary would be horrified if he were to present her with an invitation to become one of his mistresses, an invitation few women have been able to turn down."

Hugh felt his face drain of blood, but there was little he could do or say. Why should he care whether Mary became this Prince Regent's mistress? But he did care.

Lord Baynes continued: "Of course, if she were to marry, Prinny might leave her be. Though it's possible he would pursue a married woman, and certainly he has before, there are other young women to choose from who are not so encumbered."

Hugh's throat was dry. "Have you said anything to Mary?"

"No, and I think I won't, at least for the present. She does not need to be worried about the schemes of the Prince Regent. But this is one reason I am glad she will be coming with me to Paris. I would not leave her in England alone with him."

Chapter 9

One social event remained before Mary and her uncle were to leave: the next ball of the season. As Lord Baynes had informed her, it was to be held at the grand home of the Dowager Countess Claremont.

Mary remembered the countess's home from her past visits. It had the most beautiful great room in all of London, one that would provide a most excellent ballroom. The floor was white marble. Tall columns stood at one end, and six long crystal chandeliers hung from the vaulted ceiling. Mirrors covered one wall. She could only imagine them reflecting a thousand candles. It was a perfect stage for an extravagant affair.

Thankfully, she would be going with her uncle and Lizzy.

"Milly, I am late now! Hurry and help me dress or Elizabeth will be here and I will still be in my chemise."

"And I'm thinking it's a shameless chemise you'll be wearing this night, mistress."

Mary grinned. She knew the servant was teasing her. The two of them had enjoyed a fond relationship for the last several years.

The young lady's maid had spent more time than usual on Mary's hair. The devoted girl wanted Mary's crown of curls to be special this night, and so with considerable care she had drawn them up into soft layers leaving a few golden wisps curled at her temples. The gown Mary intended to wear was ivory, a color appropriate for a young, unmarried woman, but the silk was not just any ivory color. It shimmered with golden highlights. A wide, garnet-colored ribbon was tied at the garment's high waist, and small flowers at the hem were embroidered in the same color. She would wear dark red slippers on her feet, which was another expression of her own taste, as few would dare choose slippers of such a strong color. But they were Mary's favorite.

"You look like a princess tonight, Lady Mary," Milly exclaimed, standing back and giving her mistress an admiring perusal. She had been determined to have her look the part of a most elegant ingénue, even if Mary's heart wasn't in it.

"And you are too kind for words, Milly."

Just as Mary finished dressing, Elizabeth arrived. Her friend wore a white gown with a pale blue sash a shade lighter than her eyes, and with her copper curls worn up save a few left dangling over her nape she was radiant. Mary took in her friend's unusual finery and found herself willing to concede the balls did have some purpose, since they gave Lizzy such joy.

Her friend drew near and whispered, "I am wearing my new French silk chemise, Mary. The blue one. And it *does* make me feel wicked!"

Mary grinned. "You'll not be alone, Lizzy. I'm wearing one of my new ones, too. I do believe I shocked dear Milly. It's a bit like having nothing on, don't you think?"

"I do!" Lizzy's eyes were twinkling.

"I thought it would help me get into the frame of mind for Paris."

Lizzy whirled in a circle, her skirts held in her spread hands. "I've never been to Paris, Mary, but I feel French tonight."

After a moment, Mary saw her friend's eyes studying her. "What is it, Lizzy?"

"You are quite beautiful tonight, Mary. And there is an excitement in your eyes I haven't seen before."

Mary dismissed that. "Whatever can you mean? We're just going to a dreadful matchmaking event, one of the many that make up a season."

Lizzy shook her head. "I think it's more than that. You actually look excited to be going. Could it be that you're looking forward to seeing someone special?"

Mary scoffed, fighting off a blush. She'd been doing her best to suppress her interest in a certain rake about town. "Well, there are *very* few I would consider interesting. If someone like the Nighthawk were to appear—"

"That old French legend?" Lizzy shook her head. "I am talking about *real* men, Mary, and you know it. What about Lord Ormond? Could it be that you are thinking he will be there?"

"I have no idea if he will attend," Mary said shortly.

Before her friend could respond, Milly appeared in the doorway, having come and gone from downstairs. "Mistress, Lord Baynes is asking for you. He's ready to depart."

The girls hurried to the stairs so as not to keep their escort waiting.

When her uncle saw Mary descending the stairs, he smiled. "You might want to bring that gown to Paris, Mary. I think it would draw many compliments."

"I'm so glad you like it, Uncle. I'll ask Milly to pack it."

Her uncle's eyes took in her friend next. "You look quite lovely tonight, too, Miss St. Clair. Quite lovely. I'll have the two most beautiful women in London by my side."

* * *

They arrived at the Claremont Estate a short time later, and as they disembarked from their carriage Mary saw a large grin cross her uncle's face.

"It is not every man who can attend the ball with two beauties in tow," he announced. "I'm feeling very favored tonight."

Mary laughed. "Your diplomatic skills are showing, Uncle. But consider this: It isn't every lady who finds herself on the arm of such an elegant man. Your attire is quite dashing. That waistcoat and your steel-gray hair make me think of a silver fox." Mary leaned into him and whispered, "Best beware of the ladies this evening."

Lord Baynes clutched her arm tighter and whispered back, "You have just puffed up this diplomat's pride and given me a most wonderful gift. Thank you."

To her surprise, Mary immediately spotted Ormond's tall dark form upon entering the ballroom. He stood just across the room with Lady Hearnshaw at his side, her gloved hand on his sleeve. The beautiful brunette was wearing a gold brocade gown with a bodice cut low to display her ample bosom. Mary barely choked down her disappointment. She had never seen Ormond so close to another woman, and though she could not hear the conversation, the way Lady Hearnshaw leaned into him brought his reputation to mind.

"It looks as if Lord Ormond is occupied this evening," she whispered to Lizzy.

"Well, she *is* his mistress, Mary."

Then why was he kissing me? "I should have remembered that...."

Lord Baynes heard their comments, and his eyes followed Mary's gaze. "Ahem. Why don't I see about some champagne?" he asked.

Mary was relieved to move on to something else, and champagne sounded perfect. "That would be wonderful, Uncle."

* * *

"Dance with me, darling," Amanda Hearnshaw purred at Hugh. "You look so handsome in your black tail coat, and it has been too long."

Seeing Lady Mary across the ballroom, Hugh frowned and tactfully removed Amanda's hand from his sleeve. He didn't want to start again with her. Though he considered Amanda a friend and had enjoyed her company for a while, she no longer held the allure she once did.

"Dear lady," he said in a kind voice, "I am thankful for the invitation, but I don't think I'll be dancing tonight." He hoped she knew he didn't only mean on the dance floor.

It seemed she did. But the fire in her eyes belied the calm in her voice. "If you insist, my lord."

She was a beautiful woman, Hugh admitted to himself. She would have her choice of many men. She'd do fine without him.

Amanda walked away and joined a group of friends. Relieved, Hugh turned back and saw Lambeth a short distance away, his gaze reaching across the room to Mary and a young redhead standing with her. Tonight the blonde minx was otherworldly, a golden glimmer calling to him like a siren.

"That could have been better timed," Lambeth said, approaching him with a smile. Apparently he'd seen Lady Hearnshaw's advance and connected it with Mary's entrance. Across the room, Mary turned away.

"Perhaps." Hugh shrugged. He would not apologize for his past.

* * *

Standing at the edge of the dance floor, Mary saw someone headed in her direction. His eager expression caused her whisper to Elizabeth, "Lizzy, Arthur Bywood is coming toward us. I think I shall dance with him tonight. At least *he* does not have another woman draped over him."

Mr. Bywood appeared, greeting both girls and expressing his good fortune at finding them so early in the evening. Immediately he asked Mary to dance. She was eager to accept but begged him to wait for her uncle to return with their champagne.

They did not have long to wait. Her uncle rejoined the girls quickly, a servant in tow with a tray of bubbling champagne. Each of the girls and Mr. Bywood took a glass. Once they had drunk their fill, Mary joined Arthur Bywood on the floor. Her uncle and Elizabeth followed.

Her partner's enthusiasm was open and vibrant. "You are simply dazzling tonight, Lady Mary."

"And you are very kind, Mr. Bywood."

Mary loved to dance. With a rising desire to put Ormond out of her mind and enjoy herself, she smiled at the eager young man. She could get through another ball. One last ball. And she could avoid Lord Ormond and his many female admirers.

* * *

Adrian twirled Elizabeth St. Clair about the dance floor, enjoying himself thoroughly. He had not been to a ball in London in some time.

"You are an excellent dancer, Lord Baynes."

"Why thank you, my dear. I must say I am having a rousing good time."

Two gentlemen stood at the edge of the dance floor on the far side of the room, and Elizabeth's next comment was about them, surprising Adrian—but only a little. "Sir, do you know Lord Ormond and the gentleman standing with him?"

Without appearing to look, Adrian glanced in their direction. "Yes, I know them. Ormond is with Griffen Lambeth, his good friend."

"Can you introduce me?"

"I'd be happy to make the introduction, Miss St. Clair, though I cannot leave you alone with them or the gossips will buzz."

He did just as he promised. When the music stopped, Adrian casually escorted Elizabeth from the dance floor as if unaware the two men were standing in his path and it appeared they inadvertently arrived together at the spot. Adrian paused to greet the two men and introduced Elizabeth at the same time.

Lambeth smiled at her, obvious interest in his eyes. "I think I know your older sisters Caroline and Charlotte, Miss St. Clair. You look so much like them. Do they not also have your lovely red hair?"

Elizabeth blushed. "Why, thank you, sir. Yes, they do."

"How are they?"

"Very well. Both are happily married now."

Lambeth and Ormond exchanged a knowing look. Adrian did not miss it, and realizing the subject of marriage had turned the young men's interest to concern, he decided an exit was in short order. "Well, gentlemen, we must bid you an enjoyable evening. We're off to find refreshment."

The two men wished them an enjoyable repast, and Adrian guided Elizabeth away through a doorway and to an elaborate display of sumptuous hors d'oeuvres covering a long table. Reading the young woman's mind as she glanced about the room he assured her, "Don't worry. Mary will find us."

Elizabeth nodded. "Thank you, Lord Baynes, for the introduction."

Adrian wondered if it had been wise. Taking a plate, he set about selecting some tasty comestibles and asked, "What did you think of them, Miss St. Clair?"

"They are both most handsome."

"Ah, yes, I suppose they are. Despite their reputations, they do seem to be much in demand by the ladies."

"Perhaps because of it, Lord Baynes."

Adrian smiled and handed her a glass of champagne. Wise words from the young woman. He hoped she was always as wise.

* * *

Hugh watched both the diplomat and the young woman walk away, but Lambeth's eyes followed only the redhead.

"She is fairer than her sisters, and that's saying something."

Hugh chuckled under his breath. "You always were partial to redheads as I recall."

"Aye, that's true. They have been my downfall more than once, as you well know. And she is quite exquisite."

Hugh's eyes drifted to the far side of the room where Lady Mary was surrounded. Arthur Bywood was there, and other young men anxious for a dance, swains every one. He had no intention of asking her to dance, though. That could be construed as a declaration to the *haut ton* that the rake was retiring.

Lambeth followed his gaze. "Still looking at the fair Mary Campbell, I see."

"Perhaps." In fact, he could not take his eyes off her. *The Swan*. But Hugh could not allow the young debutante to consume his thoughts, for that could mean something he was not ready for: marriage.

"You'd best take care or she will become an obsession."

"Hmm…" It just might be that she already was.

* * *

By her fifth dance, Mary was quite tired of the effort required to keep up the small talk required of her. The ballroom had grown overly warm with its multitude of candles and many dancing bodies, and to Mary's mind it was too loud. She needed some air. Her friend Elizabeth had disappeared some time ago, but before she went looking for her, she thought she might just take a short walk through the cool gardens.

Avoiding the eyes of Arthur Bywood, who had been lured into dancing with Lady Harriet, Mary dodged behind a group of older men in deep discussion. They barely noticed her as she slipped by them to exit the room through the terrace door. Outside, her warm cheeks welcomed the brisk night air.

The stone terrace was lit, and the soft light on the balustrade from the outside lamps allowed her to see she was alone for the moment. She welcomed the times she was alone. As an only child, she had frequently been her only company.

There were gardens out here she remembered from her prior visit, and with confidence she took the stairs that led down to them. On the lawn she inhaled deeply the smell of clean earth, grass and flowers. Gardens. It seemed she was always escaping into them. The thought amused her, and she smiled.

A few quick turns and she found her destination, or rather, more accurately, she smelled it. The fragrance of roses was just what she needed to shake off the memory of that crowded ballroom. She was just bending down to smell a pink blossom when she heard a deep voice behind her.

"The Empress Josephine had a passion for roses, too, you know."

She started at the familiar voice, stood up from the flower and turned. Lord Ormond loomed before her like a terrible dark angel. Was he taller than she'd remembered? His dark brown hair appeared ebony in the dim light, and tonight it was smoothed back from his chiseled features. The pirate had dressed up for the evening, and he was so ruggedly handsome he made her heart ache.

Before she could say a word, he said, "I wanted to see you, but I didn't want to announce it by asking you to dance."

"And what did you want to see me about, my lord?"

He chuckled. "I've missed you."

Mary tried to control her speeding heart. How could she be so glad to see the arrogant man? Being drawn into his seductive lure could mean her demise, and she respected herself more than that, even if she thought society's strictures often foolish and misguided. He was toying with her. And despite that, she was happy to see him.

But she would not give him the satisfaction of knowing it. "Surely not, my lord. My foolish female thoughts are likely boring and—"

Ormond chuckled again and stepped closer. "You could never bore me, Lady Mary."

He moved closer still. She had the urge to back up but held her ground, determined not to show weakness. He was nearly touching her before he stopped. "Come walk with me."

It felt like a command, not a request. She knew giving in to him was unwise, but at that moment she felt powerless to refuse. "All…right. Perhaps for just a few minutes."

He took her elbow and guided her deeper into the gardens where tall yew hedges grew. She was thankful the bright moon gave some light to the darkened spaces.

"You are beautiful, Lady Mary."

A tingle went through her spine. Mary never knew what to say to compliments, knowing men just said those things as a matter of courtesy to young women, or as a prelude to seducing them. Either reason made her uncomfortable. But still, the man had called her beautiful, words she could not recall hearing before, and certainly never from this man. She couldn't fail to recognize that kindness. "Thank you."

He stopped and turned her toward him. His warm fingers held her arm just above her glove, producing an amazing shiver that sent ripples of sensation down her body. For a moment their eyes locked and a powerful force flowed between them, the same heat that had been there from the first time they touched. His dark eyes held hers as he bent his head.

Mary could hear the quaver in her voice as she asked, "Are you thinking about kissing me again?"

"Yes, I am." He continued to move toward her.

"Well, don't—"

His lips claimed hers, cutting off any further words. They were warm, oh so warm. And they moved so sensually. She began to shiver, but she stopped when he traced her bottom lip with his tongue, paralyzed by that intentionally erotic touch.

At last he lifted his mouth from hers and whispered, "I've been wanting to do that for some time." That sensuous baritone had a hypnotic effect. She melted against him, arms coming up to his chest as he nibbled on her ear.

"I find I can't stay away from you, Lady Mary."

"If you continue following me into gardens and kissing me whenever you like," she breathed, "I fear you will ruin my reputation."

He leaned back to look at her and smiled with lazy self-assurance. "I promise you that is not my intention, but with you it seems I have little control. I like kissing you."

Remembering Lady Hearnshaw, Mary was suddenly suspicious. She pulled back abruptly and dusted off her skirts. "Surely you are toying with me, my lord. You seem very smug, like the cat that swallowed the canary. If this has anything to do with my going to Paris, I can assure you that one of your kisses will not change my mind. I *am* going with my uncle."

Ormond frowned and stepped back. "I know. And I don't like it, but I can see that I will not be successful in changing your mind when everyone else seems determined you go. But that was not my intention in kissing you." The self-assured smile was back. "I simply wanted to."

She hurriedly changed the subject, happy to be back in control of herself. "How are your ribs?"

He shrugged, clearly put out by her retreat from his affections. "My ribs seem to be fine, no doubt due to your kind ministrations."

They began to walk. As they did, she found herself taking his arm, an unconscious gesture that brought pleasure nonetheless. "I'm glad. Such a fall can sometimes bring much worse consequences."

There was a brief silence. "You refer to your father?"

"Yes," she admitted. "That hunting accident reminded me..." She trailed off, not sure what to say.

"I'm sorry for your loss."

She stole a glance at him and saw genuine concern. "It was a very long time ago. I never really knew him. But I have longed to know him."

"I have experienced such feelings myself," he replied. "They can keep you locked in the past—but I don't want to talk about the past. I want to talk about us." Taking her elbow, he turned her to face him. "There is more between us than a kiss. You must feel it. Your body tells me you do."

Embarrassed by his words, she didn't want to admit how true they were. Especially not when there were other considerations. "I saw you with Lady Hearnshaw tonight. Surely I cannot be a part of that."

Ormond looked annoyed. "I assure you she is not *with* me. There is nothing there. Nor is there anything between me and any other woman at present."

"I see." Mary pondered his words. Perhaps he was between mistresses. But if he wanted her to be his next, she was not interested. She might be innocent, but she was keenly aware that she could never give her body without her heart wanting to follow. She would be no man's mistress, particularly this man's. That path would lead only to heartbreak, for she was coming to see how easily she could give him her heart.

With men like him who found it easy to take their pleasure and move on, how could a woman ever know he was truly hers? Could he ever give himself to just one woman? Elizabeth had been right. Being a rake had its consequences. But for whom? Him? The woman? Both?

They walked in silence for a few minutes, and Mary anxiously looked toward the ballroom. The light from the chandeliers shone through the windows. She needed to leave while she still could.

It was as if Ormond read her thoughts. "Shall I allow you to return by yourself?"

Her eyes darted to the light then to him. "Yes, that would be best."

She turned to walk away but stopped as he reached out and touched her arm. "It's not over between us, Lady Mary."

Her hands were shaking, but she did not look behind her as she hurried down the path to the wide stone steps and back to the ball.

Chapter 10

"Ah, Paris."

Mary sighed, her hand dangling from the open window of the carriage as she and her uncle rode down the tree-lined street in the enchanting city she loved. The breeze was a soft caress on her face. Spring had arrived, bringing with it blossoms in shades of pink and white.

"Even with all it has endured, Paris is still beautiful," she remarked. "The buildings have more grace, more artistry in their lines than those in London. Somehow they seem more feminine—don't you think, Uncle?"

"I agree it is a beautiful city." Lord Baynes followed her gaze out the window. "The cafés and the music are full of life, but it is also dangerous here."

He leaned back in his seat and sagely regarded her. "Remember that, Mary. This is the country that rejected an unworthy king to embrace an unworthy emperor, and now the world watches and worries to see what France will embrace next. Violence persists in many districts, so I am asking you to be careful. I am begging you."

Mary noted the stern look on her uncle's face, aware of the violence of which he spoke. In part it was due to the backlash of those called royalists, those who would have vengeance for the bloodletting that had characterized the Reign of Terror. The Bourbon supporters had not forgotten the horrible deaths of their family and friends. That anger had resulted in bloody riots in the south of France and even some areas of Paris.

"I will, Uncle," she told him. But even his stern reminder could not dampen her delight.

She had been in Paris for a week now, and though it had rained for several days, this day dawned clear and the brilliant blue sky stirred her spirits. She hadn't seen much of her uncle, who had been occupied in meetings during most days, meetings to which she had not been invited, but she'd enjoyed the few evenings she had spent with him at the Tuileries Palace, the seat of the French court and home of the king. This afternoon they were calling on the minister of police, Comte Elie Decazes. Much was happening in Paris since Napoleon's defeat at Waterloo and King Louis XVIII's return last year. The comte was an integral part of the king's plan to bring much-needed change to the government.

"Is it true what I have heard, Uncle, that France is still in deep financial straits?"

"The country has suffered much from the war," he acknowledged. "Our own blockade kept goods from entering the country, which slowed commerce to a crawl. It will be a while before France returns to its former glory."

"All of Paris is talking about the new Chamber of Deputies the king has created, *La Chambre Introuvable*."

"Yes, the Unobtainable Chamber. A most interesting body. Most of its members are the 'ultra-royalists' who support the monarchy and hope for the return of the *Ancien Régime*. Though Louis is a moderate with ideas for reform, even he cannot control them. Their ways can be vicious."

Mary thought about what he said and all she'd learned since their return to Paris. "They are still talking about what happened to Michel Ney, the one Napoleon called '*le brave des braves*.' What I heard is rather chilling. After we left Paris this December past he was tried for treason and executed. Was that because he was Napoleon's most famous marshal?"

"He was. But Louis had a personal reason to want him gone. He asked Ney to stop Napoleon's advance through the south of

France during the hundred days when the emperor returned to power from Elba. Instead, Ney deserted the Bourbons and rejoined his old master. He paid the price.

"But it is not just the royalists and the revolutionaries who are causing trouble now," her uncle continued. "There have been fights between the Protestants and the Catholics, too. The power of the Catholic Church has begun to grow once again. I do not overstate my concern for you. Paris holds many dangers. In that, Lord Ormond was right."

Though Ormond had never been far from her thoughts, Mary did not wish to discuss him with her uncle. She reminded herself that if Ormond had gotten his way she would not be here at all. Ire at that thought helped buffer her away from him.

"But, Uncle, surely there are reasonable men who have the ear of the king. They will set things right. What about the prime minister, Duc de Richelieu?"

"I confess I admire the man. And there is our own Duke of Wellington who still leads England's troops here. He has been a good friend for many years, and Louis listens to him. So, yes, there is reason for hope."

Mary thought for a moment. "Your business here is not just with the French, though, is it? What about the allies' ministers I have met at the Tuileries?"

"Smart girl." Her uncle gave her a small smile. "They, too, have a say in what happens in France, and they will be involved in reviewing the king's plans for changes to his new government. Louis resents their presence, of course, particularly the Prussians. But he tolerates them because they have brought stability to the country." He paused for a moment, watching her. "I trust your thoughts have not *all* been about politics. You've made some new friends, I hope? Your desire to be of assistance to me is commendable, but I also want you to enjoy yourself."

Mary nodded. "A few. Diane Brancalis, from the south of France. She is here with her father. She reminds me of Lizzy. Perhaps it is her blue-gray eyes, or maybe it is because she is kind. Diane's family lived through the riots in the south, though, so she is glad to be in Paris. I'm not certain where her sympathies lie, but I rather think she believes in the recent reforms. Why dwell on the past when the future is such a challenge? And there's another young woman I am fond of as well. An Austrian, Theresa Koller."

"That name is familiar to me. Is she the one with brown hair I saw you talking with last evening?" Lord Baynes's eyebrows drew together as if he were trying to recall the girl.

"Yes, she has brown hair and eyes. You remember her, Uncle. Her older brother—or rather half brother—is General Koller, whom you met in Vienna on my first trip with you. Theresa's mother is French and married General Koller's father after his first wife died. There is quite an age difference between them. Her half-brother is more like an uncle to her, I think."

"Ah, yes. Now I recall. General Koller is an Austrian general. He is quite popular among the allies, and I believe he enjoys a close relationship with the king."

"Theresa has been here with her brother before and has many friends in Paris," Mary explained. The two had met for coffee one morning after being introduced at the Tuileries, and the Austrian regaled her with stories of the former emperor. "Her stories about Napoleon could hold my attention for hours."

Her uncle nodded. "I think you will enjoy meeting Comte Decazes, too. He is the leader of the moderate royalists in the new Chamber, and another favorite of Louis. You will no doubt approve of his ideas. They could result in great economic rewards for France if he succeeds in seeing them implemented. I am trying to assist him in the meetings where he sets forth the reform he seeks. He brings a balance to the extreme ideas of the ultra royalists—and of course as minister of police he is the one who must rein in the ultra royalists' excesses."

The carriage slowed and Mary peered out the open window to see an elegant three-story town house with a chateau roof and decorative iron fence and gate. Behind the fence was a small but well designed garden. Pink rhododendrons bloomed on either side of the black front door, and there was a tall wisteria vine flowing down the corner of the town house like a lavender waterfall.

The front door opened as they stepped out of the coach and approached. Just outside, a butler greeted them and accepted her uncle's hat. Just behind him, standing in the entry, was a handsome man with brown hair Mary judged to be in his middle thirties.

"Welcome, Lord Baynes."

"Comte Decazes. How good of you to invite my niece and me to tea—a concession for you French, I imagine."

"*C'est bon.* We enjoy tea as well as coffee. We do." He smiled at Mary and added, "Is this your lovely niece I've heard so much about?"

"Yes, Comte, this is Lady Mary Campbell."

Mary curtsied briefly and allowed the comte to bow over her extended hand. "*Enchanté.* You are as charming as I have heard. But I have also heard of your intelligence, so it is with great anticipation that I look forward to our conversation."

"You are very kind, Comte." Mary gave him a sweet smile, but before she could say more another man approached, a slightly younger version of the comte with light brown hair curled around the edges of his face. His dark blue eyes stared intently at her.

"Your Excellence, Lady Mary, this is my younger brother Joseph, Vicomte Decazes. He often assists me in my work when he can be pried from his own assignments with the new government."

The vicomte acknowledged her uncle and then turned back to Mary. "Lady Mary, you must allow me to show you some of my favorite places in Paris."

She liked his face. Both he and his older brother were handsome men. "I would be most happy to accept your invitation, Vicomte, providing my uncle agrees."

Her uncle winked at the comte. "I think it a splendid idea. Mary has been eager to see your beautiful city. The last time we were here, she spent most of her days in our apartments."

The vicomte's expression showed his distress over learning this fact. "*C'est terrible*! Had I but known…. But of course I will make it up to you. You shall see some of the sights that Paris is best known for, and I can also introduce you to some of our more interesting citizens. With the king restored, some of those we thought lost have returned. I think you would enjoy meeting Germaine de Stael."

Mary enthused, "Oh, I would! I have read her books and find them fascinating."

The group continued talking, as the comte directed them into the parlor and offered his regrets that his wife was not available to join them. Mary was immediately struck by the bright rose brocade sofas and the elegant draped table set with tea and pastries. As they sat, her uncle elaborated.

"Mary, King Louis calls Germaine de Stael 'a Chateaubriand in petticoats.'"

Mary did not hide her puzzlement.

"It was quite a compliment, Lady Mary." The vicomte smiled at her as he spoke, or at least his blue eyes did. "Chateaubriand is considered the intellectual hero of the royalists."

"So it wasn't criticism." Mary had wondered.

"Ah, no, Louis is very fond of her," Comte Decazes interjected. "He respects her mind as well. He enjoys the wit of Chateaubriand, so the comparison only conveyed his favor."

Mary recalled the last book she had read by the woman. "I have read Madame de Stael's *De l'Allemagne*. It is an amazing study of German culture."

"Pity Napoleon didn't think so," the comte stated. "Madame de Stael believed Germany had some things to teach France, and the suggestion so inflamed the emperor he expelled her from the country."

His brother eagerly chimed in. "Once Napoleon was gone, she was anxious to return to Paris and has taken apartments here. I think you will want to hear her insights on all that has happened in Europe. Something tells me she will like you very much."

"I hope you don't find her *too* inspiring, Mary," her uncle remarked with a look of both amusement and concern. "Madame de Stael chose a difficult path being so bold."

Mary would not be discouraged. Women like Germaine de Stael were rare. "I can think of nothing I would enjoy more than meeting her."

After that, Mary sipped her tea and listened to the men talk politics. Occasionally she would make a comment or ask a question, but surprisingly her thoughts kept drifting to a tall, dark British lord who had somehow taken root in her mind—and, she worried, in her heart. He was a man of many women, however, with very conventional ideas about a woman's role: limited apparently to his bed and the home. And, he was clearly not looking for a wife. Not that she was looking for a husband.

She banished thoughts of Ormond and concentrated instead on the comte and his younger brother, both of whom were expounding on the need for certain changes in leadership. Yes, Paris would be good for her. Some time away from England, some time away from that enticing man with the brandy-colored eyes.

* * *

Adrian helped Mary into their carriage, curious to know her reaction. "What did you think of them?"

"They are men with brave ideas," his niece replied. "I can see why you find the comte's thoughts encouraging. He strikes a middle road that France appears to need sorely. And the vicomte is most charming."

"He seemed quite taken with you," Adrian noted.

"He seemed a puzzle to me. He is polished and polite, of course. Very charming, very French. But I have a feeling much lies beneath the surface. It's in his eyes."

The vicomte had a hidden life, as Adrian was well aware. The Frenchman was one of the Crown's agents in France. As such, he would have two identities and two masters, though if such became known it would jeopardize his work. And still in the back of Adrian's mind was the thought that someone had passed England's intelligence to the French. Could it have been the vicomte?

"Would you rather not accept the vicomte's invitation to tour Paris?"

"Oh, no," Mary replied. "I look forward to seeing the city with him. He is very pleasant, and I think quite safe. I can always invite Diane and Theresa, too. They will want to meet Madame de Stael if they can. Besides," she added with an impish smile, "with the vicomte's kind invitation, I won't have to spend *all* my days reading in your apartments."

Adrian sighed, but it was safer to imagine her exploring the city with the vicomte available to protect her. "At least he is a gentleman, and his carriage is accompanied by footmen with weapons, should they be needed."

* * *

The vicomte quickly made good on his promise, Mary was pleased to discover.

"Where are you off to this fine day?" her uncle asked, gazing at her over the edge of his newspaper, *Le Moniteur*, as he took a bite of sausage. In addition to the meat, the breakfast table was laden with fruit and eggs and the French pastries Mary loved, but she was too excited to eat.

"The vicomte has arranged for Diane, Theresa and me to call upon Madame de Stael. My head is spinning with all I want to ask! I have admired her for so long."

"You will find her most amusing, though her ideas are somewhat unique. If my memory serves, I met her when she was in Vienna. Like that Pascal character you love, she will encourage you to think."

"She already has, Uncle. I have read more than one of her works. Her novel *Corinne* taught me much about Italy."

Her uncle set down his newspaper and made a prediction. "Germaine de Stael may be the most brilliant woman of our time, Mary. At the very least she is the most intelligent woman in France. Her battle against Napoleon lasted for years and demonstrated great courage. You will think her a kindred spirit for her defense of individual freedoms, particularly for women."

That afternoon, Mary discovered her uncle's words to be true as she and her companions sat clustered in the Paris apartments where Germaine de Stael shared her thoughts on the changing face of Europe. The vicomte observed the show from the side, and judging by his many smiles he seemed to be enjoying himself immensely.

The politics were fascinating, but another topic ultimately became the subject of the day. They were talking of de Stael's past when Diane asked, "Madame de Stael, you are a woman of wisdom concerning men. Will you tell us of your opinion of them and of love?"

Mary had been aware of Germaine's passionate nature. She had found satisfaction in many lovers, sometimes carrying on several relationships at the same time. This was widely known, so it was not surprising the conversation eventually turned to matters of the heart.

"*Bon Dieu*," de Stael remarked, "what a question! And call me Germaine, *ma petite*," she said to the dark-haired girl. Sitting back, she grinned at the eager faces before her and relented. "I suppose I should not be surprised you ask. I have been open about my lovers, though it has been a while since I have thought much about love. While it may be the whole history of a woman's life, it is only an episode in a man's."

Mary frowned. "That is rather discouraging." It was what she feared most when she thought about Ormond.

"You may find it discouraging," said Germaine, "but I find it to be true. Perhaps it is one reason I had so many lovers." Theresa nodded agreement, and the older woman continued. "In so many things one must choose whether to be bored or to suffer. I chose to suffer."

Sadness gripped Mary at the woman's words. She hated boredom, but she had no desire to suffer, either, particularly not for the sake of love. "I do hope those are not the *only* choices."

The vicomte, who had been quietly listening, turned his intense blue eyes on her. "I am certain they are not, Lady Mary."

The only response to his encouragement Mary could muster was a faint smile.

As Decazes escorted the young women home in his carriage, his eyes watched Mary, though his words were for all three. "I hope you found this afternoon interesting, Lady Mary, mademoiselles."

Mary and the others nodded.

"She has seen so much in her life," said the brown-eyed Theresa. "It is too bad she and Napoleon were ever at odds."

"I could listen to her all day," said Mary, "but still, one can hope for a more optimistic future than a choice between boredom and suffering. I know a truly independent woman will encounter obstacles. Germaine certainly has, and perhaps it is inevitable—"

The vicomte's blue eyes sparkled. "You can be independent and still find love, Lady Mary. I promise."

Mary returned his gaze. "It seems Germaine has done just that, though I would not follow her example. So many lovers seems the way of pain to me." She wanted only one, and that one would have to be a man who would love her as her father had loved her mother or she'd prefer none.

The look the vicomte gave her made the heat rise in her cheeks. Mary realized she knew very little about him, and yet he intrigued her. She was certain he harbored secrets and wondered what they might be.

Decazes helped her down from the carriage when they arrived back at her uncle's apartments and walked her to the door. "I will see Theresa and Diane home, but I wanted to ask if you might like to see Notre Dame with me?"

"The great cathedral? Oh, yes! I would like that very much. The tales I have heard suggest it is a wondrous place."

"I am quite fond of it," the French nobleman replied. "*Bon.* With your permission, I'll call for you tomorrow morning."

She did not refuse.

Her uncle was waiting for her in the parlor when Mary came in. "Good, you're back. Did you enjoy Germaine de Stael as much as I said you would?"

She dropped into a chair next to him. "Oh, yes. She is an amazing woman, like a great cup brimming over with knowledge.

She has so much to say that one visit is not enough. I want to see her again."

"Well," her uncle replied, "you might see her tonight. We dine at the Tuileries with the leaders in the king's government. Some of the ministers I've been meeting with will be there, and I think you'll find them interesting."

"Will we see the king?" she asked hopefully.

"I think not," Lord Baynes admitted. "He has been unwell, and recently his condition has worsened, so I expect he will avoid the evening festivities."

"Do you know him well, Uncle? I have yet to catch even a glimpse of him, though I know he meets with the ministers and military leaders."

"I first met him when he lived at Hartwell House in England during the latter part of his exile. We became friends. He is well-read with a great wit, and both a charming companion and an insightful leader."

"Diane and Theresa have told me stories of him," Mary replied. "Diane especially admires the king."

Her uncle nodded. "It is too bad he is so affected by age and ill health, because his wisdom is much needed. I am afraid at this stage obesity and gout have taken their toll. Though, even with his health issues he has managed to put some good ministers in place. You should have a chance to meet them. They will all be there tonight."

Chapter 11

Mary was on her way to dress for the evening and paused on the stairs. "Shall I wear the rose gown, Uncle?"

"I think that would be very nice," Lord Baynes replied, standing near the bottom landing. "You will certainly gain compliments and yet look the young lady you are. They already consider you unique, and that is to your advantage. But do be careful if you listen in on others' conversations as you are wont to do."

She took that as license to listen in on others' conversations. After all, French wine flowed freely at the Tuileries Palace, and wine freed tongues. It would make the evening more interesting if she was engaged in a task to help her uncle, though Mary also knew why her uncle had told her to be careful. It was difficult to say what would happen if she was caught eavesdropping.

They arrived at the palace to see uniformed men at the outer doors dressed in the blue, silver and red of Louis XVIII's livery. Their white trousers and stockings were immaculate above silver buckled shoes.

Mary took her uncle's arm as they entered the large room where the reception was being held. The décor was opulent. Even the walls were gilded, and the furniture fairly glowed in reflection in the many large mirrors. White and gold satin brocade chairs in small groupings at the corners of the room encouraged more intimate conversation. The vaulted ceiling was adorned with paintings, drawing the eye upward. Exquisite crystal chandeliers created prisms of dazzling light. The art on the walls was old and classic in its style, showing scenes of France's history and its royalty.

"Uncle, have you ever seen such a fine gallery of the royal and noble?"

Her uncle smiled at her. "The allies raided the Louvre—or as Napoleon called it, the *Musée Napoléon*—just before the king arrived in Paris, eager to recover the art the emperor stole from them. Some of the museum's walls were left empty while others held only empty frames. Can you imagine? Even so, there was much art left in Paris. But some of the portraits you see were brought back with the Bourbons when they returned."

Mary surveyed the gathered assemblage. The allied military officers clustered together like proud roosters, their uniforms bright with color and rank. Diplomats like her uncle and the French ministers wore dark jackets, silk waistcoats and fine trousers. The women, dressed in beautiful silks, satins and brocades, decorated the room like flowers in a garden. Mary was reminded that, as with her trip here the December before, the colors were brighter and the necklines lower than in London. It was Paris, after all.

Conversations were already erupting into a cacophony of sound as servants passed silver trays of champagne and tongues loosened in response. From across the room, Joseph Decazes's head rose as he spotted Mary, and he quickly came to her side.

"*Bonsoir*, Lady Mary, Lord Baynes."

It is easy to smile at him. His dark blue eyes welcomed her, and Mary gladly allowed him to sweep her off to introductions to his many friends.

She enjoyed Decazes's company. His aristocratic face was not hard to look at, though he was shorter and not as muscled as Lord Ormond.

Lord Ormond? When had she had begun to compare all men to the tall British lord? While Joseph Decazes had captured her interest, she did not believe he had captured her heart. She wondered if her heart already belonged to another. It was a most disquieting thought.

Mary and Decazes were engaged in conversation with Diane Brancalis, whose blue-gray eyes stared with adoration at the French nobleman, when Cardinal Gonsalvi joined them. The prime minister of Pius VII and friend of King Louis was an elegant man, being both intelligent and charming with a rich baritone voice and dark brown hair and eyes. His dark features complemented the olive skin so common to the Italians Mary had seen at the French court, and she recalled reading that Napoleon had called the cardinal "a lion covered with a sheep skin." Perhaps that was right. He radiated power cloaked in gentle charm. Were all Italians so charming?

She suddenly had the feeling of being watched. In such a crowded room the sensation was ridiculous, so she tried to shrug it off, but the conviction would not leave her.

Seeing nothing unusual before her, Mary turned to glance behind. And there, near the door, dressed all in black except for his white shirt and cravat, hovering like a large black cloud, his piercing eyes focused darkly on her, was Lord Ormond.

* * *

At last Hugh saw Mary recognize him, and he headed straight for her. He had sensed her presence the moment he entered, but in that low-cut gown what man wouldn't? Its rose color drew his attention to her honeyed skin and the sweet mounds of her breasts rising just above the bodice. Those waves of golden hair were swept up into curls at her crown. Her slim neck rose from slender shoulders.

He suddenly had the desire to kiss the base of her throat. It was ludicrous, but whenever he saw her, his thoughts turned to what she would look like naked in his bed. He felt both possessive and protective of her, and just now he wanted her anywhere but Paris.

When he stood directly behind her, he allowed his fingers to rest on her waist in a too familiar touch. He could feel her shiver through the thin fabric of her gown.

Hugh supposed he was difficult to ignore, being at least a head taller than the other men in the room. Cardinal Gonsalvi's dark eyes darted from him to Mary. "Is this gentleman a friend of yours?"

Mary glanced up over her shoulder at him. As if remembering her manners, she said to the cardinal, "Oh, yes. Please forgive me. Mademoiselle Brancalis, Excellency Cardinal Gonsalvi, Vicomte, allow me to introduce Hugh Redgrave, the Marquess of Ormond, an associate of my uncle's."

The cardinal smiled graciously at Hugh. "So, Lord Ormond, you are a countryman of our *Bella Maria*."

Hugh nodded, fighting the jealous wave that swept him as Mary blushed. No matter that he was a man of the church, the smooth Italian had called her "Bella Maria" as if it were a lover's endearment. And others were encroaching, too. Hugh was particularly chagrined to see Joseph Decazes standing close to Mary, watching her with possessive interest. Hugh was certain Mary didn't know all there was to know about the good vicomte.

"Why are you here in Paris, Lord Ormond?" she asked. "I didn't expect to see you here."

"Business of the Crown," he replied curtly. For the benefit of the men, however, he gave her an easy smile that staked his claim. "Just now, however, I must see your uncle. Do you know where he is?"

Mary gestured toward a large doorway. "I think I saw him go into one of those rooms."

Hugh nodded. "Thank you." Then he turned to the others and said, "If you'll excuse me." He hoped that they would take the hint and disperse. His own departure surely looked like a storm leaving the sky, but perhaps that would work to his benefit.

By the time Hugh returned, Mary was indeed with other people. In the main reception room an hour later he was unsurprised to find her engrossed in conversation with two of the most fascinating people in Paris. Germaine de Stael and Benjamin Constant, both of whom he knew from his earlier years in France.

Hugh quietly approached the group and felt himself scowl when he saw Decazes standing very close to Mary. Apparently the Frenchman hadn't been scared off.

Germaine welcomed him. "Ormond! I had no idea you would be gracing us with your handsome face. When did you arrive in Paris?" Her large brown eyes flashed in delight as he took her proffered hand and bowed over it.

"Only just this week. As ever, it is a delight to see you, Madame Germaine." He nodded to Benjamin Constant, who smiled in return, and at last he acknowledged the encroaching vicomte with a tilt of his head.

"Do you know Lady Mary?" asked Germaine.

"I do." Hugh grinned at Mary, which caused color to rise in her cheeks. Good. He was disturbing her like she was disturbing him.

"Well, you must join our conversation, dear boy."

* * *

Mary had been enjoying the conversation and very relaxed until Ormond strolled up to them. She had been most anxious to meet Benjamin Constant, one of Madame de Stael's former lovers. A French Swiss author and a champion of individual liberty, he had been de Stael's companion for more than a decade and very much a partner of the mind. Now he was a member of the Chamber of Deputies and had been heard to tout Britain as a model of freedoms for France's citizens. Though an older man, Constant was still quite virile in appearance. Broad of shoulder, he had thick silver hair and an aristocratic nose. Mary thought his piercing dark eyes revealed a formidable intelligence.

He looked intently at Germaine, who continued, "Ormond, we have been engaged in discourse on the lingering effects of the Reign of Terror. I was explaining to Lady Mary what it was like to live in France in those terrible days. The ideals were noble but the end so very sad. Even I fled in the face of it."

Mary recalled the murder of the leading thinkers in France as well as thousands of the nobility. Though the Revolution had taken place before she was born, her French tutor had described the nightmare in many stories. Blood flowed endlessly from the guillotine and the streets became the grave of innocents along with the guilty. Mary was glad England had not seen such a time.

She shook off her gloom as Constant began to speak. "Not even an obscure life offered protection during that time, and many who could have led France to a better future were sacrificed to the mob."

"Who then provided a pathway for Napoleon," added Germaine, as if completing his thought. Knowing the woman's political views, Mary was not surprised.

Ormond shook his head. "A general masquerading as an emperor and running a country from his foreign war front. What a disaster for France."

Germaine agreed. "Yes, it was hard times for us. You were of great assistance to me in those days, Ormond, helping me to leave the country when the Corsican demanded I be gone. I have never forgotten it. I owe you much."

Decazes, who'd been standing silently at Mary's side, appeared suddenly anxious. "I wouldn't want you to think ill of my country, Lady Mary. We are coming out of those dark days."

Mary did not disagree, and so she nodded. And she was most curious about Constant's views of her own country. "Sir, I understand you believe Britain can be a model for preserving individual liberties in France."

"I do," said Constant. "Although not all in France share my enthusiasm for the British government. I believe a constitutional monarchy, such as England has, can serve as a model."

"What of the king? What would be his role?" Mary was curious to know what such a man thought of the monarchy itself.

Constant dipped his chin as if instructing a student. "The monarch can provide a much needed balance, my young friend."

Mary couldn't agree more. Strangely, she thought she saw a look of approval on Ormond's face. And something else. Was that desire in his eyes?

* * *

Later that evening, after dinner, Mary was deep in thought and returning from a short visit to the retiring room when she took a wrong turn and found herself suddenly lost in an unfamiliar corridor. The large hallway contained several doors, and she heard voices speaking in French behind one of them. Thinking she might ask for directions, she quietly opened the door and found herself in a small anteroom with heavy tapestry curtains covering a larger room beyond. She could not be seen but she could hear.

She recognized the heated voice. Lifting an edge of the curtain, she peeked from where she stood in the shadows into the room and saw Vicomte Decazes standing with his back to her talking to a Prussian general. She recognized the general as well. Kleist. She had met him earlier that evening.

"Not here, and not tonight!" the vicomte practically shouted. "You'll receive the information in the usual manner. I'll not be bullied here in the Palace. It's not safe to be discussing this."

The general did not look pleased. "The matter is urgent! There must be no delay."

Mary did not know the matter to which they were referring, nor why a Prussian general would be pressuring Decazes for information, but whatever the reason, the French nobleman was most annoyed. Since it seemed their brief conversation was nearing its end, Mary silently left the anteroom and ducked hurriedly through the first door she reached. She could hear the footsteps of the two men trail away down the hallway.

When it was quiet again, she carefully opened the door. As she did, her eyes fell on a piece of paper lying on the floor. It had not been there before, she was certain. One of them must have dropped it. She bent down and retrieved it.

She recognized the writing as German: *French uniforms secured in warehouse.* An address in Paris followed.

What could it mean? Had the Prussian general dropped this? If so, why would General Kleist be concerned about French uniforms in a warehouse? She tucked the paper into the front of her gown, determined she would find out herself the meaning of the message; then she followed in the direction of the men's footsteps, hoping they would lead her back to the reception.

Chapter 12

Mary woke the next morning to find a gray day and her uncle gone, but the weather could not dampen her excitement. As promised, the vicomte had arranged for them to receive a tour of Notre Dame from a priest friend, one Father Verbert.

The vicomte arrived mid morning and smiled as he helped Mary into his carriage. As she climbed inside, she noted the elaborate gold crest on the door that showed he was of a noble French family. Not that she could forget.

He seated himself across from her, but as she smoothed the skirt of her emerald green muslin gown and let the hood of her cloak drop to her shoulders, the vicomte stared, which made Mary nervous. She was thinking of the note she had found and the conversation she'd overheard the night before. Just what was the handsome vicomte involved in?

"Lady Mary, in that lovely gown today your eyes seem a darker shade of green."

"You notice everything, Vicomte."

He just smiled and corrected, "I notice everything about *you*, Lady Mary."

She smiled to herself and immediately turned to peer out at the city, catching glimpses of the river winding its way through the shops and small buildings in the center of town. It wasn't the majestic Thames of London, and she knew it to be disease-ridden, but the smaller river Seine curved in a feminine way that delighted her. It was so like the city itself.

When the carriage hit a rough patch, Mary nearly bounced into Decazes's lap. She fought back embarrassment, but he only laughed and set her back on her seat.

"I hope you are all right, Lady Mary. Though Napoleon began a number of construction projects, including fountains and parks, most of the streets remain unpaved. It can make for a rough ride."

She gave him her sweetest smile. "I don't mind. It keeps me aware of where I am. For me Paris will always be the most beautiful city in the world."

The vicomte took on a pensive air. Suddenly, he spoke. "Have you ever considered living here, Lady Mary? Permanently?"

Mary couldn't disguise her surprise. "Why, no, I had not thought of that."

The French nobleman's dark blue eyes focused intently upon her as he took one of her hands and leaned across the carriage. "You are a woman who is most alive, Lady Mary, and Paris is a city coming back to life in a country that is doing the same. You could be happy here."

Mary saw the longing in his eyes and suddenly she felt uncomfortable. "But surely it would be inconvenient for an Englishwoman to try and find her way alone in France, Vicomte."

Those blue eyes burned into her. "That could be made much more convenient, Lady Mary, if that young Englishwoman were to marry a Frenchman of good reputation who is well placed at court."

Mary could feel the heat rise in her cheeks. Was he proposing to her? Was he about to take her into his arms?

He leaned closer. The smell of his cologne engulfed her, and she knew he meant to kiss her. Just as his lips touched hers, however, the carriage pulled to a stop. He sat back, clearly deciding in favor of propriety, and relief flooded Mary as the footman opened the door. The vicomte stepped out and turned to assist her.

They had crossed the Pont-Neuf Bridge to the Ile de la Cité, the island in the Seine at the center of Paris. Before them, the cathedral of Notre Dame rose as a grand monument to an earlier age.

Father Verbert greeted them, his black robes blowing in a cold wind that suddenly descended. He was a middle-aged priest whose kind eyes suggested to Mary he had a gentle spirit. They were hazel, a color very complementary to his soft brown hair. He had a few gray hairs at his temples and lines at the corners of his eyes said he smiled often.

The trio strolled down the central aisle of the cathedral toward the main altar, Mary walking between the father and the vicomte, her eyes raised to absorb the tall gothic architecture and the sweeping arches high above. The brilliant stained-glass windows cast blue, red and gold light into the cathedral even on this gray day. The experience was stately, beautiful, otherworldly.

Father Verbert explained the cathedral was first commissioned in the twelfth century by the bishop of Paris, Maurice de Sully. Dedicated to the Virgin Mary, it quickly became a place for the growing population of Paris to worship. It had taken one hundred and eighty years to complete.

Most fascinating to Mary was the fact that, because the common people did not read, the cathedral had been designed to tell the story of the Bible through its very portals, paintings and stained-glass windows. Although Mary's French tutor had told her about the old church, it was quite different to experience it herself. Mary sensed the history of the place. Crusaders had prayed here before leaving on their king's holy war. It was a wonder to her such a place had survived.

"Well, there's at least one good thing the French can say about Napoleon," she spoke aloud. "He saved this cathedral."

"*Oui*, he did," said Father Verbert, "though perhaps for selfish reasons. He wanted his coronation here." Mary recalled from her lessons that Napoleon had crowned himself emperor within its walls, and immediately crowned Josephine his empress.

As Father Verbert commented on the two rose-shaped stained-glass windows gracing the north and south walls, out of the corner of her eye Mary saw Decazes gradually drop back and to the side. She and Father Verbert walked on toward the altar, the father explaining the history of the cathedral and gesturing above.

Pretending to pay attention to the lesson, Mary watched the vicomte take a small paper from his coat and slide it into a recession behind one of the statues. If she hadn't seen him do it, she would not have known the paper was there; it was well hidden behind the stone. She was still staring up at the north rose and listening to Father Verbert when Decazes returned.

"What do you think, Lady Mary?" he asked.

The windows were overwhelming, their Gothic structure majestic, and she again experienced an immense sense of history. "Magnificent. It gives me such a feeling of the ages."

"Ah, *oui*," agreed Father Verbert. "The grand lady of the French church has stood the test of time and remains to remind us to look beyond this life to the next."

Mary glanced at the vicomte, who did not seem affected by his short excursion to hide the paper. He faced her and asked, "Did you know the early Celts held their services on this very same island in the Seine?"

"No, I was not aware of that," she said.

"*Oui*. This land has always drawn those who desire to worship."

How smooth he is, Mary thought, moving as he does from secret messages to romantic notions. A man of many faces. She thought him a very good choice for a spy.

Father Verbert seemed unsuspicious, however. He smiled at Decazes, his eyes full of mirth. "You've been listening to me too much, Joseph."

"As I should, Father, as I should."

When the tour was over, the priest bid them good day and the vicomte went to call for their carriage, leaving Mary at the door. She realized she would have only a few minutes alone, so she turned back into the cathedral and moved quickly to the place where the paper was hidden. Making sure she wasn't seen by other passersby, she retrieved it, tucking it into her reticule.

Just as she returned to the door, Decazes entered, looking for her.

"I dropped my glove and went back to find it," she said, holding up a glove. Though she was a little breathless, he did not seem to take note. She breathed a sigh of relief.

The carriage ride back to her apartments was dull, and the vicomte did not return to his earlier subject. He seemed preoccupied. Mary was relieved, though. She hoped he did not try to kiss her again. Not wanting to encourage him, she chatted about other subjects, particularly of her visits with Madame de Stael and the book by Pascal she was reading.

The vicomte smiled as she talked. Mary sensed his pleasure in the fact that she admired Madame de Stael and was reading the works of Pascal, a Frenchman. She wondered again if he wanted to marry her. What would her uncle think of such a match? Decazes was mature but not old, still in his early thirties. He was handsome, intelligent, and from a good family. He clearly would allow her independence, too; in fact, he seemed to delight in it.

Perhaps if she'd met him before Lord Ormond....

Chapter 13

Mary had just finished a letter to Elizabeth when her uncle joined her for tea in the parlor of their apartments. They sat on either side of a small round table next to the large bay window looking out on the tree-lined street. A few blossoms still clung to the branches, but with the recent rains she realized sadly that they would soon be gone.

Turning her attention to a silver tray laden with tea and pastries, she waited until the servant left and raised her teacup to take a sip. "Do you remember I told you I thought Joseph Decazes might be hiding something?"

Her uncle studied her with keen interest. "Has something happened?"

Mary nodded. She then recounted the conversation she'd overheard the night before with General Kleist. She had already determined not to tell him about the writing in German she'd found in the hall at the Tuileries. Not sure what it might mean and determined to see for herself, she would keep it secret for now.

Pulling from her sleeve the small paper she'd taken from the cathedral, she passed it to her uncle. "While we were touring Notre Dame this morning, when he thought I was otherwise engaged, the vicomte hid this behind a statue. Your German is better than mine, but I believe it speaks of troop placements."

Her uncle took the note and read it quickly. His face grew strained. "You were not seen?"

"No, I am quite certain I was not."

Her uncle reviewed the paper, and his countenance grew grim. "Indeed it does speak of troop placements. *Our* troop placements."

"There is something else about it that occurred to me," Mary said.

"What?"

"The writing," she pointed out. "The hand is not the same. I know the note I read on the minister's desk the last time we were in Paris was in French and this one is in German, but the letters are formed quite differently. Assuming Joseph Decazes wrote this note, he did not write the other."

"Ah. Thank you. That gives us much to consider."

Though she did not understand all the ramifications of her information, she was pleased she had contributed.

Her uncle's brows furrowed, and he spoke almost to himself. "At the moment, the fact the vicomte is willing to share knowledge of British troop placements with the Prussians is troubling."

"Uncle," she asked, "how would he know the movements of English soldiers?"

He sighed and glanced at her. "It could have come from a French source, I suppose. Wellington reports our troop numbers and general activities here in France to the king."

"Assuming we are correct that the use of German indicates its intended recipient, why would the vicomte be giving that information to the Prussians?"

Her uncle paused. "I don't know. I can speculate, maybe. If the Prussians were planning something they knew we would oppose, they would want to know how many soldiers we have near Paris that can be called upon. I suppose you might have guessed, but if not...I should tell you: Joseph Decazes is one of England's agents."

"A Frenchman?" she said.

"Yes, but working for us."

"Good heavens." She considered the idea, and a thought suddenly occurred to her. "*Only* for England, Uncle?"

"Ah, you are perceptive today. That is the question Ormond has been asking. Certainly it seems now that Decazes is involved with the Prussians. Those damned Prussians. If only we knew what they were up to…but we have no spy in their camp."

Mary fingered the other note in her pocket, the one she had found on the floor of the hall in the Tuileries. She couldn't say why she had kept it back, but she wasn't quite ready to divulge everything to her uncle. "From his conversation with Father Verbert, I had the impression the vicomte is a frequent visitor to the cathedral. Perhaps the message he left there is not the only one."

Her uncle looked worried. "Mary, this could become dangerous. I am concerned you are taking too much of a risk. What if you had been seen?"

"I do not believe I was, and Decazes will not know it was me who took the hidden message. Others could have discovered it. As long as he is willing for me to travel about the city with him, I might as well keep my eyes and ears open for what I may learn." Maybe she could make a contribution to the welfare of both France's king and England. That was what she'd hoped for all along.

"I won't argue your point," her uncle allowed. "You *are* in a unique position to see and hear things to which I am not privy. When are you to see him next?"

"Other than tonight?" There was another reception and dinner to be held that evening at the Tuileries. The vicomte had told her he was looking forward to seeing her, and there was talk the king might even attend if he was feeling better.

"Yes," her uncle said, "other than tonight."

Mary thought back to their last conversation. "He said something about wanting to show me a gallery of some favorite painter tomorrow. I expect he may mention it to you tonight."

Her uncle took a drink of his tea and set down his cup. "I must meet with Comte Decazes tomorrow to discuss the French budget. It seems there is concern the French deputies may renege on payments owed the allies, and the allies are threatening to remain in France unless the king dissolves his Chamber of Deputies. As a result, I will not be available to escort you. Are you comfortable being with Decazes in such a setting? If you feel at all strange—"

"Of course I don't! Your business is too important to worry about me. And we will not be alone. The vicomte intends to ask General Koller if Theresa might join us. I like her. She is interesting, and I really want to see the gallery."

Her uncle sighed. "All right, I will allow it, but please be careful."

"I will, Uncle. Paris really is an education all in itself." She blushed as she thought about what she'd realized just before Joseph Decazes dropped her off. "Oh, and I think I should tell you the vicomte may have a personal interest in me."

Lord Baynes barely reacted. "I would not find that surprising, Mary. Not with all the time he has given you. He is beginning to look less like an obliging Frenchman and more like one of your suitors."

She felt embarrassed to be discussing it, but she had raised the topic and so she continued. "Today he asked me if I have ever considered living in Paris."

"I see," her uncle said. "But you do not appear smitten."

"No. I am not," she agreed. "Still, I enjoy his company."

Her uncle looked thoughtful. "Hm. Though it would be unusual for a vicomte to ask for the hand of an English noblewoman, it isn't out of the question. It could happen. Indeed it might. But you will have other options, perhaps better ones."

"I am in no hurry, Uncle."

He shook his head, and she wasn't sure if he was serious. "This is precisely what has me worried."

* * *

She gave a last tug on the bow of her dark red sash as her maid helped her with the final touches on her appearance for the evening, then she went downstairs to meet her uncle.

"What a lovely gown, Mary," he remarked, offering his cravat for her to straighten as she so often did.

"It's the one I wore in London; you suggested I bring it to Paris."

"Oh, yes. I remember now. And I like your hair done up with pearls. It's quite attractive."

"My maid labored over it for some time. She thought the style made me look French. What do you think?"

"I hadn't thought about it, but yes, I can see the Parisian influence. I approve."

Mary winked at him and took his arm. "Our carriage awaits!"

* * *

Hugh had been in many of the impressive palaces of Europe, but the staterooms in the Tuileries Palace were among the finest.

Huge oil paintings of bewigged French aristocrats decorated the walls, reminding him of an earlier era. The gilding the French so loved was displayed on the walls, chairs and side tables, and of course on the crystal chandeliers and large mirrors. The wooden floors were inlayed with different-colored exotic woods, and the wallpaper in many of the rooms appeared to be gold brocade cloth, which he supposed it was. Extravagant, for a country that had endured a people's revolution, but he reminded himself, this was once again the home of a French monarch.

He and Lord Baynes stood together at one corner of the elegant reception room. Each had a French cognac in hand; thank God Napoleon had been fond of the drink and assured a continuing supply. He scanned the room and saw Mary some distance away drinking champagne while talking with that damn vicomte and the Austrian girl, Theresa Koller. When Mary laughed at something the vicomte said, Hugh had the sudden urge to drag her out to the gardens.

"Does he never leave her alone?"

He hadn't realized he spoke the thought aloud until his companion chuckled. "Not often." As Hugh continued to glare at the Frenchman, Lord Baynes leaned in to whisper, "I think he may be in love with her. He seems quite besotted."

Hugh's eyes narrowed dangerously. Decazes was smiling at Mary now. Stupidly.

"Take a walk with me, Ormond. I need to tell you what has happened," Lord Baynes remarked.

The two of them strolled out of the hall and onto a wide terrace. Alone at one end and mostly hidden in shadows, the older man explained to Hugh what Mary had observed and the message she'd recovered from Notre Dame.

"So, he is not merely an agent for us and the French, he is also working for the Prussians?"

"We have to at least consider the possibility." The diplomat's tone was serious. "But even with that, he could be acting for France. Who his real master is remains a mystery."

"It is good Martin has limited his information to that which we are willing to reveal."

"Yes," Lord Baynes agreed. "I would say it was a wise move. And is your friend—Sir Martin Powell, was it—the vicomte's only contact now?"

"Yes, for some time. Oh, and by the by, in France he is known as Martin Donet. He takes his French mother's name as part of his disguise." Hugh pondered the new information he'd learned. "I wonder what the Prussians are planning."

Mary's uncle appeared grim. "There has been bad blood between Louis and the Prussians for some time. I witnessed some of that bile during my work with the Congress of Vienna. It wouldn't surprise me if they were hoping to undermine Louis's new government, or even the king himself."

"There is more to this than the Prussians," Hugh decided, thinking about his recent conversation with Martin.

"Mary is to see the vicomte again tomorrow—a trip to a gallery, I believe, with General Koller's younger sister. Perhaps she will learn something more."

"Is that a good idea?" Hugh didn't like Mary involved in what was becoming more than just an indirect observational role.

Lord Baynes shrugged. "Though I have my reservations, you cannot deny these circumstances are an excellent opportunity for you to gain information. Based on how he feels about her, and on his family's standing with the king, I do not believe he would put Mary at risk. Besides, she is determined to go. I think we have little choice but to play this out and see what she discovers. Unless you want to tell her no...."

Hugh frowned. "Her love of adventure and her attraction to danger do not bode well." How could her uncle allow her to take such a risk? What kind of a guardian would be so cavalier about a young woman's safety?

As if her uncle read his thoughts, he said, "Mary thrives on this, you know."

"My concern exactly."

Lord Baynes pinned him with keen eyes. "Ormond, you have reminded me. A series of meetings with the allies will have me outside of Paris for a few days. It cannot be avoided. The allies are up in arms about the French following through on commitments, and I must be there to preserve Louis's point of view and allow Comte Decazes room for his needed reforms. Mary will have her friends to occupy her during the day, particularly Germaine, who has taken a great interest in her, but since your work with Martin Powell—or rather, Monsieur Donet—will keep you here…would you be willing to watch over her, especially in the evenings?"

"Of course," said Hugh. He didn't see how he could say no, though more time alone with Mary would severely test his restraint. Especially as she was set upon a dangerous course of action.

"I'd be most grateful. Your protection of her would give me peace of mind while I am away."

Hugh wondered if he would find any peace of mind, himself.

Chapter 14

Mary was keenly aware of Lord Ormond each time he came near, which thus far had been only during evenings at the Palace. She had no idea what occupied him during the day, but she supposed it was some business with her uncle. He certainly hadn't been seeking out her company.

She wondered if he was avoiding her. Much to her dismay, in her evenings at the Tuileries she found herself scanning the room for his tall imposing figure. It disturbed her that her heart beat more rapidly when he came into sight and that her eyes sought out that dark head of hair rising above the others. She still feared his reputation and thought his designs on her dishonorable, but despite all that she found herself wanting to be near him. Perhaps Elizabeth had been right when she suggested he was yet another adventure. But no. Mary knew it was more. How much more was what worried her.

Just now he was nowhere to be seen. She had been talking with Theresa Koller and Joseph Decazes for some time and relishing some very good French champagne. The subject was their planned visit the next day to see work by Jacques Louis David, a favorite French artist of the vicomte, though as Mary recalled he was somewhat controversial.

"Wasn't he a supporter of the Revolution?" she asked, surprised the vicomte would want to see David's paintings if that were true.

"Yes, Lady Mary, you are correct. He was quite enamored of Napoleon, but King Louis has granted him amnesty, even offering him the position of court painter. He is a splendid artist."

"Has he accepted the king's offer?"

"No. Much as we might wish otherwise, he has chosen instead to live and paint in Brussels. We can still enjoy his paintings, though, for some are here in Paris. I thought you might like to see them."

"Oh, I would." Mary was genuinely eager. She had heard about David's art. She also wanted to observe the vicomte's activities; she was beginning to think his visits around the city with her were more than just interesting diversions or even an attempt at courting her. "I am looking forward to it." She smiled at Theresa and Decazes and added, "But just now I need to find my uncle. Please excuse me."

As she started to walk away, the vicomte stopped her. He seemed anxious. "Would you like me to accompany you, Lady Mary?"

She laughed, amused. "No, please stay with Theresa. I'll only be a few minutes."

Though it was obvious to Mary he wanted to join her, he stayed with her friend and they resumed their conversation as she turned to go. Mary hurried out of the room and down the corridor, passing walls lined with paintings of French aristocrats. How different they seemed than the noblemen of England. Even their dress was more flamboyant: more lace, more ruffles. Many of the men wore powdered wigs that were no longer in fashion.

She rounded a corner and spotted a set of tall, paned glass doors leading outside. Just as she was thinking about going through them, they opened and her uncle and Lord Ormond stepped into the corridor.

"Look who we have here!" exclaimed her uncle. "Mary, are you alone?"

"Yes, I was hoping to get some fresh air. It's very hot in the main room."

"Well, I am certain Lord Ormond would be happy to escort you out."

Ormond said, "It would be my pleasure." He looked a bit uncomfortable, however.

Still he offered Mary his arm as soon as her uncle left, turning back toward the doors. "Shall we?"

"Yes, thank you." There was little Mary could do but take his arm. Her uncle had reminded them dinner would soon begin, so they didn't have much time.

As they stepped through the doors, Mary felt lightheaded. Just putting her hand through the crook of Ormond's elbow sent chills down her back. He was so close and so warm. Once again she was reminded of how powerful his body was, how she liked touching him, but the sensation was also disconcerting, like taking a stroll with a pirate. A very handsome pirate. A pirate who at any time might take what he wanted.

There were others seeking the night air. Couples walked the terrace, and some lingered at the surrounding balustrade. Toward the disciplined hedges bordering the Palace gardens Hugh led Mary down a set of stairs.

"You seem to always be escaping into gardens, Lady Mary. Why is that? I shall have to call you 'Lady Mary of the Gardens.'"

She thought about that. "I guess I eventually find myself more comfortable outside with my thoughts than with all those people, much as I enjoy some of them." She was embarrassed at how it sounded, but she tired easily of large crowds and longed for quiet after a time.

"You might be surprised to learn we have that in common."

She caught his smug look. "I see I have become a source of amusement for you."

"Not at all. Even you admit to liking gardens, Lady Mary. Is it wrong that I should as well?"

She smiled. "No. No, I suppose not."

"Are you enjoying yourself in Paris?"

"Very much." She had grown to love the city and the richness of its culture, despite the unsettled nature of the place—which made her think of the war and her conversation with Germaine. "You seem to know Madame de Stael well. Have you met her before?"

"I have known her for some years, from when I was here…"

"Before?" she finished.

"Yes, I have traveled to France before, and Germaine de Stael and I have met on several occasions."

She did not look at him as he guided her along a path deeper into beautifully landscaped gardens blooming with pink and red roses. The perfume of the flowers lingered faintly in the air, and Mary wondered what he wasn't saying. The last time Germaine was in Paris, Napoleon was emperor. But Germaine had said he helped her leave France. What was a British lord doing in France while Napoleon reigned?

"Your uncle has told me of your recent adventures involving Joseph Decazes," he said, disrupting the silence. Mary thought there was an edge to his voice. "You must be very careful, Lady Mary. It would not go well for you if you are discovered…interfering."

So, they were back to that. She felt like a scolded child. And why would her uncle tell Ormond the information she'd obtained?

"I am well aware of the danger, my lord." She knew she sounded irritated, but at the moment she didn't care.

Ormond pressed her gloved hand to his lips and kissed her fingers. "I am concerned you might be harmed."

Her flesh quivered at the touch of his lips, and so she withdrew her hand. Even through her gloves she had felt the effect deep in the most intimate part of her body. His kiss had been a tender but possessive gesture, and her reaction to it unnerved her.

She held her head high as she turned to face him. "I have been careful, and I will continue to be. You need not be concerned."

"But I am. You must know I am."

His eyes were dark glowing pools of heat in the low light of the garden, his deep voice as smooth as rich port. Their gazes locked for a long moment. Suddenly, they were like two powerful magnets brought so close that the force to pull them apart did not exist.

In an instant so fast she did not see it coming, his lips were on hers. His tongue pressed for entrance to her mouth and she surrendered. Despite her good intentions, she kissed him back and reached her arms to his shoulders. The kiss grew fiercer still, as passion was loosed that had been long reined in. His lips were demanding, his tongue dueling with hers and fanning the now familiar flames of desire. His arms wrapped around her waist and pulled her into his body.

His lips moved away from hers only to follow a hot trail down her neck to the pounding pulse at the base of her throat, to her collarbone where bare skin was exposed to his hunger. He nibbled there, making Mary shiver at his touch. She clung to him. Involuntarily her fingers moved into his thick locks of his hair as she held his head close. Her breath grew ragged, and her woman's center throbbed. That longing returned, that pleasant yet painful ache she experienced each time he kissed her. She was alarmed at how her body recognized his touch and so readily responded, but his hand moved to her breast, gently cupping the fullness and causing her to tremble.

A groan loosed from him just before he whispered her name. To Mary, that was a call to a place of secret retreat. She wanted to go with him wherever he led. Her heart was pounding so loud that she was sure he could hear. She was swimming in his masculine scent, overcome by the power of his tall, muscled body pressed to hers; his fingers rubbing her nipple were driving her mad.

Alarms began to sound in her head at the unprecedented intimacy. "Ormond...Hugh...we must...stop," she breathed in a ragged whisper, and with the last remnants of control she pulled his hand away from her breast.

He drew close once more, kissed her softly and whispered, "You said my name. I like it on your lips." He hesitated before adding, "I cannot stay away from you, Mary. And frankly, I don't want to."

He held her close, her head just under his chin. Her breasts rose and fell against his muscled chest. Fear gripped her at what he might be contemplating and all she was feeling; she had to guard her heart, and at this moment that seemed an impossible task. After all, hearts could give themselves away.

Suddenly, he stepped back, holding her out with his arms. Mary wanted to reach for him. Her whole body ached for him, yet she knew she should not.

"I'll take you back." With those words, his face changed, as if he'd donned a mask. His dark eyes grew cold, and the longing and desire she had seen in them moments before vanished. Was he having the same difficulty controlling the passion as she was, or was there something else going on?

"Thank you," she replied, praying her own mask was as good. She took his arm and they walked back in silence, the coolness of the night air calming her still-racing heart.

Apparently the vicomte had been looking for her. He came down the corridor toward them, and as Mary and Hugh drew near, the Frenchman called, "Lord Ormond, dinner is about to be served, and I was hoping I could see Lady Mary to her seat."

"By all means," said Hugh. "I was merely escorting her through the gardens at her uncle's request. She wanted some air."

Decazes seemed relieved, and he reached for her hand. "*Bon.* I'll be happy to escort you from here, Lady Mary."

She went with him, but as she did she turned back to Hugh. "Thank you, Lord Ormond. I trust you will have a good evening."

His face betrayed no sorrow for their interrupted passion. "You as well, Lady Mary."

Chapter 15

"I can hardly wait to see!"

The vicomte, too, was obviously enjoying himself. His face sported a grin as he said, "*C'est bon.* We will soon be there."

Mary had been thrilled at the chance to see the paintings of the celebrated artist she had heard so much about, but Theresa had not said a word on the journey, so Mary was startled when her friend suddenly spoke. "I am anxious to see David's paintings of Napoleon."

"There will certainly be some of those," agreed Decazes. "David was a favorite of his." He gave the brown-haired girl a curious look.

The gallery was in a part of Paris housing shops nestled along narrow winding streets that were dirty and crowded with horse and cart traffic. Though new streets were being constructed to accommodate the growing population, none were new in this part of town. The added burden of horse droppings only made the situation worse, making it difficult for the carriage to move along with any speed.

They had traveled for some time when the carriage pulled up at a corner and a footman opened the door. Decazes helped Theresa and Mary down, explaining that they would need to walk a bit to the narrow street that held the gallery, but both Mary and Theresa had been prepared, wearing dresses suitable for day travel and hooded cloaks to shield them from the damp afternoon. Though there was occasional sun, it had turned cold again in Paris.

Mary wore a blue gown with a warm, dark blue woolen cloak. Theresa wore a dark green garment that complemented her rich brown hair. The vicomte stayed the prominent French aristocrat, dressed in a gray waistcoat and trousers with a black frock coat and hat.

The first thing Mary noticed as they stepped into the gallery was the rainbow of colors. "Oh my."

The richness of the oils on canvas was a welcome assault upon her senses. All around her, a striking display of reds, browns, yellows and oranges pulled her attention in various directions. Large paintings hung on cream-colored walls. They were glorious to her thinking, the figures life-size, the colors vibrant and the scenes inspiring. The gallery had a high ceiling, and the light from the windows above illuminated each of the works of art. Many of the paintings were as tall as she was, displaying historic and mythic subjects.

Theresa seemed to recognize all those that had been a part of Napoleon's France, and she patiently explained them to Mary. It was wonderful to walk among the paintings, for David, she recognized, was truly a master.

One painting in particular drew Mary. It was very large, taking up nearly the entire wall. Entitled *Leonidas at Thermopylae*, it told the story of brave Leonidas, who led three hundred Spartans to sacrifice themselves, defending Greece against Persian invaders.

The vicomte stepped to her side as she admired the painting. "Has this one captured your interest, Lady Mary?"

"Yes, it has." She read the title plate. "He only completed this painting a few years ago."

Her eyes examined the beauty of the human form as only a master could call it forth on canvas. But while she found the noble cause uplifting, what drew her most was the sensuality of the men of battle. Instead of the bold warrior before her, she saw Hugh Redgrave and his masculine earthiness, the muscles of his naked chest.

Was the man she now thought of as "Hugh" never far from her thoughts? She hoped Decazes standing beside her did not notice the flush in her cheeks.

Mary continued to admire the painting while listening to Decazes describe its complexities. Theresa joined them to comment as well, pointing out that the painting represented a change in David's style. At this point the vicomte left, however, and out of the corner of her eye Mary watched.

He stood off to one side, several feet away as a man dressed like a tradesman approached. She could only hear snippets of their conversation, but it sounded as if they were speaking German.

When the tradesman left the room, Decazes returned to Mary and Theresa. "Please excuse me, Lady Mary, Mademoiselle Koller," he said, "but I must attend to a small issue. I will return shortly." Theresa just shrugged, gave him an odd look and turned back to the painting.

Mary followed Decazes with her eyes, watching as he passed through the crowd and then stepped around a wall dividing the front of the gallery from the rear. As soon as she could, Mary left Theresa pondering another painting to follow. She peeked around the corner of the wall to see the vicomte talking with two men only a few feet away, his back to her. They were speaking German in harsh whispers. Again, she heard only snippets of the conversation, but enough to know the Prussians were demanding some promised information. Mary was reminded of the hidden note she'd taken from the cathedral the day before.

Concerned she would be noticed, she returned to Theresa. Soon Decazes rejoined them, but his face bore an anxious look that quickly became a forced smile.

"Would you ladies enjoy some coffee? I know of a place not far from here. We can walk."

"That would be very nice," Mary said. She had seen enough for one afternoon, and the coffee served in Paris would be a welcome change from tea.

"Yes, let us do have coffee," agreed Theresa. "A cup of something warm would be most welcome."

They left the gallery and plunged into a cold wind. Mary drew her cloak more tightly around her, glad for its warmth, but they had traveled only a short distance before they heard shouting behind them. Turning back, she saw two groups of men, their faces twisted in anger. The men shouted taunts at each other, and from the exchange it was clear the altercation was between ultra royalists and liberals.

The shouts became more heated. Suddenly, a group broke off and began to run toward them. "He has a gun!" came the shout in French of one of the men, a liberal dressed like a dockworker and wearing a dark knit cap on his head.

Decazes attempted to move them away, but before he could, several of the well-dressed royalists drew pistols and fired shots at the retreating group. A few liberals came running toward them, and Mary stood frozen in horror. More shots exploded around them. Bullets whooshed by, and Mary ducked, fearful of being shot.

"Henri's been hit!" cried a man with a knife.

What was happening? *Oh my God.*

Still frozen, Mary saw a man fall to the ground not far away. He was holding his chest, blood oozing over his hands. Another shot was fired, and another man fell. Liberals and royalists both yelled; confusion reigned all around. Mary was knocked to the ground as a man pushed roughly by her trying to escape. Bodies were scattered on the paving stones. Men lay everywhere groaning.

The vicomte lay on the ground a few feet away holding his left arm to his chest. Blood spilled over his dark coat sleeve and onto his light gray trousers. Mary searched frantically for Theresa, found her several feet away pressed up against a building, a horrified look on her face. The conflict was still erupting around them, but now it had devolved into several fist and knife fights.

Still lying on the ground, Mary jerked to one side to avoid a falling man. As she did, strong arms suddenly lifted her. She whipped around to see her captor, but the sight was entirely a surprise as she stared into the face of Hugh, his stern dark eyes mere inches from her own.

"Hugh…?"

"Are you hurt, Mary?" His eyes roved over her body.

"No, I'm…fine." She was simply stunned.

Hugh looked past her and shouted, "Decazes, can you walk?"

"Yes." The vicomte's voice was weak, though, and she saw him wince as he struggled to his feet.

"Where is your carriage?" Hugh called, still holding Mary to his chest. She felt like a child in his strong arms.

"Just around the next corner and down another street."

By this time, the combat was moving away, leaving only the bodies of the dead or wounded strewn about the narrow street. Hugh lifted Mary and set her on her feet, but he kept his arm tightly around her. He called to Theresa, and she came eagerly. With the vicomte following, Hugh escorted the women to the waiting carriage.

The footmen, who had not realized their charges had been caught in the fighting they'd heard at a distance, gave cries of alarm when they saw them approach.

"Vicomte, you are wounded!" one of them exclaimed, reaching for his injured master who still bled profusely.

"Vicomte," his coachman urged, "we must see you to a doctor."

Hugh guided Theresa toward the carriage. "Take Theresa, too."

"I don't think the wound is deep," Decazes was saying, gazing down at his arm. "It all happened so fast." But Mary could see his bloodstained jacket and wondered just how badly he was hurt.

The coachman agreed. Grave concern in his eyes, he said, "We should leave."

Mary stared Decazes's wound. "I should go and help."

"No," Hugh said sternly. "You're coming with me."

She started to move toward the carriage anyway. He took firm hold of her arm and drew her back to his side.

Indignant, she pulled on her arm. "What if I don't wish to come with you?"

"Madam, what you want just now is of little concern." His dark eyes were full of anger, at least until he turned to the Austrian girl who regarded him with huge brown eyes of her own. "Theresa can go with him. Are you in agreement, Theresa? You will make sure that he is seen by a doctor?"

"Of…of course," she replied in a halting tone.

"I will see her safely home," said the vicomte, looking at Theresa and still clutching his arm. He was obviously eager to return to the role of protector.

The coachman was happy to be moving away from the scene of the violence, and he rushed to help Theresa into the carriage. Decazes followed, using his good arm to lift himself in. Once inside, he peered out the window to where Mary stood at Hugh's side.

"Lady Mary, I'm so sorry."

Mary was only concerned for his wound. "This wasn't your fault. Just take care of yourself."

"May I call upon you tomorrow?" he asked.

"Yes, if you're well enough," she said, surprised he would ask such a thing given his condition.

Hugh scowled and began to pull her toward him, and Decazes's carriage sped away even as the British lord continued to drag Mary in the opposite direction. The street was still littered with bodies, and curious people had begun to check who was left alive.

"You don't have to pull me so. I can walk!" Mary was cross and becoming more annoyed by the second.

Hugh was brusque. "I want to get you out of here."

Mary didn't reply.

She allowed him to pull her down the street and struggled to keep up with his long strides. At last they reached a broader avenue where he hailed a carriage. He quickly assisted Mary into the vehicle that stopped.

Her hair had fallen out of its pins and her clothes were covered in dirt on one side from her fall to the ground. Hugh climbed in behind her and directed the coachman to an address she didn't know as he watched Mary brush the dirt from her cloak. Then, without warning, he grasped the top of Mary's arms and shook her once.

"You must not take such chances!"

Shocked and angry, Mary spat fire at him. "Take your hands off me!"

He yanked her into his lap and his lips crushed hers. It was a kiss of fierce possession, as if he could bind her to him. As if he were afraid—

As she began to respond to his kiss, he withdrew and buried his face in her hair, pulling her tightly to his chest. She stilled in his arms. She'd never seen such a rush of fierce emotion from him. He held her tightly for a few moments, breathing heavily. Eventually she felt him relax; his breath returned to normal. Mary moved to sit next to him, but he kept his arm around her. She began to feel a sense of wonder as he looked down at her.

The carriage slowed, and Hugh got out. Mary watched through the window as he retrieved a horse—his own, she assumed; he must have left it here earlier—and tied it to the back of the carriage. When he returned, his anger had, too.

"This is not a safe part of town, Mary, not that any place in Paris is entirely safe right now. Thieves and pickpockets roam the streets."

Mary scoffed. "Those were not thieves or pickpockets. They were yelling about revenge."

"Even worse. You could have been killed. Such men would not think twice to take your life…or your virtue."

Mary had seen the pain in his eyes as he let her go. Her concern for him had calmed her, but now his words were making her feel like a scolded child again. "It was a gallery!" she nearly shouted. "Artists don't always live in the best part of town."

His face twisted in anger. "That is why it was not the best choice for an outing." He added, "For which I blame Decazes."

Mary's lips stung from his kiss, and his body so close to hers was unsettling. Suddenly a thought occurred to her, and in an unsteady voice she asked, "How did you know where we were?"

Hugh's eyes flashed just for a second. "I was aware you were visiting the gallery and I happened to be near when I heard the shots."

Mary thought that too great a coincidence. "Were you following me?"

"Let's just say I was concerned about your destination today. As I mentioned, that district is not safe."

"You *were* following me!"

"Get used to it," he insisted in a harsh voice. It was a final pronouncement, allowing no debate. If she hadn't been so angry, she might have been thrilled at his caring for her.

He took her hand, regret in his eyes. "Mary…"

His voice was a whisper, and she had the impression he wanted to say more. A great tenderness swept over her and she did not pull away. His warmth and strength were comforting, and she had to admit she had been shaken by the disaster in the street. It was all she could do to resist the overwhelming desire to crawl into his lap and revel in his warmth. But fear held her back, fear of what it might mean if she gave in to her desire for him.

In a calmer voice he said, "Promise me you will not go there again."

She could see he was genuinely concerned, and she had no desire to return to the gallery. For that reason, she gave him what he wanted. "I promise."

The carriage moved on, eventually returning to the central part of the city and following the river Seine. When the vehicle finally stopped, Mary was surprised to see Luxembourg Palace, a massive chateau with wings on each side of a central building.

"Why have you brought me here?" Mary asked after Hugh got out, helped her down and instructed the driver to wait.

"There is a place on the other side of the palace I sometimes come when I want to be alone to think. It's a very special place and…I thought you would find it calming after what you have just been through."

She didn't know what to say to that, so they walked in silence on the wide dirt path leading around the right side of the palace. The only sounds were from Mary's shoes and Hugh's boots on the hard-packed earth. At last he took her hand and led her into what appeared to be a grove of trees. His grip was warm and comforting.

Off the path, she could see ahead a long rectangular pool of dark green water and a tall stone fountain at the far end. They were in a grotto. She could hear water falling and birds in the trees. Her eyes traveled the length of the rectangular reflecting pond to the large stone at the other end, not recognizing the carved images except to note one was a coat of arms. The trees lined both sides of the pond. The sun had emerged from the clouds and filtered through the leaves, casting a soft glow of green around them. It was very peaceful, like a place out of a fairy tale. A fountain with two streams of water and a white marble statue graced a niche of the grotto. The running water made a gurgling sound.

"It's so…beautiful. I was not aware this place existed."

"The fountain was built nearly two hundred years ago by Marie de Medici, the Italian mother of King Louis XIII. I think she must have been missing her home in Florence when she had it designed."

"What is the statue?"

"It's supposed to be Venus in her bath."

"Oh." Mary looked closely at the white marble form in the distance, imagining it to be the goddess. The sound of water flowing over the stone blended with the chirping of the birds, and she felt calm enveloping her. "It is peaceful here, restful."

"Napoleon restored it after the Revolution. We can give him credit for that."

Mary nodded. "He did some good—at least for Paris." Her mind conjured up Notre Dame once again.

Hugh had a faraway look, too. "I used to come here to think…about my brother."

"Your brother?" Mary had never heard Hugh Redgrave had a brother.

"I was eight when he was born. I had been the single child in the family for many years. I doted on him, and I allowed him to see me as a hero. I guess I wanted to be one. His, at least." A boyish smile crossed his face.

"He was just a younger version of me." Hugh shrugged. "Whenever I was home, we were inseparable, he was my shadow. I suppose it wasn't surprising he came to share my passion for horses. I taught him to ride." He paused, an expression of pain crossing his face. For a moment Mary thought he would be unable to go on.

"I was away from our family estate one day and Henry decided to ride my stallion, a horse much like your Midnight. It was foolish of him, but no one was around that afternoon to stop him. Likely he planned it that way. Anyway, he took my horse. How he…" Hugh paused again before continuing. "He must have been riding him too fast. The men who found him believed he was pulled from the saddle by a low-hanging branch. He was killed in the fall. A broken neck. I arrived home just as they were carrying his body back."

His expression broke Mary's heart. She had always thought his eyes masked something deep in his soul. Now she knew it was pain. "I am so sorry, Hugh. But it was not your fault. You could not have known."

Hugh sighed. "Perhaps not, but I encouraged him. His death drove me away from my family for many years and into the service of the Crown. For a while I cared little for anything, even my own life. I was willing to take any assignment. It is very hypocritical of me to accuse you of being reckless; few have ever been more reckless than I was in those days. But in France I found myself again. And I found purpose. It was like coming back to life."

Mary was silent. He'd explained so much and yet still she was left wondering. One thing was certain, however. Hugh Redgrave, the Marquess of Ormond, was more than a rake. Much more.

He stepped close. "Mary, I'm sorry if I was rough with you. It's just that when I saw you on the ground it made me think of Henry. And when I heard the shots…well, it…" He closed his eyes, unable to go on.

She cupped his cheek with her hand. "It's all right. I'm glad you found me."

He opened his eyes. They were obsidian pools reflecting only pain, and while she was suddenly aware of how close he was, she wanted him closer. Without thinking, she leaned toward him and rested her head on his chest. It felt so right, like this was the place she was meant to be.

He wrapped his arms around her but spoke not a word. A moment later, he pulled back and she looked up, their eyes locking. Mary knew her expression gave away everything she was thinking, everything she was feeling. She wanted to comfort him, but more, she wanted to love him. And she wanted him to love her.

Hugh lifted her chin with his finger and brought his lips to hers. Gently he kissed her, as if she were the most precious thing in the world. But the kiss was gentle only for a moment. He soon parted her lips with his tongue and his hands pulled her hips tightly to his. He had taught her how to kiss, how to want his body close. She could feel the hard ridge of his arousal. Her tongue tangled with his as her fingers tangled in his hair. She couldn't hear the birds any longer, only the sounds of their breathing.

Hugh broke the kiss, and without a word he took her hand and led her around the grotto. Confused and aching for more, she searched for something to say, anything to break the silence. "Wasn't this the place where Michael Ney was executed by a firing squad?" She realized it sounded a bit absurd given what they'd been doing.

He chuckled. "Only you would remember such a fact." His thumb stroked the back of her hand, a lover's caress. "The answer is yes—and no. It was not here in the grotto but on the grounds in front of the Palace."

"It seems a terrible deed to occur in such a lovely setting."

"Yes, it was, but I don't think about that when I'm here."

"Do you come here often?"

"No, but when I do, it seems to restore me. I guess that is why I thought of it today…and I wanted to share it with you."

She considered the man holding her hand. Strong and silent at times, deeply passionate at others. Always sensual. He was an enigma, but God, how she could love him.

It seemed, as it had before, that he fought for control whenever they kissed. She knew if they persisted it would lead to a place she was not ready to go, though her body yearned for a joining with his. She supposed she should be grateful for his not taking advantage of the passion between them. More the gentleman, he.

"Thank you for sharing this with me, Hugh, and for telling me about your brother."

* * *

The ride home was silent, though he did not let go of her hand. When he dropped her off at her uncle's apartments, she curled up in front of the fireplace with a cup of tea to think. There was indeed much going on in Paris. Somehow both Hugh and Decazes were involved. And what of her uncle? There were too many pieces of the puzzle missing. And around it all swirled the growing passion between her and Hugh.

The next afternoon, Mary was sitting in the parlor when her uncle's butler Pierre announced the vicomte. The French nobleman's left arm was in a sling, the white fabric prominent over his dark blue jacket.

She frowned in concern. "How is your arm?"

He grinned. "I'll live. It's only a flesh wound, more embarrassing than painful. I am so sorry Lady Mary that—"

"Come," she interrupted, "sit down and I'll order some of your wonderful French coffee for us." Then she called the servants and did just that, requesting both coffee and pastries. As they took seats in front of the fireplace she inquired, "How is Theresa?"

"Shaken, but she seemed fine by the time we arrived at my town house. She was mumbling something about Paris being safer under Napoleon—probably a hysterical reaction to seeing blood spilled. My coachman took her home."

The coffee and pastries arrived. Mary peered at Decazes over her cup and asked, "Does that happen often? The violence in the streets, I mean."

"More often than I would like. The streets of Paris still present opportunities for those whose ambitions would see them control France." His face reflected worry. "But it is getting better, Lady Mary. The city will one day return to a calm and tranquil place."

Mary did not share his certainty, but being in the center of history appealed more than violence repelled her, so she smiled and took a swallow of coffee. "Well, it certainly made for an exciting afternoon."

Decazes chuckled. "I admire your courage, Lady Mary. You are taking all this in stride, and that tells me you are not the meek sort."

Suppressing a laugh she said, "No, I've never been accused of being meek."

After a few moments of pleasant conversation, Mary made a decision. As long as they were alone, she might ask about his work. With all that she'd observed, she knew he was involved in something surreptitious. Perhaps he was a spy for some government…but which one? It seemed unlikely that he would tell her all but she might learn something that would explain what was going on. At least, so she hoped. It was clear that he had a fondness for her.

"Tell me what consumes your time here in Paris, Vicomte. Tell me all you are doing."

Over the next hour, he told her details of his work with the new government and his brother the comte. He seemed proud of his contributions, working hard to instill new reforms that would, as his brother put it, "royalize France and nationalize the monarchy." Decazes did not talk of other assignments, however, and Mary found herself getting impatient. What he had shared had been interesting but it was also all above board. She wanted to know the rest.

"Have you many dealings with the Prussians? I see them at the Tuileries each evening, and they seem a strong presence in Paris."

He seemed surprised. "Well, they have troops still in the city, of course. You must know that no Frenchman particularly likes the Prussians, however. There has been bad blood between us since the clash in Berlin years ago. Their desire to annex Saxony was a particular annoyance to King Louis."

So he didn't think much of the Prussians. Then why was he passing them information? It was all so confusing.

As his expression grew pensive, Mary poured them more coffee. "Is there something wrong?"

"No," he said, "I was just thinking of our visit to the cathedral the other day. I think I lost something there."

Her heart stopped, but she kept her face blank. "What?"

"Oh, just some notes to myself. Did you happen to see them?"

"No, I was looking up the whole time at the windows and arches. I only looked down when we went to leave, when I realized I dropped my glove." She forced herself to laugh, trying to convey how silly she'd been.

Decazes examined her over the rim of his cup. "Lady Mary, will you be free this Saturday evening?"

That was three days away. Her uncle would be back, which meant she would have the added benefit of his advice if anything difficult developed. And there was always Hugh. "Why, yes, I think so. There is no affair scheduled that evening, at least not that I have heard."

"I was thinking you might like to go to dinner and the theater. Have you ever been to *La Tour d'Argent*—The Tower of Silver, near the cathedral? It's my favorite restaurant, and they serve wonderful veal."

Well, what he offered was yet another chance to get closer to him and to discern where his loyalties truly lay. Then, too, she legitimately liked Decazes. If he wasn't a spy and a traitor, they might be good friends. For that reason, she answered in the affirmative.

Chapter 16

Martin Powell gazed across the desk at Hugh Redgrave, watching him read the missive. It reminded him of something he had once heard: A country can make a man. That was certainly true in Ormond's case. A country *had* molded the man. His duties in France had changed him, required things of him, and after each conflict a different man moved forward. Like a rock being weathered by tides and rain, Ormond had been shaped by war. No, not all of Britain's heroes in the war with France were celebrated. Some had served in secret. Ormond was one of those, a man of stealth and strategy. As long as Napoleon had remained in France, the British lord remained the thief of the emperor's secrets. Ormond and Martin had survived many narrow escapes and worn many costumes. Along the way, they had become friends.

Martin's Paris office was not large, though it was all he needed. It had a good-sized wooden desk, now covered with maps and papers piled in neat stacks. A few bookcases held various government documents and records, and a large black safe stood in one corner. He and Ormond often retreated here to think and to plan just as they did this night.

Ormond looked up from the paper. "What does all this tell you?"

"You will find the story amazing, my friend." Martin reached into the bottom drawer of his desk to pull out the French brandy he kept there. He poured the amber liquid into two glasses he took from a shelf and handed one to Hugh. "It seems we are not yet finished with those who resent the Bourbons. We've identified some Napoleon supporters who want to return the Nightmare of Europe from yet *another* of his exiles. Now of course it is St.

Helena. From what we've uncovered, they are willing to undertake drastic measures to see it done."

Ormond sighed. "We've been down this path before." He took a big swallow of brandy. "What kind of people would join such a group?"

Martin almost laughed, grim though the answer was. "Napoleon's former soldiers, his officers now on half pay, government workers ousted by the ultra-royalist Chamber, enemies of the monarchy, liberals objecting to the revenge of the ultras… The list is a long one, I'm afraid."

Ormond grimaced. "I guess I shouldn't be surprised. The king will face treachery for years to come."

"Louis is a wise leader, one who can weather the storm."

"But he is an old one. I wonder if he will be able to deal with opposition like this."

Martin tried to bolster his friend's spirits. "The men he has attracted to his government—men like Decazes and Richelieu— will bring stability. It gives me hope, Ormond. England will one day benefit from the friendship it offered Louis when he was in exile. You shall see."

Ormond gazed into the distance. "I hope you are right. France needs a stable government. Hell, Europe needs one."

Martin nodded. Leaning back in his chair, he put his hands behind his head just as his eyes caught some papers upon his desk. They reminded him: "Oh, there is something else I wanted you to see. It adds a strange footnote to our concern about Napoleon's friends lurking in the wings, a rather bizarre connection to our own English poet, Lord Byron."

"What?" Ormond said.

Martin nodded. "I know it sounds strange, but when the dethroned ruler escaped from Elba, Byron admitted he was dazzled. Now the poet is stirring the fires of revolt with poems extolling Boney's virtues." He picked up a sheet and began to read.

> "'Farewell to thee, France! but when Liberty rallies
> Once more in thy regions, remember me then
> The Violet still grows in the depth of thy valleys
> Though withered, thy tears will unfold it again
> Yet – yet – I may baffle the hosts that surround us
> And yet may thy heart leap awake to my voice
> There are links which must break in the chain that has bound us,
> *Then* turn thee and call on the Chief of thy choice!'"

Martin finished reading and shook his head. "Think of it! 'The Chief of thy choice'? Is it any wonder Napoleon's supporters are inspired?"

"Just what we need." Ormond grimaced. "A poet urging a return to insanity. I had hoped, perhaps unreasonably, that Napoleon was finally gone from the hearts of the French. The king will not be able to bring all the factions into the fold. Not if such treachery succeeds."

"It bears watching, certainly."

Ormond took another drink as Martin stared at the brandy he swirled in his glass. "I've had my hands full dealing with information coming from the new government and watching Lord Baynes's niece, who has become a major project, so I've lost track. Have you uncovered anything involving the Prussians?"

Martin raked his hand through his hair as he considered the question. "There have been Prussians in the mix at the meetings of Napoleon supporters we've infiltrated, but for what purpose we do not yet know. They have never been fond of the French, so it seems a strange alliance."

Ormond nodded. "It takes little imagination to see what a tangle this could become."

"Just now it is a bit of a maze," Martin agreed. He picked up his pen and circled Paris on their map. "The prospect of a military action by Prussians in Paris is worrisome, so we cannot dismiss it easily. Do you know something I do not? Has my agent in the French government, the Vicomte Decazes, been leading you on a merry chase?"

"Not really. I've given you what little I've learned," his friend replied. Then: "No. Nothing you don't suspect."

"Do you have time to join me in the hunt?"

Ormond laughed. "Oh-ho. Not so fast. You are the spy. I am a mere thief."

"'Mere'?" It was Martin's turn to laugh. "It seems to me that your accomplishments moved you past 'mere' long ago."

"We digress, Monsieur Donet," said Ormond. You well know I've left that role behind. At least, that is what Prinny would have. My role here is purely as an aid to our diplomat…and it seems that role is expanding with each day. Which leads me to my next question: How do you assess the threat to the British in the city?"

Martin fought back disappointment. More than once he had called upon his friend and fellow Englishman, and the British lord had always been there, once even saving him from death by another's blade. "Knowing we are allied to the Bourbon monarchy? Napoleon's supporters will expect us to protect the king, so I imagine they will try to neutralize us. They would have to."

The two men sat in silence, pondering all they knew and wondering what they did not.

At last Martin shifted his gaze from the map to Ormond. "It is not difficult to imagine that the supporters of the deposed emperor and the disenfranchised might well join forces with the Prussians."

"The enemy of my enemy is my friend," Ormond muttered under his breath.

Martin nodded. "Quite so." Which led him to something else. As his friend rose to leave, Martin raised a hand to stop him. "One last thing. Our man posing as one of the Napoleon supporters has learned they are searching for the Nighthawk again."

Hugh looked surprised. "The Nighthawk? Why?"

"I suspect it is a matter of both unfinished business and revenge." He paused and gave Ormond a wry smile. "I suppose he should not have kissed the general's daughter when he stole those plans. She well remembered him."

Hugh shrugged. After a moment, he gave a great sigh. "It was a whim. I should have exercised more control. Something I'm surprisingly finding harder and harder to do."

Chapter 17

"Germaine, how do you feel about having an adventure?"

Mary's excitement was spilling over. She had traveled to the older woman's apartments for morning coffee and good conversation, and she had come alone for a reason. The paper she'd found in the hallway of the Tuileries Palace was burning a hole in the pocket of her gown. She had a plan, and if she were successful Germaine would be a part of it.

The coffee was hot. Germaine drank deeply and set her cup down. "An adventure, my dear? What kind of an adventure?"

Mary handed Germaine the note and explained her interpretation, and the woman seemed intrigued. "What exactly are you suggesting, Lady Mary?"

"I want to see what is being kept in that warehouse. If I can verify that it holds French soldiers' uniforms—if I can see them for myself—well, the French government might be interested to know. Don't you think?"

"I love a good adventure, but it sounds dangerous. Should you be correct, it seems like something the government should handle on its own."

"It isn't as if I haven't thought about the danger," Mary replied. "I have. But think of it, Germaine! I can only imagine what nefarious use the Prussians would make of French uniforms. This could be of great importance to both France and England."

"What precisely do you propose to do?"

"If such a warehouse exists, I'd like to see it for myself—to get inside. I think I could do that without drawing too much attention…if I were dressed as a lad and had a bit of help."

"Dressed as a lad, you say?" Germaine bit back a smile. "This bold suggestion of yours both alarms and amuses. You are a brave young woman. A bit impetuous, perhaps, but it occurs to me you may have done this before."

Mary blushed. "Well, actually...I *am* rather comfortable in such garb, though usually it is for purposes of riding."

"I daresay you must shock your English peers. But do continue. What would be my role in all of this?"

Mary smiled. "Cover...and perhaps one of your footmen?"

Germaine listened intently as Mary spilled her plans like milk from an overfull pitcher.

"I've been thinking we could take a carriage, a common one that would not raise any suspicion. We could leave it a street or two away, and you could stay with the carriage while I take a footman with me into the warehouse. He could help me open any storage containers and perhaps afford some protection should we encounter someone unexpectedly, and we might have to deal with a guard, and of course the warehouse will be locked, but I'm sure we can figure out some way around that. With a bit of planning it could work. Oh, say you agree, Germaine! Think what it could mean if I'm right."

"It's quite a daring idea," said Germaine, "not to mention illegal." But her brown eyes told Mary the older woman was intrigued. "Perhaps I do need some excitement. Things have been rather dull since my return to Paris. When would we do this?"

"I would like to ride by the place this afternoon, just to fix the location and see the area. We first need to know if there is a warehouse at this address and if it is being guarded."

"Yes, that seems reasonable," Germaine agreed.

"We would need a plain carriage for this, nothing fancy," Mary continued. "If all goes well, we could plan for our examination of the warehouse tomorrow. That is, if you have the time." She gave the older woman a look that she hoped was her most convincing.

"Well, yes," Germaine said, "I think I do have time just now."

The conversation quickly led to plans for the carriage and clothes for Mary and the footman that might provide a legitimate disguise. Mary felt in perfect form, and she felt certain that this adventure would be worthier than any of her past achievements. She just hoped they wouldn't get caught. She knew that, if she were, this time the consequence would be much worse than embarrassment at getting caught with a lady's chemise or a week confined to her room.

* * *

That afternoon, Mary and Germaine dressed simply and climbed into a rundown carriage pulled by horses that appeared to have spent many years on the road. The warehouse was in a different part of town near the river, and so they had to cross the city. They traveled some distance, and at times the unpaved streets rendered it a most uncomfortable journey. But Mary was determined.

Her gaze drifted out the carriage window, but she barely noticed the city, her thoughts consumed with their plans and what Hugh might think of them. She had been reminded of him when she tried on the boy's clothes to make sure of the fit. No, he would not like her plans at all.

"Germaine, the other night at the Palace you seemed to know my countryman, Lord Ormond. Had you met him before?"

"Oh, yes," the woman said. "I know him. Ormond is an old friend."

Mary felt her heart skip a beat, surprised at the jealousy even a woman of Germaine's age could stir in her, knowing the two had been close. "Might I ask how long you have known him?"

"For several years, my dear."

"When Napoleon was ruling France?"

"Yes." The woman paused, and a sly look crossed her face. "You seem quite interested in my friend Ormond. How well do you know him?"

Though they had been together in several settings and he had kissed her more than once, Mary knew there was a great deal she still did not know about the man. "Not well, really."

"Ah." Germaine glanced out the window. "Hugh Redgrave was an only child for many years. That is why he plays the piano so well. Did you know he played?"

"Yes," Mary said, though music was not what she wanted to hear about. "I heard him play at a house party. It was beautiful…as if he could feel the music in his soul."

Germaine nodded and smiled. "He told me his mother taught him."

"He must have a close family," Mary said.

"He did at one time." Germaine's brown eyes observed her closely. "Did you know he had a younger brother?"

"Yes," Mary admitted. "He told me about Henry."

Germaine paused. "He must consider you special. He doesn't speak of his brother to many people. It was a great tragedy. He came to France to forget the past, I think. That is when I first knew him. For a while it seemed he cared little for his own life. He was—and is—very daring. I believe he still carries the pain of little Henry's death. I have sometimes thought it keeps him from caring for anyone else."

The two women rode together in silence, and outside the scenery changed from tree-lined streets with elegant town homes and large buildings to a more commercial part of the city, tall ramshackle warehouses. Old and weathered, their peeling paint reflected years of neglect. A few were so tall they all but blocked the sky. Trash lingered in front of the buildings. A gutter ran down the center of the road, bringing with it foul smells. Fewer people were in sight, only an occasional workman hurrying off to complete some task. There were no women in fine dresses. There were no women at all.

Soon the carriage turned onto the street they were looking for, and the warehouse that was their destination loomed before them. There was little activity and no guards that they could see. By plan, the carriage traveled past the warehouse and stopped some distance away, and the footman Jacques, whom Germaine had earlier introduced to Mary, climbed down from the top of the carriage and went to the warehouse to survey the large doors leading into the building.

He knocked, but as they anticipated there came no answer. They also expected to find it locked, which it was.

"I wonder if it's always left unguarded," Mary mused after Jacques returned and relayed all he'd discovered. He then climbed back up onto the carriage and they were again in motion.

Germaine did not seem concerned one way or another. "I have no idea, but this is the best scenario, no? It will present the least danger for us."

Mary lifted a curtain to glance out the carriage window. "I suppose you are right." But, whether there were guards or not, there was a problem that remained: "We still need to find a way to get inside."

Germaine smiled. "I think I have someone."

Mary grinned in return. "Wonderful," she enthused. She had chosen her partner well.

Chapter 18

"She wants to do *what?*" Hugh shouted.

"As I said, she believes the Prussians may be storing French army uniforms in a warehouse, and she wants to be sure her information is correct before letting the authorities know."

Hugh ran his hand over the back of his neck, his other hand resting on his hip. *Good God.* The girl was becoming a full-time assignment, putting herself in danger with every step she took. This thing she contemplated could have grave consequences, and it wasn't even the bad luck of stumbling onto a random riot.

"She goes from one disaster to another," he exclaimed, venting his fury. "What can the little minx be thinking? It is ludicrous!"

Germaine shrugged. "Ormond, she wants to see this through. I, for one, would feel the same. You cannot deny that Lady Mary may have discovered some nest of intrigue."

Hugh glared. "You're both daft is what I can't deny. You shouldn't be encouraging her, Germaine. She has a taste for danger and too much time on her hands. This is not one of her foolish little adventures. This could end badly. Very badly. For many more people than her."

Germaine nodded. "Actually, I think that's why she cares so much. But Lady Mary also worries that she may not have the full picture, and she wants to make sure her suspicion is accurate. Why would the Prussians be holding French uniforms in a warehouse, Ormond?"

Hugh didn't answer her final question. Instead he said, "Well, I will not allow it! I'll see that this is checked out by the appropriate parties."

Germaine appeared amused, which irritated him further.

"She could get herself killed," he mumbled when Germaine gave him a knowing smile.

"I remember a young man who would risk anything, dare anything, to help his country. To prove himself. I once accused him of being too reckless with his life. Do you remember?"

"I remember," he admitted. "But this is different, Germaine. She's a woman."

"*Mon Dieu!*" she gasped. "Is that the crux of it? Always it is because we are women. What, we cannot take risks for a grander cause? You never used to feel this way. At least, you never said so. In light of recent happenings, perhaps it is reasonable for us to at least look inside the warehouse, no?" When Hugh said nothing, she scrutinized him carefully. "You like the girl, don't you?"

"What makes you say that?" he asked.

"The way you looked at her at the Tuileries…and your anger now. You cannot fool me. Ah, but if you intend to offer for her, *mon ami*, you'd best hurry. The Vicomte Decazes means to have her."

Hugh had seen the vicomte look at Mary, but the possibility of an offer of marriage came as a surprise. "How do you know that?"

"It is obvious to everyone who knows him, and he has said some things to his brother of which I am aware. You realize his family would welcome her. A beautiful and engaging English noblewoman as a hostess for the rising young Decazes? Yes, they would like that. I expect he will speak to her uncle before they leave Paris. Maybe even as soon as Lord Baynes returns."

Hugh stared out the parlor window as a wave of jealousy swept him. "No. She will not accept. I cannot see her wed to a Frenchman."

"Perhaps you are right," Germaine allowed. "I do not know her heart."

He turned. "This plan of hers worries me."

Germaine nodded. "And yet, I like her fearless character, Ormond. I would let her see this through. I think it can be done without harm. And she wants me to join her. I have seen it can be done and I've agreed to do it."

"I cannot have Lady Mary dressed as a man and combing through warehouses. It's unseemly and dangerous. Her uncle would be appalled."

Germaine looked unimpressed. "This reminds me of the many men who have told me I could not do something I thought important. Napoleon was such a man."

"Yes, I remember," Hugh replied, "and you know how well that turned out."

She sighed. "One thing I've learned about Lady Mary, Ormond. If you tell her she cannot do something, that is the surest way to see she does it."

Hugh recalled the arguments about not going to Paris. Germaine was right. Mary would do this whether he counseled against it or not. Maybe even because of it. "Damn rebellious chit!"

Germaine laughed. "Perhaps. But so was I."

"She does remind me of you. From the first time I met her."

"I think she would take that as a compliment. You won't change her, Ormond. Best try and protect her. She would not like it that I told you her plans, but I did so for a reason."

"I'm listening," he said. He felt himself frown.

"We need to get past the lock. My footman tells me it is a complicated system, but you would know better than I. We could also use some protection also. It was my thinking you or some of your friend's men could be near. You could even go with us if you like." Her lips quirked. "We need your old talents."

Hugh remained unconvinced. "I can't believe you're really suggesting I do this, Germaine."

"Ah, Ormond, Lady Mary is intelligent and courageous. She's also young and too daring for her own good, and perhaps sometimes unwise. But with you as a part of this escapade, it would be safer. She need never know you're involved. You can ride on top of the carriage with my coachman. Wear a disguise! She won't look up. When we arrive, I'll keep her occupied while you attend the lock. Once you return, she and Jacques can proceed to the warehouse to see if her theory is correct. With luck she will never know you were there."

Hugh shook his head. He felt like he was encouraging Mary's wild schemes just by entertaining them. "And how can I justify my part in this when I should be turning the information over to the French—and turning her over my knee for even suggesting it?"

"Can you not see that Lady Mary so wants to be a part of the world you thrive in? She wants adventure, and to be useful. So few young women do, you know."

Hugh saw no need for adventures with so much at stake. Not with Bonapartists planning some treachery to bring down the king. "I can see it. I just don't like it. I don't want her in danger."

"I see, too."

"What?"

"Your feelings for her."

He ignored the comment. "I can't believe I am letting you talk me into this, Germaine."

"Think of it as a favor for an old friend."

He sighed, exasperated. "Oh, hell. I guess I could ask Powell to help. Though it would likely be better if he and I did it entirely on our own. But if Mary learns of this little conspiracy, she won't like it."

"Ah," Germaine promised, "but she won't."

Chapter 19

Mary arrived at Germaine's apartments the next afternoon dressed in worn trousers, a muslin shirt and faded blue jacket. Her long golden hair was tucked under a cap. Being tall, particularly for a woman in France, added another dimension to the disguise. She'd smeared her face with a bit of dirt and hoped it would take a close inspection to detect her sex. When her friend opened the door, Mary was pleased to discover Germaine wearing a simple brown traveling gown and eager to be off in their rented carriage.

The sky was overcast, and there was a chill in the air as they returned to the warehouse district. Still, Germaine seemed to be enjoying herself. Knowing she was loyal to the king and believing she could be trusted, Mary told her all she had learned of the Prussians and the vicomte. Germaine expressed surprise at what the vicomte's actions suggested, but told Mary it was not impossible. Mary was just thrilled to be engaged in a task she felt would be significant to the stability of France, which was so important to England at this time.

The carriage stopped a street from the warehouse as the man Germaine had hired to attend the lock did his work. Mary was anxious to get inside. At last a tap on the roof of the carriage signaled the lock was open and it was time to depart.

Mary and Jacques hurried to the front of the warehouse. For a moment Mary's heart stopped, for a worker appeared on the other side of the street coming in their direction. He was dressed in worn brown trousers and jacket with a dark cap pulled down low over his forehead, and he was carrying some heavy rope. He did not seem concerned with them, however, and as he passed, Mary soon forgot he was there as she focused on the task ahead.

This warehouse, like most of the others, was a structure that evidenced long use and poor maintenance, with peeling gray wood and dirty windows high in the building. A cold gust of wind blew dust from the street as she and Jacques stepped up to the large wooden structure.

Jacques slowly opened the rough doors and peered in. It was quiet. Mary followed him inside, blinking at the dimness. Some tools and rope lay on the dirt floor. Shafts of light from high windows fell onto some crates lining a back wall. The inside of the warehouse mirrored the outside and smelled of dirt, tobacco and some animal, perhaps rats. A few chairs and a small table with a half burned candle sat just inside the door, which proved someone had been there during the night.

"Let's open some of the crates," she urged, eager to discover what they held.

Jacques brought a large knife, but instead he reached for one of the tools lying on the floor, a metal bar of some sort with a flat end. As he began to pry up one of the tops, Mary peered over his shoulder to see the cropped gray jackets of the French military she had seen so often around the Palace. At last she let out the breath she'd been holding.

"We have found them! Let's open another crate from over there."

When she pointed to a stack farther along the wall, Jacques proceeded there and opened another crate. Just as the last top had given way to show the jackets, this one held the dark blue breeches of the light infantry soldiers.

"It is as you said, my lady," the footman admitted. "Exactly as you said."

* * *

At Hugh's request, though they had not entered the warehouse, Martin's men had been watching the building since this morning, assuring him no guards had shown up for work. From his post across the street, dressed like one of the common workers, his friend kept surveillance himself, ready to assist Hugh should such be necessary.

Hugh was still on top of Germaine's carriage, thinking about the secret supply of uniforms. Grudgingly, he gave Mary credit for leading them to the hidden stash. While he didn't know the specifics of the Prussian plans, he could guess. And they could now keep a watch on the warehouse to identify and possibly interrogate its visitors.

He had suggested to Germaine that she be the one to inform French officials of the note and where it led. He did not want Mary involved any more than necessary. She had done her part and could take pride in it, and he hoped Germaine could persuade her to stay out of the affair from this point on. After all, this could lead to the arrest of General Kleist, a military leader of one of France's allies.

Surely she would see the danger.

* * *

Burning with the pleasure of success, Mary hastened back to Germaine to tell her friend what she had found. Jacques had re-secured the crate tops to hide that they had been disturbed, and the locks were now back in place on the front door. She'd brought one of the jackets as proof of their discovery. A single jacket would not be missed among so many crates.

They were riding back to Germaine's apartments when a broad smile crossed the older woman's face. "That was simple enough."

Mary considered. Yes, it had been simple. Easy, even. "Perhaps it was too easy."

The older woman just shrugged. For a moment Mary thought Germaine looked nervous, but a moment later she asked if she might be the one to report their discovery to the French government. As Mary had never been interested in taking credit, just in getting the job done, the suggestion made sense. After all, she had her hands full trying to follow Joseph Decazes.

* * *

Hugh arrived that night to escort Mary to another affair at the palace. She had not seen him since the incident at the gallery and their visit to the grotto. He was polite but distant as they rode along in the carriage.

After her first few attempts at conversation drew only short replies, Mary settled back and peered out the window, watching the passing lights from the homes they passed. Some cast a bit of light inside the carriage, limning in gold the amethyst satin gown she wore. The garment was elegant, with a low-cut V bodice that, while still modest, displayed the edges of her full breasts. The silken fabric clung to her curves and dipped at the high waist. She wore her hair up with just a few loose curls dangling over her bare shoulder. The drop earrings hanging from her ears were perfect as well, the oval amethysts just a shade lighter than her gown and surrounded by tiny diamonds.

Hugh found himself staring. Her transformation from stable boy to temptress in one day was nearly a miracle. She had been adorable in those pants and faded jacket, but as he gazed at the enticing vision that was Mary Campbell in lavender satin, it was all he could do to tamp down his desire and resist pulling her into his lap.

"How was your afternoon, Lady Mary?" he finally asked.

"Not very eventful, just a carriage ride with Germaine."

"Oh, really?" If he weren't so disturbed by the danger she'd put herself in, he would have laughed at the mundane nature of her description. "Where did you go?"

"Just around the city."

Around the city, indeed. He found himself grimacing. The clever young woman had likely uncovered a Prussian plot against the king and now sat there as if it were afternoon tea and a carriage ride in the park. Damn. She was a pistol. Lambeth had only the half of it when he guessed she'd be "difficult to manage."

He said nothing of that. "You look lovely tonight. That color becomes you."

"Why, thank you. And you look quite handsome, my lord. I understand there will be dancing tonight. Will you dance with me?"

She was flirting with him and he liked it. If the young innocent only knew the danger that put her in, perhaps she would not. He was very close to kissing her, and given what had already transpired between them, they would never make it to the palace. He wanted very much to dance with her. And to do much more.

"Would you want me to dance with you?" he asked with an easy smile.

"It would be novel," she replied.

He could see that her eyes were daring him. "Good. Save me a waltz."

She smiled as if she'd had her way with something important. "I shall…and I shall look forward to it."

Her green eyes were sincere. She might have encountered a waltz or two at her first balls, but this was Paris where the waltz was truly admired. And here it would not create the scandal there would be in London if he were to dance with her.

Her response produced the desire again to kiss her but he refrained. He was now certain they would not make it to the

Tuileries if he did. Instead he thought about holding her as they danced.

They arrived a short time later, and Hugh entered the ballroom with Mary on his arm. A server dressed in a royal blue jacket with gold braid quickly offered them champagne. Each of them accepted a glass and turned to observe the room.

Decazes and Theresa Koller were the first to join them. The Frenchman's eyes were ablaze with desire. "Lady Mary, you are *tres jolie* this evening in that lovely gown."

Hugh's jaw tightened. The look in Decazes's eyes was one of a man who'd seen what he wanted and intended to have it. Hugh would not make a scene here, though, much as he wanted. Instead he diverted his attention to Theresa Koller and her stay in Paris. "Have you recovered from the shock of the altercation at the gallery, Miss Koller?

"Why, yes. Vicomte Decazes was very kind and made sure I was safely back to my lodgings."

"Will you be staying in Paris long?"

Theresa's brown eyes flashed. "For a few weeks only, I think. Just until my brother's business is completed."

Hugh perused the young woman. What had he heard about her? Her brother was General Koller and her mother was French, but there was something else, something nudging at the back of his mind. Whatever it was, he could not recall. But thoughts of the young woman's brother's schedule suddenly made him wonder how long General Kleist would be in Paris.

He searched the room and spotted Germaine, who was talking to Benjamin Constant. Turning back to Mary he asked, "May I leave you with your friends a moment so that I might attend to a small matter of business?"

"Of course," she said, but he felt her eyes following him as he made his way across the crowded room.

Not only was Germaine in a deep debate with Constant, but also with the Duke of Wellington, head of the British army in France.

Wellington nodded when he saw Hugh. "Good evening, Ormond. I didn't know you had returned to Paris." The English general and hero of Waterloo had his own spies and was well aware of Hugh's work during the war. They were friends.

"I am working with the diplomats now, Your Grace. Lord Baynes at the moment."

The duke casually gazed about the large room. "Ah, yes. Baynes. I was aware he was in Paris. I haven't seen him tonight. Is he here?"

"No, he is outside of Paris for a few days."

"Well, then, I will see him when he returns. We need his help with some of the allies."

Hugh nodded, promising to help arrange a time for them to meet. Then he faced Germaine and said, "Forgive me, Madame de Stael, but could I have a word?"

After she'd made her apologies to Constant and the duke, she and Hugh walked to a more private corner of the ballroom. Hugh took two glasses filled with champagne off a passing tray and handed one to her, saying, "Germaine, can you find out how long General Kleist will be in Paris? Has he told anyone? That may indicate the timing of anything he might be planning."

"I can certainly try, though the generals jealously guard their schedules," she explained. "Perhaps I can tease him about how he will be missed when he departs. He is a vain man and will enjoy the flattery." The older woman winked, and it seemed to Hugh that she was enjoying her new role as spy. He hoped Mary's reckless sense of adventure wasn't catching.

Still, he admitted, "That might just work."

The dancing began several minutes later. It seemed they would start with a waltz. Hugh found Mary, who was still with Decazes and Theresa Koller. Lady Mary's friend Diane Brancalis had joined them, and the pretty brunette's blue-eyed gaze seemed fixed on the vicomte, which pleased Hugh. Another man stood next to Mary. Hugh recognized him as a French officer attached to the Palace.

Introductions were made; then Hugh let his hand rest on Mary's back. He said, "I believe you promised me a waltz?"

Mary looked up and smiled. She had clearly not forgotten, which brought Hugh some pleasure. Decazes, on the other hand, looked unhappy. Mary tried to soothe him. "Dear vicomte, you have already asked for two dances and they are yours. Surely you do not mind if I grant one to my own countryman?"

"No, of course not," he replied. "Forgive me. But do hurry back. I shall miss your company."

Hugh did not scowl, but he could not refrain from clenching his teeth.

He took Mary's hand in his and swept her onto the dance floor. Gliding across the wood, his hand firmly on her back, he held her closer than was perhaps proper. This was their first dance, though, and since it would not be repeated in London, Hugh decided to enjoy it. He finally had the woman he wanted in his arms.

* * *

Mary was sorry to see the evening draw to a close, though it had been a long one and she was tired from the day. She had given many dances, and the room still whirled in her mind, but above all was her waltz with Hugh. They had moved as if their bodies were perfectly matched to each other as the eyes of those standing at the edges of the ballroom followed them.

He helped her into the carriage for the ride back, and settling onto the velvet seat she turned to stare out the window and allowed her mind to drift back to her carriage ride with Germaine that afternoon. She was just beginning to put the pieces together as she became aware that Hugh was watching her.

Her eyes suddenly narrowed, and his eyebrows lifted in question. "What?"

It was as if a candle had been lit in a dark recess of her mind. This was why, when she'd noted their exploration of the warehouse had been too easy, Germaine had been nervous. Then, too, Ormond and Germaine had been good friends for years, even during Napoleon's reign, and his words spoken when she'd complained of his following her to the gallery came back to Mary: *Get used to it.* She shook her head at her own naivety. She'd been duped.

"You knew."

"Knew what?" he asked, appearing slightly uncomfortable.

"You knew what Germaine and I were doing this afternoon. I'd even wager you were there."

His face wore no expression. "Yes."

Mary was furious. Once again she felt like a child who had been indulged, but she resisted her desire to shout at him. Instead, she let out a heavy sigh and carefully controlled herself. "You probably found it amusing, seeing me go through the motions of an investigation when all the time you were working ahead of me while I was in the dark."

"Mary," he began, "I could not let you put yourself in danger. There could have been armed men in that warehouse. Your uncle asked me to watch over you, and Germaine wanted my help."

"I see. But you felt no need to tell me you were going to be involved?"

"Germaine thought it best if you didn't know. She wanted you to be able to confirm your intuition. And let me remind you, you mentioned not a word of your plan to me. I allowed it against my better judgment."

"You *allowed* it?" The arrogance of the man. Silence hung heavy in the air and she turned to stare out the window into the darkness, wishing she could be somewhere else, anywhere else. All right, she admitted, perhaps he was concerned about her safety. And he had been given responsibility for her. But must he always have the upper hand? Another question occurred to her. "What was *your* role?"

"I'm good with locks."

"Locks?" she repeated. Then: "Of course you are. You were the one Germaine got to open the door." Silence settled back around them like a heavy cloak before she announced, "My uncle returns tomorrow, my lord. I see no reason for you to continue to follow me."

Her voice was calm. As was her resolve to keep him as far from her as possible.

* * *

Hugh didn't want to fight with Mary, not when she was so adorable, pouting beautifully like an angry princess. Instead, he wanted to drag her into his lap and kiss her until she acknowledged what was between them. All those curves! What was her uncle thinking, putting her in his charge?

He was becoming obsessed with the girl. With great determination, he controlled his desire. "I make you no promises."

When they reached their destination, Hugh escorted Mary to her uncle's apartments. Pierre opened the door and Mary quickly stepped through, turning back to Hugh and abruptly thanking him for the evening. Before he could respond she closed the door in his face. The sound of the heavy door slamming still rang in his ears as Hugh walked away, but oddly he wasn't angry.

No, there was even a smile on his face. The minx might not know it, but she would soon be his.

Chapter 20

Theresa Koller stepped out of her carriage and walked toward the tavern, drawing her cloak tightly around her against the cold night air. The establishment was one of the better options in this bad part of Paris, a place frequented by working men and transients. It was not a place one often found gentry, so she felt safe from discovery. Still, while night had fallen and she expected the tavern would be crowded, she did not intend to enter through the front door.

The older man by her side was dressed simply, blending in with the tavern's customers. He spoke with insistence. "You really shouldn't be here, mademoiselle."

"I know, Henri, but tonight our leaders gather. This is the most expedient way to tell them what I have learned, and I need to hear of their plans. I need to be a part of the discussion. Our time draws near."

Henri's pained look proved he knew it was futile to argue. "Does Maurice know you intended to come?"

"I sent word to him this afternoon."

The guard at the back door nodded, so her message must have arrived. She and Henri entered and found men already gathered and sitting at small tables. As usual, they were reminiscing about the days of Napoleon and grumbling about the king. Their conversations quieted as she stepped over the threshold, however. The air was heavy with the smell of smoke, sour wine and unbathed men. It was not a place a lady would come unless she was in the wrong place—or involved.

There was only one other woman present. Theresa's eyes spotted the buxom brunette as soon as she entered. Her swaying walk said she was aware of her allure. It was apparent she was the companion for the night of one of the men. Theresa's face twisted into a look of disgust.

She approached the aide to their leader. "Franz, where is Maurice?"

Casting her a leering glance, he drew close. "He will be along *ma petite*. Do not worry."

The door opened and a well-dressed, dark-haired man in his late thirties entered. He smiled when he saw her.

"*Bon*, you've come."

Looking around, she drew him aside and whispered, "Maurice, I think it would be best if we have a smaller group."

Maurice took off his coat and his gaze followed hers. The crowded room had once again grown quiet. "Perhaps you are right," he whispered after a moment. "There are too many here."

Theresa was content only after Maurice summoned Franz and instructed him to let all but a handful go. "Franz can tell the others of our decisions—those who are essential to our plans."

Franz agreed before Maurice spoke. "*Oui, d'accord.*" He turned and went about gruffly clearing the room. There were protests and affirmations of loyalty, but all who were told to leave eventually did. Theresa felt better. It was safer to deal with only a few.

* * *

Hugh sank into a soft chair and accepted the brandy Martin handed him, and his friend slid into the chair across from him. It had been a long day, and the night held a damp chill, even in the parlor of the house that was home to Britain's agents in France.

"You have something for me?" Hugh was anxious for information.

"Well, it's not what I'd hoped for, but it moves us along I think. We believe the Napoleon sympathizers may be planning an attack to try and demonstrate the ailing king is weak. That would, of course, be a prelude to bringing back their emperor."

Hugh considered. "That could fit in with the Prussians storing French military uniforms for more than two hundred men. They obviously mean to use them, and they have never been friends of Louis. Do we have any idea of the timing?"

"No, my man was thrown out with most of the crowd before the details were revealed, but it must be soon."

"Germaine tells me General Kleist is planning to leave in a few weeks, as are many others. That may indicate a deadline for whatever they are planning. They'll want diplomats carrying this news back to the allied leadership."

Martin nodded. "There's another interesting development, too. A young woman is involved. My man thought she might be Austrian."

Hugh blinked. "There is a young Austrian woman at court. Theresa Koller, half sister to the Austrian general."

"I have heard of General Koller," Martin replied, "though I have not heard of a sister. But I don't travel in your circles."

Hugh suddenly remembered more. "Her mother is cousin to Napoleon's mistress, Countess Marie Walewska, the mother of Napoleon's son Alexandre." How could he have forgotten?

"Countess Walewska. The one who visited Napoleon during his first exile on Elba," Martin noted.

"The very one."

It had been a passionate affair of the heart for Napoleon. Though she had resisted the emperor at first, the pressure from Polish leaders overcame her objections and the countess succumbed to the man who could control Poland's fate. The blue-eyed blonde became his mistress, and the affair burned hot for years, becoming something of a scandal. Hugh stared into the distance thinking about this strange turn of events.

Martin frowned. "That family connection might be enough to give the Austrian girl sympathy for Napoleon, perhaps even an inclination to join those seeking his return. The countess would want her lover back in power if for no other reason than for the sake of her son. If this Austrian woman we observed is truly the Theresa Koller you speak of, her involvement makes things more difficult."

Hugh agreed. "So, they have someone on the inside of the Palace. Someone no one suspects. She can make use of whatever information she hears from her brother."

Martin shook his head. "That is all we need, another player on an already crowded stage."

Hugh wondered what Mary would say if he suggested her choice of friends was not the most ideal.

Chapter 21

Mary's uncle returned as expected the very next day. She was happy to learn he was not immediately opposed to Joseph Decazes's invitation of theater and dinner that evening, especially when reminded that many guests of the French court took in the opera. He agreed things were different in Paris and that she was not under the same restrictions as in London. And whatever plots he might be involved in, the vicomte's intentions toward her retained all appearance of being honorable.

She did not tell her uncle about the incident at the gallery, nor that the vicomte had been wounded. Nor did Mary tell him of her findings at the warehouse. She worried that if she did, he would withdraw his permission.

For dinner Mary selected a sapphire silk gown with black beading at the neckline. A black velvet cloak provided a dramatic counterpart to her white gloves and golden tresses, which she wore up at her crown—perfect for a night on the town in Paris.

Dinner at *La Tour d'Argent* was an experience Mary would not soon forget. The atmosphere was one of elegance and lively conversation, mostly in French, but she could hear some English and German, and even some Russian as well. Many of the allies frequented the restaurant, and it was even said that royalty had dined there. Her uncle's butler told her that men had even fought duels over certain tables.

Decazes was watching her with a new, curious expression. She wondered at its source, especially as he was more quiet than usual, his blue eyes giving no hint of what he was thinking. There was certainly a keen intelligence there, however.

"You seem quite pensive this evening," she teased.

"I suppose I am," he replied. "Do you like the mutton?"

Mary was just putting another bite into her mouth, and she briefly noted that her appetite did not suffer in the presence of the vicomte. She supposed her loss of appetite with only one man—Hugh—was another indication that her feelings for the British lord were more than she had acknowledged. "It's splendid. The béchamel sauce is unusual, very delicious, and this place is livelier than any restaurant in London, at least the ones I've been in. Hearing so many different languages, it is a bit like King Louis's own court."

"I am pleased you find it to your liking," Decazes replied. He took her hand and kissed her fingers, and his eyes gazed intently into hers. "You see, Lady Mary, life in Paris can be most enjoyable."

"I have become quite fond of all things French, good sir, and Paris is central to that."

"I hope I am one of those things of which you are quite fond," the vicomte sallied.

She didn't respond but just smiled, realizing that she would indeed miss Joseph Decazes when she and her uncle returned to London. The vicomte was a man whose company she truly enjoyed, assuming he was not involved in some underhanded plotting, which she reminded herself every day was indeed a possibility. But either way, her mind, her heart and her body wanted Hugh Redgrave. She couldn't deny it any longer.

What a predicament, to be in love with a rake. Not only that, he was a bossy rake who would likely take her virtue and then tell her how to deal with her broken heart.

She determined not to let her sad thoughts take away from a wonderful dinner, though, and perhaps one of her last evenings with a handsome and considerate Frenchman whose company she enjoyed. Decazes was taking her to see a popular burlesque opera,

Bombastes Furioso, written by the Englishman William Barnes Rhodes. How thoughtful of him to seek out an opera written by one of her own countrymen. Reaching for her wine, she took a sip of the dark red liquid and smiled at the vicomte. He smiled back, a charming and wonderful expression.

"I have heard this opera is very entertaining," he said later as he helped her into the carriage. "We still have some time before we are due at the theater. Since we are close to the cathedral, I was wondering if you would mind if we made a brief stop. I must convey an invitation to Father Verbert."

"Not at all," said Mary. "I love the cathedral, and I would welcome any chance to visit the good father again."

It was dark when they left the restaurant, and though clear, the night was cold. Glad for the warmth, Mary drew her velvet cloak around her after the vicomte draped it over her shoulders. Was it her imagination, or had his hands lingered on her shoulders?

It was a very short trip across the now familiar bridge to the Ile de la Cite and Notre Dame. The air inside the immense stone cathedral was cold, so she kept her cloak on as they walked down the central aisle. They were nearly to the main altar when Father Verbert appeared from the side. His greeting was warm, as it had been on her first visit.

"Good evening, Lady Mary. I'm so glad Joseph brought you back. But surely this is unusual given the hour."

Decazes answered for her. "Father, we are here only for me to convey an invitation for you to join my family one evening next week."

And it was indeed that simple. The vicomte and Father Verbert concluded their brief conversation, agreeing on a time with little hesitation. Father Verbert invited them to linger and enjoy the cathedral if they could spare the time, though he himself would bid them *au revoir*.

"Thank you, Father," Decazes replied. "You are most kind, but needs must it will be a short visit. We are on our way to the theater."

Father Verbert left them, heading toward the back, and the pair strolled slowly toward the front door, stopping occasionally to look at the statues to the side of the central nave. They took their time and pondered different pieces. Mary had just begun to admire a painting when she felt Decazes move from her side. Out of the corner of her eye she watched him approach the same statue where he'd left the note before. Very quickly he slid a paper into the same crevice. Just as quickly, she turned back to study the painting.

"It's a touching scene of the Virgin and Child, is it not?" the vicomte remarked, moving to stand close behind her. "A favorite of mine, in fact."

"Is it? I think it is beautiful."

Decazes walked a few paces away, seeming to study a sculpture. It took him closer to the cathedral entrance, and at the same moment Mary heard the sounds of others entering the cathedral. Turning, she saw a group of three men. They stood near the door whispering. The vicomte moved farther from her and toward the trio.

It would be close, but Mary thought she might be able to retrieve the paper without attention being drawn to her. She backed slowly toward the statue and reached for the hidden paper…then she tried to still her heart as she hurried to join the vicomte.

"We should be going so we are not late," he said, suddenly serious as he turned from the sculpture before which he stood. The three men at the front of the cathedral were leaving.

"Of course." Mary took his offered arm and walked with him to the entrance.

They had just stepped outside the cathedral when Mary saw a plain carriage waiting in front, and she was instantly aware it was not the vicomte's. The conveyance was black as night, the curtains drawn over the windows, and it bore no crest, no markings.

Decazes did not move, just stood giving the carriage a questioning look. Mary turned and saw a man in common clothes come up behind the vicomte. The man raised a pistol and slammed the butt down on the back of Decazes's head. Mary screamed as her companion sagged to the ground.

"Grab the woman!" shouted the man to two others who had suddenly appeared on either side of her. Mary knew just enough German to understand. She gasped as one of the two men grabbed her, opened the door of the waiting carriage and roughly shoved her onto its dirty floor. The smell repelled her senses as she struggled to rise.

The man climbed in behind her and pulled her up onto the seat. The one who had hit Decazes picked him up and shoved him onto the floor of the carriage. Mary started to reach for the opposite door, but another ruffian climbed in and formed a barrier to her escape. A moment later, the man who had hit the vicomte shouted "*Gehen Sie!*" from outside the carriage, and the vehicle sped off at his command.

"Who are you, and why are you doing this?" Mary demanded in French, looking anxiously for signs of life from the unconscious vicomte lying in the shadows at her feet.

"Shut up, wench," the man on her right replied in French. "The question is, who are you and why did you take the missive?"

Horrified he had seen her, she did not answer. The two men flanking her were the ones who had spoken to the vicomte at the gallery, she suddenly realized. *The vicomte knows them.*

"What are you going to do with us?" she asked.

"That is none of your concern." The man's eyes raked her and then settled on the gap in her cloak that revealed the tops of her breasts. "But I am certain we can find something to do with you until then, eh, Anton?"

The man sitting on her other side surveyed her body and agreed with a nod of his head. Then he reached inside his pocket and pulled out a length of black cloth, tying it over her eyes. She felt him grab her hands and tie another cloth around her wrists. At least he had left them in front of her.

"Where are you taking us?" Mary asked desperately. But she was to have no answer. They traveled on in silence; the only sounds were the wheels of the carriage and the horses' hooves hitting the ground. Decazes did not stir.

Less than an hour later, the carriage slowed to a stop. Mary could hear nothing but the horses moving in their harnesses and a dog barking somewhere in the night. The sound of footsteps on stone captured her attention, then the carriage door opened and she felt cold air rush into the small space. The man on her right side moved. She could hear him climb from the carriage, as a man outside asked in German, "Franz, what happened? Did she take the message?"

"Ach, yes, the bitch betrayed him. What a fool he was to trust a woman."

Another voice spoke. "Do you have them?"

The man called Anton sitting beside her rose and left the carriage. Someone began to drag Decazes's body out, tugging on her skirts as his body slid past.

Franz spoke again. "Here's the Frenchman. The woman is still inside."

Rough hands pulled her from the carriage. She stumbled, nearly falling as she tried in vain to keep her balance without her hands free to hold on to anything. The damp air was chill and caused her to shiver.

Still blindfolded, she was pushed into some kind of building. The warmth of the room immediately brought her senses awake; she could hear a fire crackling and smelled food permeating the air. Perhaps they'd just finished dinner? She stumbled on the rug beneath her feet as she was pulled forward. One of the men mumbled an oath under his breath, grabbed her and tore off her blindfold.

"Enough! You can walk on your own."

Once her eyes adjusted to the light, she saw she was in a large house. She wondered whose and where it was. Crystal sconces and dark polished furniture in the entryway indicated a person of means, so it did not belong to Franz or Anton, whose coarse attire and speech did not speak of wealth. The carpets were fine Persians, with ornate red, blue and tan designs. The floors were of polished dark wood.

Two other men walked in from the next room. One of them wore a cap and a red scarf around his neck with a gray woolen coat and brown trousers. The dress was French, but he too was Prussian; of that, she was certain. The second was dressed in similar fashion, but she thought his clothes were perhaps newer, finer.

Franz turned to the newcomers. "Get the Frenchman."

The vicomte was carried into the house and unceremoniously dumped at Mary's feet, then her captors began to speak in German, discussing what had happened at the cathedral. As she watched them, a door to the hall opened and a woman stepped through.

"Theresa!" Mary exclaimed in French. "What are you doing here?"

The young woman sighed. "You have stumbled into something that is none of your affair, Lady Mary. I feared your meddling when I saw you watching Decazes at the gallery. I am sorry for it, because you have now become a problem. We cannot have you in the middle of this. Our work is too important."

Mary was in shock. She'd been kidnapped, the vicomte was unconscious at her feet and now Theresa Koller was somehow involved. "Theresa, how could you be a part of such treachery? Your brother is an officer!"

"My brother is a fool—and he is only my half brother. He has no respect for the emperor." She turned and began to instruct the men in German. "Franz, I must leave. Maurice won't be home until tomorrow. It is most unfortunate this occurred tonight. You will have to handle the situation. Find out how the general wants to deal with them. Guard them well until you hear from him." Then she left without a backward glance.

Mary was just thinking it was likely not a good sign she had been allowed to see their faces and hear their names when Franz grabbed her and informed Anton in German, "I'm taking her upstairs. I'll come back to help you with the Frenchman in a bit." He pulled her by her elbow past the entry to a set of wide stairs leading up. She tried to climb as he prodded her forward, but with her hands bound she stumbled and fell backward onto him.

Franz set her back onto her feet. "Stupid Englishwoman, with all these skirts." He untied her hands, though, allowing her to lift her skirts to climb the stairs.

Once upstairs, he shoved her down a hallway and into a large room. It appeared to be a study with a desk and chairs. One wall was lined with books. A low fire burned in the fireplace. She was glad there was no bed.

Roughly Franz retied her hands behind her back and silently deposited her in a chair at the center of the room. He then found a rope lying in a corner and secured her. It was painful having her hands tied tightly behind her, but she knew her discomfort was unimportant to him so she said nothing.

When he left, she examined the room for weapons. There was the fire poker, but it was too far away even if her hands had been free. She saw no knives or pistols. A large-paned glass window was set between two cases of books. The tapestry curtains were drawn.

Soon Franz was back with Anton; the two carried the still unconscious vicomte between them. Without a word they dumped him on the rug and tied his feet and hands. Then they began to discuss her in German. She supposed they did not know she understood, as she had intentionally spoken to them only in French. She tried not to react to what they said.

"Franz, she's an English lady. We can ransom her."

"No, Anton. The woman knows too much, and she's seen the messages the Frenchman was to deliver. Bah! He was a careless idiot." His eyes fell on the vicomte lying crumpled on the floor. "She may even know about the plans for the palace. No, she cannot be allowed to live."

Anton's eyes shifted anxiously from Franz to her. "You can't kill an English lady; it will be noticed."

"People die in the streets every day, my friend. It would not be difficult to arrange."

Anton shook his head. "We should do naught for now. We should wait to hear from the general. You heard the mademoiselle. He may want to question this one."

"Fine," said Franz, exasperated. "Send one of the men to seek word. Find another to guard these two. I have not had my supper."

Anton moved toward the door. Franz stepped close to Mary, his breath foul and reeking of tobacco and sour wine. He lifted one of the curls at her nape and ran it through his fingers. His voice was gruff.

"Perhaps her condition is not so important as long as she is alive for the questioning. We can enjoy the wench while we wait, eh?"

His smirk revealed brown teeth, and Mary winced and pulled back as far as her bindings allowed. When she did, he grabbed her chin in his hands, pinching the skin and forcing her to look at him. "*Oui,* we could enjoy you very much, English."

Anton still looked anxious. "First we send a message to the general. Then we eat, Franz. Leave the woman."

Franz seemed to consider as he continued to play with her hair. Finally: "Yes, some food and wine first." He chuckled as he left the room.

This was all so surreal, like she was watching herself from somewhere else. A cold sweat broke out on her skin, but her mind was strangely calm as she began to consider the pieces of the puzzle. What did they think she knew? Whatever it was, it was apparently enough to condemn her to death.

She was aware of the messages concerning the British troops. She had listened to Decazes's conversation with General Kleist. Was he the general they referred to?

She knew the Prussians were storing French uniforms, but they would not necessarily know she was aware of that.

Her gaze dropped to the vicomte lying unconscious at her feet. What exactly did he know? Was this all a part of a plot involving the Tuileries Palace? That was what they'd said, but while her mind tried to sort out the puzzle, she could not arrive at an answer. She was surely missing information.

A new thought gripped her, and one that was harder to take. She could expect no help from anywhere. No one knew where she was. The stop at the cathedral was not a part of the itinerary she'd left her uncle. He would be frantic with worry…and then there was Hugh. For once she wished he had followed her, and she was overwhelmed by the desire to be once again in his overprotective arms. What would he do when she did not return home? What would they do when her body was discovered?

Chapter 22

Lord Baynes paced in front of the fire. His butler appeared at the open door, bringing with him a silver tray bearing steaming coffee. "My lord."

Adrian absentmindedly reached for a cup. "Where can they be?"

The servant had no answer.

"Has there been any word from Lady Mary, Pierre?"

"No, my lord."

Adrian went over the details in his mind once again. Vicomte Decazes and Mary had gone to the theater, but that had ended some time ago. The nightlife in Paris could continue until morning, but his instructions to Mary had been to return as soon as the performance was over. She would have sent word if she'd intended to change her plans, no matter how headstrong she was. She had always been good about that. No, something had gone very wrong.

"Please send a messenger to Lord Ormond and ask him to join me immediately."

"At once, my lord." Pierre turned and left the room.

* * *

It was after midnight when Hugh knocked at Lord Baynes's door, answering the summons he'd received two hours earlier. "I would have been here sooner, but I had guests and moving around Paris at night is always difficult," he said by way of apology. Worry ravaged the older man's face.

"Ah, yes, the meeting with the French liaison and his staff was tonight. I'd forgotten."

"What has happened? Your footman said it concerns Lady Mary."

"She and Joseph Decazes went to dinner and the theater. They should have returned long ago, but I haven't the slightest idea where she is."

"Was she alone with him?" Hugh felt his stomach sink.

"Yes, but they intended to visit very public places. Dinner and the theater. He's been most honorable with her, Ormond."

Hugh didn't think he could criticize, not when he had been alone with her himself. And he had been somewhat less than fully honorable—though he had not done nearly as much as he wished. And now that he thought of it, he wasn't truly worried about Decazes. Mary wasn't likely to run away with him. However, some of the vicomte's associates...

"I'll retrace their steps and see what I can learn."

"Good idea," said the statesman. "I'll come with you."

A few hours later, Adrian and Hugh had been to both the restaurant and the theater. At *La Tour d'Argent,* guests were still partying, and many remembered the couple there. They spoke to a night watchman at the theater who directed them to a place where theatergoers partied after the performance, but none they spoke with remembered the well-known Decazes attending. Nor did anyone recall the beautiful girl with golden hair Hugh described. Stumped, they returned to Lord Baynes's apartments to consider their next step.

"Something happened after they left the restaurant," Hugh decided.

"It is certainly odd they were not observed," Mary's uncle replied.

"Would she have gone to Decazes's residence for any reason?" Hugh didn't like the thought, but he had to consider the possibility. Maybe the vicomte had exerted more influence and attraction over Mary than he realized.

To his relief, Lord Baynes seemed to think that unlikely. "No, I cannot imagine she would. But his household staff might know something about his plans for the evening."

"Yes," Hugh agreed. "But before we ask them, I'd best wake Martin. It would be good to have some men at our disposal."

Within fifteen minutes they had arranged for instructions to be conveyed to Martin to gather what they might need and to meet them at the vicomte's town house. Rather than take a carriage, Hugh and Lord Baynes rode horses, since it seemed unclear where the hunt might lead and versatility seemed paramount.

On the way, Hugh filled Adrian in on Mary's adventure with Germaine at the warehouse, then he told him all he had himself discovered. Unsurprisingly, her uncle was not pleased.

"It seems my niece has been busy in my absence."

"You have no idea." Hugh shook his head. "I found it a difficult task just keeping up with her."

Lord Baynes expressed surprise at Germaine's participation in Mary's scheme to get inside the warehouse. "Mary has always sought adventures beyond the ordinary, but this is more dangerous than anything she has so far ventured. I would have thought her wiser than this, at least given the state of affairs here in France."

Hugh kept his response to: "She is definitely a challenge."

It didn't take long for them to travel to the elegant town house that was Joseph Decazes's residence in Paris. It was a prominent home near the palace, built of tan stone with a slanted, gray slate roof. They let the brass knocker fall loudly on the front door, expecting it would take quite a while to rouse someone, but almost immediately the door opened and a portly butler with wrinkled face and thinning gray hair peered out. He held his candle high, and his expression was worried. Surprisingly, he was not dressed in nightclothes.

"Is one of you Lord Baynes?" the man asked.

"I am," Lord Baynes offered.

"Please do come in, my lord." The butler waved them inside. "Our footmen have just gone to your apartments to inform you they were set upon by men with clubs as they waited for the Vicomte Decazes and Lady Mary at the cathedral. You must have just missed them. They and the coachman were hit over the head and left unconscious for some time. When they revived, the vicomte and Lady Mary were gone. They had hoped to find them at your apartments. I can see from your face that is not the case."

"The cathedral? You mean Notre Dame?" asked Hugh. Now it was clear why no one had seen the vicomte and Mary at the theater.

"*Oui*, my lord, that is the one."

"Why would they have gone there?" asked Mary's uncle. "They had plans for the theater."

"We don't know, my lord. The vicomte only told the coachman they'd be making a short stop. He wasn't told why."

Hugh's eyes danced between Lord Baynes and the butler. "Did they say anything else?"

The servant stared off into the distance, thinking. "*Oui.* One said he heard the men speaking in German, telling the others to hurry."

The note Mary had retrieved from the cathedral was in German. The note about the French uniforms was also in German. Decazes had been dealing with the Prussians, apparently providing them information on the British troops garrisoned around Paris. Hugh let out a breath. His worst fears were realized. If he hadn't let himself believe it before, now there seemed little doubt. Mary had been found out.

Taking Mary's uncle aside, Hugh whispered to him, "The Prussians must have discovered she took the note. Decazes's dealings with them must have gone amiss. I think your niece is with the Prussians who are working with the supporters of Napoleon."

Lord Baynes's face paled, clearly sharing his conclusion. "Where could they have taken her? We must get her back."

Hugh watched the butler leave as he recalled a list of locations that Martin had told him Prussian agents in the city used in their dealings with supporters of the deposed emperor. Many were public locales for random courier rendezvous, but there was also a tavern and...

"There is a house they use as a base. They may have taken the pair there. It is owned by one of the men they have been seen dealing with, a Frenchman named Maurice. It is well guarded."

"How long before your man can be here, do you think?" Lord Baynes asked.

"Martin will be here soon, and he knows the location of the Frenchman's house. Perhaps we'd better take another man with us." He called out for the butler. When the man returned, he inquired, "Is there one of the vicomte's men who can handle a weapon?"

"The most likely one of those still here would be Georges, my lord. He is one of the men who attend the vicomte's carriage and horses. I can wake him."

It took several minutes for the butler to fetch him, a beefy man in his early forties with big hands and a thick muscular neck that indicated he did heavy work. Hugh was glad for his presence, though he might have preferred someone adept at bearing arms. Also, by the time Georges arrived, so had Martin and his younger assistant, Jerome.

The house they wanted, Martin said, was on the east side of the city. "It will take us some time to get there and there will be guards," he added, handing Hugh a black shirt. "Thought you might want to change. That white shirt will draw attention."

Glad for Martin's foresight, Hugh took the shirt without a word and assessed their weaponry. He had the pistol with which he'd arrived and the knife he always carried in his boot. Lord Baynes had brought a pistol as well. He knew Martin and Jerome would carry both pistols and knives. Spies were always well armed.

Decazes's butler managed to find a pistol for Georges, and Hugh considered the large man for a moment. "Georges, do you know how to use that?"

"Er...*oui*, monsieur, I do."

"Good," Hugh said, handing the large man the weapon. "Let us hurry."

He changed his shirt right there, anxious to be on the road. They would again take horses, which would be faster and allow them better maneuverability on the dark, narrow roads. His men had brought their own, and Georges took one of the vicomte's.

The five men rode fast through the still dark city toward their destination. The horses' hooves pounding on the dirt road sounded like thunder in the still night. At one point they passed a man who was clearly in his cups and was singing his way home. He just stared open-mouthed as they flew by, his song choked off in his throat.

They reined their horses to a slow walk as they drew near, then left the mounts in a copse of tall pine trees and tackled the last bit on foot so as not to alert anyone standing guard. Their destination was the last house on the street. The moon cast shadows from the surrounding trees onto the large, gray, two-story building, and light leaked from the closed shutters on the first floor. One side of the house was hidden in the heavy branches of a tall tree.

There was a guard out front keeping watch. Crouching low to the ground across the street, Hugh turned to Martin and whispered, "I'm going to circle the house and see if I can get access to the second floor. Stay here and watch for anyone coming or leaving."

"Do you want company?" Martin asked.

"No. If Lady Mary and the vicomte are here, they could be on either floor. Give me ten minutes, then deal with the guard out front and any in back, and then go in through the front door. Warn Georges and Jerome not to fire unless they are sure of the target, though." Then he turned to Mary's uncle. "Lord Baynes, you must promise me you will not go in with Martin. I want you to stay here until we have secured the house. We cannot risk you."

The statesman nodded. "I will wait, Ormond. It has been a long time since I've seen any fighting, and I do not wish to get in your way."

"Take care," Martin said. Lord Baynes echoed those words, and Hugh slipped off into the night.

If she were there, he would find her.

* * *

Mary's arms and shoulders ached from being tied behind her back, and her wrists were sore from her efforts to loosen her bindings. The hours of night had brought her no sleep. Fear had held her awake, as she knew her captors could change their minds and do something terrible to her and the vicomte at any moment.

The guard, who had watched her closely at first, eventually drifted off, and the room echoed with his dull snores.

At one point during the night the vicomte moaned and began to wake, but the guard had been stirred by the noise and summoned Franz, who'd dealt the French nobleman another blow that knocked him back into unconsciousness. Franz had then pawed her, running his wine-soaked mouth over hers. Nauseated by his foul smell and the stubble that scratched her delicate skin, Mary had nearly vomited before he stopped, interrupted by the guard asking in German about plans for the Tuileries and wondering aloud how much she knew. She immediately thanked God he had been deflected from his threat to "enjoy" her. As the men talked, Mary again pretended to be ignorant of what they were saying.

They then asked her in French what she knew about the Tuileries operation. She didn't have to feign ignorance. She truly knew nothing and said so.

Whatever it was they were planning, she expected from their conversation that it would soon occur. In her pocket Mary still had the paper she'd taken from the cathedral, but since the Prussians showed no interest, she decided it was unimportant. Only her theft of the paper was of significance to them. It had been a trap into which she'd willingly fallen. Her thoughts wandered to vicomte. Had he been party to the scheme? Was he testing her? Since he had placed the message, she thought it possible, but he could not have anticipated the result or he wouldn't be lying on the floor at her feet.

The fire had died to glowing coals long ago, and the two candles burned low. Mary watched her Prussian guard, guessing an hour had passed since he had last fallen asleep; his heavy breathing and snoring were the only sounds in the room. Even if she could free herself, however, the pistol tucked into the man's waist was a deterrent. He was a hard man with dirty brown hair and dark eyes. Cruel lines etched his face, and she guessed he wouldn't hesitate to shoot a woman.

She heard voices from downstairs. They were faint, mostly, making it impossible to hear what was being said, but occasionally the voices rose in loud argument. She wondered if the fight concerned her and the vicomte, and that thought made her again begin to work at the knot tying her hands.

The knot gradually loosened enough for her to slip her hands free. *Success!* Keeping her eyes on the guard, she worked her hands around to the front of her body still bound to the chair, her arm muscles protesting at being left so long in one position. Now to see herself free. Working on the rope wrapped around her and the chair, she was finally rewarded and the rope fell away—just as the guard woke.

He blinked then narrowed his eyes, staring at her as his mind roused from the haze of sleep. "Hey! What are you about?" he demanded, still groggy.

Mary froze as the guard rose on unsteady legs and approached, his face turning ugly. Anger burned in his dark eyes, and he lunged toward her like a madman. She was quick, though, rising and backing away past the overturned chair. He kicked it aside and stalked her.

She had no weapon, for the fireplace tools were behind the man. "Stay away from me," she said in French, but the man kept coming and drew his hand to one side. Before she could duck, he backhanded her so hard she crashed to the ground. Searing pain gripped her temple and her vision blurred as she slumped to the floor and remembered nothing more.

Chapter 23

Hugh left the three men and Lord Baynes to make a wide circle to the right of the house, creeping toward the tall pine whose branches reached above the second story. Arriving at the base of the tree, he paused in the shadows and scanned the windows above. Curtains covered them, preventing detection of any movement.

As the guard at the front of the house could not see him, and he'd seen no movement at the back, Hugh swung his leg over a low branch and began to climb. The first bit was easy, as the heavier branches were easily scaled, but when he crossed to the thinner limb touching the house, it swayed with his weight. He grabbed the ledge to steady himself and checked the window. It was not locked, and the room behind looked dark. Relieved, he climbed inside.

Crossing a rug, he carefully listened and then opened a door to a hall. Voices in muted tones came from below stairs, but no sounds emerged from the room just a bit farther down the corridor where light spilled from a door left ajar. Hugh crept forward and peered into that light.

The first thing he saw was Mary. She lay on the floor, her eyes closed and her body at an odd angle. Was she alive? He took a quick step in and found his eyes drawn to another set of legs, those of a man wearing fine cloth trousers and lying on the floor. The vicomte?

He had seen enough. He suspected if Mary and the vicomte were alive, there might be a guard. Surprise was his only friend. He steeled himself for what he might discover and, drawing his pistol, kicked open the door.

The guard who had been seated behind the door rose abruptly to meet him, pistol extended. "Drop it!" Hugh shouted. He eyed Mary with an anxiety he could not hide.

The guard recoiled but did not lower his weapon. Then suddenly he jerked the pistol from its aim at Hugh to Mary where she lay on the floor. "I can see yer fond of the woman. She's alive, but unless ye drop that pistol I'll shoot the bitch in the head."

A loud crash sounded from the first floor, then shouts and pistol shots. The guard was distracted for only a moment, but it was all Hugh needed. He fired and sent the guard's weapon sailing from his hand and across the room. The guard cursed and drew his bleeding wrist to his chest, so Hugh cast his own pistol aside and smashed him in the face, knocking the Prussian to the floor.

Hugh heard someone running down the hall toward him, and Martin rushed into the room. "Need any help here?" He glanced down at the guard, who was unconscious. "I'm thinking the answer is no."

As Hugh knelt beside Mary, he said to Martin, "Are things under control downstairs?"

"Yes, well in hand." Martin pushed the Prussian forward, keeping one hand on the man's shoulder and a pistol in his back. "There were four of them besides the guard. Three men are wounded. One is ours. The guard is out cold on the front steps."

Hugh took in his friend's words as he drew close to Mary, not believing what he saw. His golden girl lay quiet. Panic tore at his heart. He could not lose her.

Feeling for a pulse, he allowed relief to flood his mind when he found a steady beat. He slapped her gently on the cheek. Mary moaned and slowly opened her eyes.

"Hugh?" she whispered on a ragged breath, as her green eyes looked into his.

"Mary," he said, relieved. Carefully, he lifted her head and cradled it against his chest.

"Oh, Hugh." She threw her arms around him and pulled him close. "It was so awful. Those men—"

"They can't hurt you now, you're safe." Hugh held her for a long moment then reluctantly pulled back to search her face. "Are you hurt?"

"He…he hit me." She touched the side of her face and winced. "But I'm all right."

Behind them, Martin cleared his throat, reminding Hugh he was there. Hugh helped Mary to stand, his arm tight around her, and turned. "Lady Mary, allow me to introduce you to my good friend and colleague, Sir Martin Powell. In France, however, he is known as Martin Donet. Sir Martin, may I present Lady Mary Campbell, Lord Baynes's niece."

Mary smiled shyly. "Hello, Sir Martin—or shall it be Monsieur Donet?"

"My pleasure to meet you, Lady Mary," Martin said, smiling warmly in return. "And you can call me Monsieur Donet. Best not to mention I'm a Powell while you are in Paris."

Hugh grew impatient. Mary didn't need another suitor, especially not one so attractive to the ladies as this ebon-haired, blue-eyed spy. "Martin, can you deal with that one?" He gestured at the Prussian lying unconscious on the floor.

Martin stepped forward and nudged the Prussian roughly with his boot. The man groaned and then awakened and gripped his bleeding wrist.

"Get up," said Martin. There was no sympathy in his voice. He forced the man to rise, pulling him up by his good arm.

Hugh held Mary to his chest. She was still wobbly on her feet.

"You came for me," she whispered. "How did you find me?"

"It was Martin's good work. The Prussians and Napoleon supporters have been using this house for some time as a kind of headquarters. We were fortunate our friends here did not take you somewhere else. But the important thing is that you are safe and I'm going to keep you that way." He kissed the top of Mary's head where it lay against his chest in what he knew was a possessive gesture.

Martin spoke from behind him. "I will take this one down. Georges, though he is wounded, and Jerome are covering the others."

Hugh turned to watch his friend prod the Prussian through the door then regarded the one man still lying unconscious on the floor. "I suppose I'd best deal with Decazes," he said.

"They hit him twice, once over the head with a pistol," Mary remarked as he let go of her to bend over the unconscious man. Hugh unhappily detected worry in her voice. "He's been out the whole time since we were taken."

Given a good shake, Decazes woke with a moan. Hugh untied his hands and feet, and the vicomte reached up to his injured head.

"You have a knot but you'll live," Hugh said, not sure he was pleased by the prospect.

The vicomte addressed Mary. "What…happened?"

"Your plan seems to have gone awry," Hugh muttered.

"I didn't plan this." The vicomte examined the small study and sat up. "Lady Mary, have you been harmed?"

"I'll be fine," she said. "I'm glad you are with us again. You had me worried." She turned to Hugh and announced, "They were expecting others, though, and soon, I think. They sent a messenger to some general when they first brought us here. That was hours ago. The messenger was to seek instructions as to what to do with us, and from what they said, I don't believe they intended us to live. They think we know of their plans and we have seen their faces."

"Then our time here must be short." Hugh helped Decazes to his feet and began to lead Mary toward the door. The vicomte followed.

Suddenly Mary stopped. "Theresa Koller was here." Then looking at Hugh, "She's…she's one of them!"

Hugh frowned. "I knew her involvement was a possibility. It is most unfortunate."

Lord Baynes met them coming down the hall. The older man looked much relieved.

"Uncle!"

The diplomat reached for his niece, and Mary fell into his welcoming arms. "Thank God you're safe," he said.

"No thanks to present company," Hugh said, turning his glare upon Decazes.

The vicomte shrank back. "I would never hurt Lady Mary," he said softly. "I care for her immensely."

Hugh turned away. He had nothing but disdain for the French nobleman, who was clearly at the root of this mess. He intended to find out exactly how, and then he would deal with him, but for now some things would have to wait. "We'd best get you out of here, Lady Mary," he said. "It won't be long before they are hunting for you, especially because Theresa knows where you live."

Crossing the hallway, they descended the stairs. Hugh's arm once again supported Mary, and her uncle followed with Decazes. Waiting downstairs was further evidence of the fight Hugh had only heard from above. Two Prussians were lying on the floor, bloodied from the scuffle. Above them stood Jerome, Martin's assistant, and Georges. Though the latter had a wound in his upper arm, with his good hand he held a pistol.

When the vicomte saw his servant, he looked serious. "You have my gratitude, Georges, for joining in the rescue effort."

"I'm only glad we were in time, Vicomte. This bunch here"¬—he gestured to the Prussians on the floor with his pistol—"is nasty."

Hugh took charge, giving orders. To Martin he said, "We'll need to question these men or see that the French do."

"Jerome and I can handle that," said Martin. "Up with you!" he ordered the men on the floor. His voice brooked no dissent, and they rose without assistance.

"I'll see Lady Mary home," said Hugh, but he had no intention of taking her there. Now that he had her, he wasn't letting her go. Though, he would be having words with her for the risks she had taken.

The sun was rising as they walked outside, Hugh's arm around Mary's waist. When they reached his horse, he lifted her into the saddle then mounted behind her, lifting her legs over his thigh. She leaned against his chest. Though she was fighting it, Hugh could tell she was near collapse. His wilted flower—she was so beautiful, and now she was safe. Anger lingered just below the surface of his calm, however. He'd come too close to losing the little adventurer.

Lord Baynes had followed, riding next to them. Decazes, who still appeared somewhat dazed, rode with Georges some distance behind.

Before long, they neared the road that led to the vicomte's town house. Hugh glanced at Georges and asked, "Will you be able to see your master home?"

"*Oui,* my lord. My wound is slight, and the master is much better."

"Very good," Hugh said. "His head should be seen by a doctor—and your arm as well. Be careful to avoid any who might follow you. Our Prussian friends will be looking for the vicomte once they see no one at the house. It would be best to post a guard or two once you are home."

Georges nodded. "I will see to it, Sir."

Mary cast a concerned look at Decazes and said, "Take care of yourself."

"Don't worry about me, Lady Mary," the Frenchman replied. "It is you I'm concerned about."

Hugh saw the longing in the man's eyes, but Decazes would never have her. In fact, he might never see her again. She had to leave to country. He could not risk the Prussians finding her. If they had planned to kill her, they would continue their hunt. He did not have enough men to guard her here. And, there was good reason for the Nighthawk to leave as well. He wondered what she would say when she learned he was not taking her back to her uncle's town house.

He turned to Lord Baynes as soon as the two Frenchmen had bid them *au revoir*. "I assume you agree it is not safe for her to return to your apartments. Our enemies will expect to find her there. With your permission, I think we should take her to my quarters first. They will not know to search for me. From there we can discuss what to do."

Lord Baynes nodded. "It seems the only wise course at this point. I'll follow you."

They took side streets to avoid being seen. Mary leaned silent against his chest, her eyes closed. Her hip was pressed snugly against his groin and he had to fight his desire. He must think what next to do, for he had no idea how he would keep his hands off Mary in the days ahead. Having her so close was tempting him even now, despite the fact that her uncle was riding right beside them.

Mary raised her head. "I just remembered. They talked of some plan involving the Tuileries Palace. They believed I knew what they were planning."

Hugh shook his head. "No. Stop. Martin will find out more when he questions them, and the French royalists have other ways of getting information. Trust me. You have done enough, Mary. More than enough. I'll not have you involved in this any longer."

She seemed not to have heard. "But—"

"No buts. You need to focus on doing what your uncle and I think best. It is only your safety that concerns me now."

She might have been exhausted and nursing a blow to her head, but she was ever the rebel; she would not give up the topic. "I don't know how much the vicomte knows. He was never conscious. But they spoke as if they knew him. Do you think they mean to attack the Palace?"

Hugh sighed. He supposed he would have to give her some answers if he was to gain her obedience. It was a price he would willingly pay for an intelligent woman. He supposed he would even pay more. "I don't know, but that would not surprise me. If that is the case, your uncle can alert the king." He glanced at Lord Baynes, who appeared exhausted as well. "They will go after General Kleist, I am certain, as well as the Frenchman Maurice. It was his house you were held in," he reminded Mary. "We believe he is the leader of the Bonapartists. But one thing we know: You are in great danger."

* * *

Glad for his warmth as they rode, Mary sank back against Hugh's chest and drifted into a restless sleep. She woke only when they arrived at his lodgings. Hugh gently pulled her from the saddle and carried her into his town house. Immediately, she was offered a hot bath and allowed to sleep for a few hours. Now, clean and dressed, she sat in front of a fire. But awake all night, too afraid to fall asleep for long, she was still tired as she drank the cup of hot coffee Hugh's manservant brought her.

Hugh stood in front of a large window near her uncle. Mary watched. Sometime between last night and this morning, he had become her protector. She drank the hot liquid and listened to the men speak in low voices. Huddled before the crackling fire, she felt like a small child being ignored and discussed but was too tired to object

Hugh's face was serious. "She cannot remain in the city. From what she told me, they planned to kill both her and Decazes because they had knowledge of a planned attack of some kind on the king. And she has seen their faces. She is too easy a target remaining here. Then, too, Theresa Koller knows where you reside."

"Yes, of course you are right. She must leave Paris. I will need to stay at least for another day or two to deal with my obligations, though. I still have that meeting with Wellington. If you think it advisable, I can take some lodgings in a different location until I leave."

"That would be wise, until this is sorted out."

"Will you see Mary safely gone? You can travel sooner and faster without me."

"I could take her on horseback using safe houses—on side roads to Calais. I had Lambeth arrange for them before I left London, just on the chance we might need them."

Mary's uncle nodded. "I'm glad you did. It is probably the best choice now. You won't be able to take the public coaches, nor any private ones. We do not know how many are involved in this treachery, nor where they might crop up. They will search the main roads."

"There is still the matter of Decazes," Hugh said. "It is not clear what he knows or how deep in this he is. His own people can question him, but I want to have one of Martin's men talk to him as well."

"No one knows the identity of the Nighthawk, do they?" Mary's uncle asked.

"No. But Martin tells me they are still searching for him." Hugh glanced over at her. "I think we should leave as soon as we can. I'll get Lady Mary some men's clothes, which will help disguise her identity and allow her to ride astride for speed. I would like to make Beauvais tonight."

As the men talked, Mary's gaze drifted around the room seeking some hint of Hugh in the furnishings. The colors reminded her of him; they were dark and very masculine. The chair she sat in was one of two French chairs flanking the fireplace. Its seat and back were covered in rich brown suede leather, and between the chairs stood a small round pedestal table holding two glasses and a crystal decanter of brandy. Cases lined the walls with leather-bound books.

Though Mary would have liked nothing better than a bed, she suddenly realized the adventure was not over. What had Hugh meant by "safe houses"? She wanted to ask, but right now she was too guilty for her own actions that may have precipitated the Prussians seizing her and Decazes. She set down her coffee and addressed the two men.

"I'm sorry to have caused you all this trouble."

Her uncle gave her a kind look. "Though I'm as displeased with the risks you took as Lord Ormond, the result of your efforts is admirable," he said. "Your motives were good, and for my own part I did not discourage you as I should have. I'll not dwell on the past when just now my concern is to see you safely home. I trust Lord Ormond to do that."

Hugh's gaze fixed on her, his dark eyes determined. It would have been fair for him to remind her of his warnings, and she suspected she'd not heard the last of his ranting, but for now he desisted. She was glad. If she had to do everything over again, she would not have changed anything—except for getting caught. But she could not forget that he had come for her. He had saved her. She loved him for that. She'd never had a man to lean on like that before and it felt right. He felt right.

Her uncle spoke up. "The thought of Mary and you on the run being chased by Prussians is not a comforting one, but if anyone can see her safely back to London, it is you. Guard her with your life, Ormond."

Lord Ormond nodded. "I will not fail you—or her."

Leaning in closer, her uncle added something else that Mary barely heard. "I expect you to guard her honor as well."

"I will," Hugh said.

"If I'm asked," her uncle continued, speaking normally again, "I'll explain she had to leave suddenly due to an illness of her mother." A slight smile crossed his face then, one that Mary did not understand.

She rose and went to hug him. "Thank you, Uncle, for not scolding me. I love you."

Hugh stepped forward and patted her uncle's shoulder. "If all goes well, we will be in London when you return. Safe and sound."

Hugh's friend Martin Donet arrived shortly after that. He greeted Mary and then asked to speak privately with Hugh, leaving her with her uncle. Mary began to revive with breakfast and changed into the stable boy's clothes Hugh's butler managed to find. Arranging her hair in a single plait, she tucked it into a cap that came with the clothes. There were also nicely fitting boots, but the breeches were a bit snug. Hugh smiled when he saw them.

There wasn't time for her to retrieve her toiletries, so a maid gave her a comb and a toothbrush. After that, all was done that could be done, so she kissed her uncle goodbye and exited with Hugh through a side door to find two horses saddled and waiting.

Hugh efficiently took charge of packing the saddlebags. He had changed from his previous garb to dark brown breeches and muslin shirt, a dark brown coat and his black Hessian boots. His hair was tousled, one stray sable lock falling onto his forehead. Just inside his coat she could see a leather brace holding what looked to be two pistols. They were odd, as they also appeared to be daggers. She'd never seen anything like the black-handled weapons, and strapped to his broad chest they made him seem all the more dangerous, not at all like a British lord. He made her feel safe and protected, and that was all that mattered.

After packing their supplies, he turned to face her. "Mary," he said, "you've made some foolish decisions in the recent past. I need you to obey me as we set out on this journey if we're to arrive in London unscathed. Will you trust me to look after you?"

Mary at first resented his bringing up what had happened in Paris, but then she saw something new in his eyes, an unspoken need. He truly cared about her. And he was asking for her trust rather than commanding her to do his bidding. It made her realize that she did trust this man. She trusted him and…she loved him.

"I will."

So many emotions stirred as those dark eyes fixed on her. Oh, how she wanted to trust him with her heart. Could he be the one to give her the love she had always wanted but never thought she'd find?

Steadying herself, she stepped toward the chestnut gelding she was to ride and stroked its forelock. When she began whispering under her breath, Hugh raised his head, glancing over his horse at her.

"What are you doing?"

"I'm telling him what I expect of him and how we will do this together."

Hugh raised an eyebrow. "And, does that work?"

Mary smiled. "It works with Midnight."

Hugh laughed. "Yes, I've seen you with that stallion. It certainly does."

Chapter 24

Dark gray clouds billowed above Hugh and Mary as they rode from Paris. Hugh considered the swirling sky and frowned as the wind picked up. The scent of rain was in the air, but the road was clear so he drove them hard. Though he saw no signs they were being followed, at any time that could change.

An hour north of Paris, a streak of lightning cut the sky, deafening thunder roared, and the clouds finally loosed the torrents of rain they'd been holding back. Hugh glanced at Mary where she crouched low over her chestnut gelding, its mane flying into her face. The swan had turned into a fierce bird of prey, her eyes fixed straight ahead as she clutched the reins. Hugh marveled at her stamina and courage. She had not slept. Neither had he, but his body was hardened from years of fighting Napoleon. Hugh was determined to make Beauvais that night, though it would mean hours of riding in what had become a cold, persistent downpour.

The roads soon turned muddy, the cold brown ooze splashing their boots and legs and even their horses' bridles, forcing them to slow their breakneck pace. Hugh could see Mary was coming to the end of her strength. His concern was for her. By now her clothes would be soaked through, and her muscles would ache from being in the same position for so long. He knew she had to be spent, but he was proud that she still did not complain. She would push herself until there was nothing left. Mary Campbell had a strong heart.

Finally Hugh drew rein, Mary following his lead. The rain had not subsided, and what had been a gray brooding sky was now descending into darkness. They left the road and walked the horses through dense woods until at last they arrived at a small tan cottage

Hugh had used as a safe house for British agents during the reign of Napoleon. He himself had taken refuge here and knew the place well. It would be a welcome shelter.

As Hugh dismounted, he saw that Mary had laid her head on her gelding's mane, obviously drained of her last strength. He observed her shivering and clenching her teeth, so he helped her down after gently prying the reins from her stiff hands.

"You're exhausted and freezing," he whispered. "Let me get you inside."

"I've never been this cold or this wet," she murmured.

As her feet touched the ground, her knees gave way and she collapsed against him. Her eyes closed and she was out. Hugh swept her up in his arms.

The door of the cottage opened. A young man rushed out, and Hugh yelled, "Simeon, hold the door!"

He carried his burden inside the cottage, moving quickly past the main room to the bedroom, where much to his relief a fire blazed in the stone fireplace. He carefully set Mary in a large chair, her head lolling against its upholstered back; then he tossed his cloak aside, stripped off her wet coat and cap and allowed her long braid to uncurl. Bone-chilling rain ran down her cheeks. In quick order he pulled off her boots, desperate to warm her. She was soaked to the skin and very pale.

"Simeon, get me some hot water to clean off the mud—and some brandy, please," he said to the boy who'd returned and was now staring wide-eyed at Mary. When Simeon didn't move, Hugh urged, "You can stop gawking at the lady."

"Yes, sir," the young man said, coming to his senses. "I knew you might be coming, sir, but I did not know when. I've kept the fire going each night, the provisions stocked and the spare horses here and ready."

"Good man, Simeon. After you bring the things I've requested, you can tend our mounts."

The young man hurried off. Hugh was thankful for his alacrity.

When Simeon returned, Hugh took the water and brandy. He then dismissed the lad, turning his attention to Mary, pulling off her breeches, which were splashed with mud. She didn't stir as he worked to rid her of the wet garment. As her long well-shaped legs came into view, only partially covered by underdrawers, he was captivated by the honey-colored skin and the allure of her body.

When her shirt followed the breeches to the floor, Hugh drew in a sharp breath. The only covering of her chest was a silk chemise, transparent, and not just from the rain; it was *designed* that way. A sliver of gossamer silk over a goddess's body. Her pale, full breasts clung to the damp fabric; those peach nipples made his mouth water. She was so beautiful. What he had only dreamed before was now a reality. And he wanted her all for himself.

Shaking his head, he grinned. "Is this what young debutantes are wearing under their gowns these days?" Somehow he didn't think so. But he liked it all the same. He liked to imagine she'd worn it just for him.

But she was tired and cold and unable to enjoy—or rebuff—his appreciation. He forced his wayward mind to stay focused on his primary task of assuring her health. Tamping down his desire, he removed the soaked drawers but decided to leave her in the chemise, which was quickly drying; and quickly he cleaned the mud off her hands and face. Then, after drying her skin, he took her long golden strands out of their plait and carried her to the large poster bed.

He was just lowering her to the soft linens and beginning to pull the cover over her when his restraint failed. Her body... She was more fascinating than he had ever imagined. Her skin glowed in the firelight, and her slim waist was the perfect complement to her curves. The honey-dark curls where her thighs met enticed him once again almost beyond sanity.

Not wanting her to wake naked in a strange bed, he set aside the bedcover and took one of his shirts from a saddlebag. The shirt was sufficiently large to cover her, and he quickly slipped it over her head.

Leaving the velvet bed curtains tied back at the bedposts, he pulled the cover to her chin and stood watching her for a long moment, his heart and his body drawing him toward her. After a moment, he bent down and gently kissed her on the forehead. The sleeping girl was oblivious.

Simeon returned, albeit briefly. After Hugh told the youth what they would need for the next morning, he let the boy go back to his home, not far away, then slid the lock into place on the door. Drained of his last bit of strength, Hugh cleaned himself off and changed into dry breeches and a clean shirt he left untucked and open at the neck.

God, he was tired. He reached for some brandy but was too weary to stand, so he stretched out atop the bed far from Mary and took a swallow. It had been a long day and night. Setting the empty glass aside, he let himself lie back against the pillow. Perhaps if they just got some rest, they could get something to eat and recover a bit.

Sleep quickly claimed him. A few hours later, however, Hugh woke with a start to find Mary curled into his side like a kitten looking for warmth. Her head had moved from her pillow to rest on his arm. Golden hair spilled out behind her, capturing the light from the dying fire. Her oval face was angelic in sleep. He breathed in the faint scent of gardenias.

His body reacted as it always did to her, and a desperate urge rose within him to take her in his arms. But that would not be wise. After all, he'd promised to preserve her honor. She was not even conscious! He needed some distance before he forgot those things; it would be too easy to reach down and kiss her, to seduce her from sleep—

Carefully, so as not to wake her, he slipped out of Mary's embrace and went to the fireplace, took the poker and stirred the glowing coals to life. Flames burst forth, casting a warm glow about the room and bringing similarly incendiary thoughts in their wake.

He leaned one arm on the mantel and gazed into the fire. Should he seduce her? Wasn't that what all his actions had been leading to? Somewhere deep inside his mind he'd always known what he wanted. His lips had trained hers to return his kiss. His touch had drawn such innocent responses from her, innocent but passionate, yearning for more. Though they'd had their disagreements, he thought she wanted him as he wanted her.

Did she want him as he wanted her? He wanted her in his bed, but he also wanted her as his bride. It was a bit of a shock, but he believed he'd finally met the one woman who had no equal. Whether he could control her or not, she was the only one he wanted. *I love her. And I don't want to live without her.* He was amused to realize that he, a grand thief, had allowed love to creep up on him unaware. She had stolen his heart.

He was confident, too, that she felt more for him than she realized. She was responsive to his kisses. Her eyes lit up when he walked into the room. Even when she was angry he saw the passion she could not hide. But the independent Mary Campbell wouldn't come easily to marriage. If he took her, she'd have no choice. But he did not want the strong-willed Mary Campbell that way. He wanted her willing. He couldn't give Mary a chance to think too long about losing the independence he knew she prized, however. The idea of obeying a husband's commands would not come easy.

Amused, he reached for the poker and adjusted a log. All those years as the Nighthawk, and never once had he been presented with a task as difficult as convincing Mary Campbell to be his wife. He had grown deeply attached to the girl, free spirited as she was. Mary was the most amazing woman he'd ever met. She drove him crazy, he admitted, but she also made him feel alive. Never had he been so attracted to a woman. Never had he been so obsessed with a face. He could not get her out of his mind. He still remembered how panicked he had been seeing her lying on that street in Paris, then again that very morning with the Prussians. Seeing her like that had reminded him of his brother, of losing someone who was everything to him and being entirely unable to change it. He couldn't lose her.

He shuddered, realizing it wasn't possible to love without risking loss. Isn't that why he had resisted love all these years? But sometimes gambles were worth the risk. That's what Mary had taught him. She *was* worth the risk, for he would have little life without her now. But could he be the one to successfully manage the difficult Mary Campbell?

* * *

Mary woke in a strange bed. Hazy memories of riding hard in the cold rain while struggling to fight off horrible fatigue were swimming in her head, but she was warm now. Her last memory was Hugh pulling her from her horse.

She could smell Hugh on the pillow, a mixture of horse and sweat and man. Had he been lying next to her? She touched the bedclothes, her body, and realized happily she was not naked.

Though she recognized the thin chemise, the shirt that covered it was not hers. Who had taken her clothes, and where was she?

Lifting her head, she surveyed her surroundings. The light from the fire was faint but she could see the room was fairly large and comfortably furnished with dark wood pieces. There was a window with curtains to her right but no light seeped in. Outside it was night.

She could hear rain falling gently. A round wooden table with two chairs sat in front of the window. She turned upon hearing a crackling noise from the fireplace. There was some kind of painted landscape hanging over the stone mantel, and a dark figure stood to one side with his forearm resting against it as he gazed into the fire.

Hugh.

She was reminded of Midnight: tall, broad-shouldered, so powerful that he seemed moving even while at rest. Hugh's thick sable hair was like a mane curling into waves at his nape. A wall of lean muscle was outlined by the fabric of his shirt. Even now she was drawn to the man. He would never be tamed, but perhaps like Midnight she could love him into accepting and wanting only her. God help her. Though she feared he would break her heart, she wanted to try.

She slipped out of the bed and silently crossed the thick rug, coming up behind him. Later she would remember this moment, wondering at her brazen behavior, but not now. Without a sound she slipped her arms around his waist and leaned into his heat. Her breasts and face pressed into his muscled back and she sighed, content.

Hugh started then relaxed into the softness of her body. After only a moment, he turned in her arms to face her. "You're awake."

Mary's hands encircled his waist, and she looked up to see him smiling down at her. His eyes were dark pools of desire.

"You took care of me, didn't you?"

"Yes." His smile became a grin.

"You took my clothes off?"

"Yes. But you were very wet, very cold and you fainted."

Mary turned her head to look into the fire, thinking back across the last few days. "It is certainly a strange path that has brought us here, isn't it?"

"Perhaps," Hugh replied, "but you were determined to walk it."

Still feeling guilty for all she'd put him through, even though she believed she was right, she didn't want to argue. Instead she pressed closer to his heat and rested her head on his chest. "I knew it was important."

Hugh was silent a moment, then his fingers drew her face up to his. "You must not take such risks anymore. You are important to me."

He lowered his lips to hers, and their touch was gentle. Mary wanted more, though. She craved his touch, craved his love, craved everything about the man. She did not fight when he pulled her close, wrapping his arms around her; she pressed closer. His kiss changed, devouring her mouth. His tongue fiercely claimed hers. Mary could feel the hard ridge beneath his breeches and her shirt. It was exciting and alarming, for she realized they were alone in a bedroom. They were in a place where her heart's desires could be realized.

His kiss grew more demanding, and he rocked his hips slowly into her. His hands cupped her bottom, drawing her against his arousal. She was both frightened and attracted to his masculine, virile strength. Drawn down this path, she wondered what lay at the end of it.

Like the other times, Hugh ended the kiss, leaving both of them breathless. He pulled back to look at her, the light from the fire casting a golden light over his face. She was keenly aware that all her curves were still touching him, the linen shirt a thin barrier between them. His erection was hard and insistent.

"I am tired of fighting you, Mary Campbell," he said, leaning forward. His lips brushed back and forth over her forehead as he spoke. "I am tired of fighting your suitors. I am tired of fighting my desire for you. I want you, in my life and in my bed."

He kissed a path down her throat, and Mary's body responded. The heat of his mouth burned a path to her breasts, and her hands reached up into his dark hair. She felt herself being swept away by feelings she had never experienced, and so she determined to speak while she could still formulate words.

"Hugh, I…don't want to be one of your women."

He lifted his head from her breasts. "No, Mary. Not *one* of my women, my *only* woman. My wife. I want you to be mine. Marry me."

She was shocked to realized she needed no time to think about the answer. She wanted him, too. For some time her heart had been telling her he was worth it, that Hugh Redgrave was the only man to make her want marriage, the only man to stir true passion within her. Like Midnight, he would not be easy, but she believed he could be hers alone. And yet she wanted him to be sure of what he was saying.

"Are you certain?" she asked. "I'm not like other women you may have known. I can be…well, I have my own mind, as you know. I will want to live a different life than most women."

He chuckled. "Yes, sweet Mary, I've known that from the beginning."

"You have?"

"Yes, I have. And I'm coming to see that I cannot change you. I don't believe I want to. As I think of it now, it's what drew me to you—since the first day I saw you riding that horse of yours like no proper woman would. After our first conversation at that luncheon, with your pointed remarks no debutante would ever utter, I have not been able to keep you out of my thoughts, not even for a day. And while you drive me crazy, taking risks that make me shudder, you are the woman I want, the *only* woman I want. What I feel for you I have never felt. For so long I have been afraid to care for anyone I would fear losing—"

"Because of Henry?" she interjected. He was silent, so she touched his cheek. "Hugh, we have both lost people we love. We must remember them but also let them go."

His hand covered hers. "I believe I have finally let him go, and I think I've forgiven myself. I agree that we can have a life. *Together*." He turned his face to kiss her palm.

"Oh, Hugh," she whispered softly, and she recognized her words as an invitation.

Apparently, so did he. This time his kiss was immediately one of passion and possession, and full of promise. It went on and on before Hugh finally paused, his breath ragged, giving them one last shot at decorum and honor. "Mary, I want you now but I can wait."

Mary was breathless, and her heart pounded in her chest. She wanted him in all the ways a woman could want a man, but she pulled back and stared into his dark eyes. She saw exactly what she needed there. "I want you, too," she said breathlessly. "And, yes, I'll marry you."

He swept her into his arms and to the bed, gently laying her down atop the cover. Doffing his shirt and breeches, he climbed onto the bed and lay beside her.

The sight of his naked body took Mary aback. She'd never before seen a fully grown man completely naked. He *was* beautiful, long and lean, all hard muscle covered by warm smooth skin, and her eyes followed the trail of dark hair leading from his chest down past his waist. His arousal was large and imposing.

Though she had seen horses breed, she'd never seen a man naked and fully aroused. Forcing her eyes to his chest, she remembered tending him after his fall. Her fingers reached out to touch the coarse hair on his chest.

Passion flamed in his eyes, and Hugh pulled her to him, running his hand over her bottom. As she shivered he promised, "I'll be gentle, sweetheart. I'll cherish you."

Mary reached up and kissed him, her heart and soul full of trust and love.

Hugh took command of the kiss, claiming her lips, kissing her neck and sweeping his tongue over her ear. The warmth of his naked flesh made her nipples harden beneath her thin muslin shirt. His hands were everywhere, cuddling her, caressing her, touching her. He covered her with his body, pressing his arousal against her upper thigh, and her heartbeat accelerated, her body tingling all over. He lightly ran his lips over her collarbone, and his hand dipped into her shirt to explore her breasts.

"I want you naked," he said, pulling back and drawing her into a sitting position to tug the shirt off and cast it away. His eyes feasted on her breasts, and his mouth soon did the same. Pressing her back into the pillows, he nuzzled one gently, drawing her nipple into his mouth and stroking it with his tongue. The heat of his mouth released a damp flow at her woman's center.

Her breathing rapid, Mary moaned. The feel of him sucking gently on her breast was intoxicating, and she writhed as shimmers of arousal echoed through her body. He rose above her, settling himself between her thighs. Her gasps increased as his aroused flesh pressed against her warm core. The feel of that hard flesh was both arousing and a little frightening, especially when he began to rock his hips, sliding his erection back and forth over soft folds that were now wet and slick with wanting.

Mary moved her hands up the sides of his body, memorizing the contours of his back and shoulders that had so long held such fascination for her. His warm skin was smooth and taut over flexing muscles. He was so much man, the smell of him masculine and earthy, and she repeatedly whispered his name. She rubbed her woman's flesh against him, parting her legs in further invitation.

Hugh's mouth claimed hers once again, ravishing it. His tongue presaged his body's movements to come. Shifting to one side, his hand roamed her abdomen and down to the curls at the top of her legs. He slid one leg over her thigh, imprisoning her leg while slipping a finger into her. Mary inhaled sharply.

"Oh." It was the touch for which her body cried out.

Hugh moved his finger slowly, softly, finding a tiny bud of sensation within her and calling forth a honey-like liquid. It felt so good, Mary began to move with him, and he slipped a second finger inside, stretching her. His mouth returned to hers, and he kissed her deeply until her hips rocked in time with his moving fingers.

Mary marveled at the building tension, but she craved more of the sweet feeling. She almost cried out when Hugh removed his fingers; then he covered her with his body and placed the head of his aroused flesh at her opening. She lifted her hips in response.

"I want to be inside you."

"Yes," she breathed in a heavy whisper.

He captured her mouth with a kiss and pushed inside her body. There was only him and the feel of his flesh inside her: stretching, filling, moving slowly in and out, each time pressing deeper. The gradual stretching became a sweet torture. Her muscles flexed around him, trying to hold him inside her as he withdrew. He was large but she was wet, and he slid easily in and out. He felt so good, so warm, and she began to move with him. His slowness was nearly driving her mad. She wanted him deeper.

As if in response, he suddenly thrust hard into her tight passage and stilled. She inhaled sharply, a stab of pain taking her breath. He was lodged deeply within her.

"Mary, are you all right?"

"Yes," she said, in a voice higher than her own. "Just a bit...surprised."

He was so large, she felt impaled, but his voice was gentle. "It is only the first time that this hurts, my love."

Her breath came in short pants, but Hugh kissed her deeply, softly, and her body responded and relaxed, growing wet again. His lips trailed down her throat, then to her ear where his tongue circled, setting off delicious sensations of pleasure. Slowly he began to move inside her again. Mary could feel every inch. In response, she wrapped her arms around his neck and slid her legs over his. She was moving with him, swimming in feelings she had never before known. She felt so much a part of him, felt an intimacy she had been incapable of imagining.

I love you. The words spilled through her mind though she'd not dare speak them aloud.

Hugh began thrusting faster. His voice was a ragged whisper. "God, you feel so good. I knew it would be like this with you."

The pain diminished, and Mary felt the tension building as they moved together. This time, she tried to encourage it. Hugh thrust again and again, slowly at first then faster. Her muscles gripped him, just as before. Suddenly a sensation swept over her like an ocean wave breaking. Her muscles convulsed, spasms deep inside her. A soft cry left her throat, and Hugh made one last thrust. His body went rigid as a warm flood filled her, sending her afloat on a wave of ecstasy. It was more than she'd ever imagined.

Hugh's body relaxed, and he gently pressed a kiss to her throat. She kissed his temple in return, her arms wrapped tightly around him. They remained entwined like that for a while, each holding the other. She loved the heat of him resting on her, inside her. She even liked the weight of his body. She was content to stay there forever.

Hugh pulled back to look at her face. As he did, she smiled. "I love you, Hugh."

He slid off to one side, taking her with him. Pressed into his warm body, she sighed. He kissed her forehead in response.

The fire died and the coals no longer glowed. As they fell asleep in each other's arms, Mary had never felt so protected and desired. From this moment on, she did not want to sleep without him.

But he had not said he loved her, had he?

Chapter 25

Hugh began to stir a few hours before daybreak, his body awakening to the warmth of Mary lying so close. She had turned in the night to lie on her side, her back against his chest and her bottom tucked into his groin. His arm was draped over her ribs and his hand possessively cupped one breast.

His body instantly came alive, and his fingers circled her silky nipple. Though she still slept, that nipple responded to his touch, tightening into a hard bud. His hand moved from her breasts to her stomach, sliding across satin skin. She was so soft, so warm. His woman…and soon, his wife.

He reached the soft curls between her thighs, and his fingers moved slowly over the soft folds there to the sensitive nub, coaxing her awake and to arousal. His finger slipped into her, warm liquid welcoming the intrusion. Mary made sounds of contentment and began to move her bottom against him, with no clothing between them. He was growing harder with each movement. The feel of flesh on flesh was enticing.

Hugh nuzzled her neck, kissing and nibbling on her ear. "I want you."

She turned her head to kiss him. "I want you, too."

He entered her in one swift movement from behind, causing her to catch her breath. Though she was likely still sore, Mary slowly began rocking her hips into him, arching her back and pushing her bottom into his groin to take more of his length. His heart beat faster with each driving thrust, sliding in and out of that warm flesh. And her unbridled responses drove him wild.

Still inside her, he lifted up on his elbow and shifted her beneath him, turning her to face the pillow. Moving above her and resting on his knees, he pulled her hips back into him and thrust until he was entirely sheathed within her. Then, still holding her hip with one hand, he moved his other hand to her breasts, slowly kneading her nipple between his thumb and forefinger.

Her breath accelerated to short pants as his hand traveled down to her soft folds, and there he stroked the sensitive nub until her inner muscles gripped his hard length, a wave of spasms overtaking her and she called out his name. Hugh continued to thrust until finally, pulling her hips tight to his groin one final time he filled her with his warm seed. The muscles of Mary's passage gripped his flesh, he let out a deep groan and they collapsed together, sated.

Hugh drew her close. "My love, my treasure. Such a passionate woman, I am indeed a fortunate man."

They both fell back asleep, and sometime during the night the rain stopped. Hugh woke to the sun streaming in the window where the curtains did not quite close. Sounds of birds welcoming the morning intruded on their silent haven, and Mary turned to face him, her golden hair sprawled across the pillow and his shoulder. He loved the feel of it on his skin, like silk. The faint scent of gardenias drifted to his nose, along with the musky smell of their lovemaking.

His arms around her, he held her close, one leg between hers. He smiled and kissed her forehead. "My love, we need a vicar." He would not give her time to reconsider. "There will be one at the English Chapel in Calais. Are you willing to forgo a large wedding?"

"Can we take time for this? Aren't you worried about us doing something so public while still in France?"

"There are thousands of English living in Calais," he replied. "We won't be noticed if we're careful, and they won't be looking for us in a church. More likely they'll be waiting at the channel crossing."

"I like the idea of being married in France," she mused, running her fingers through the hair on his chest. "It's an adventure."

He captured her hand, holding it over his heart. "You and your adventures. We still need to talk about those."

"But adventures are the spice of life!"

He wasn't sure he liked the idea of their wedding being an adventure, but he was glad she was not reconsidering. "What I think, my love, is that we have both had enough adventures for a while. And I don't want to take you back to England unwed. As it is, your uncle will be unhappy with me. Assuming he will accept me as your husband, he may want another wedding in England just to assure himself we're really man and wife."

Mary turned her face up to his and kissed his jaw. "As many weddings as you like." Then she rolled atop him with a kiss.

Hugh chuckled. "I see I have created an appetite in you for more than food." Drawing her close, he relished the feel of her naked body. Just to hold her was heaven. She was in his life to stay.

An hour later they sat at the cottage's small table eating the cheese and fruit Simeon had brought. Hugh took a drink of coffee, its rich aroma reviving him.

Mary reached for a piece of yellow cheese. "What will happen to the vicomte?"

"It remains to be seen. If the Prussians don't get to Decazes, I expect King Louis will. Treachery is not well received by the Bourbons. They've had enough of it. Whatever Decazes has been a part of will soon be known. Martin will get to the heart of it. He's an exceptional agent."

"The vicomte was kind to me," Mary said thoughtfully. "Even at the end."

"To my mind he was a bit too kind." Hugh frowned. "He was besotted with you. It was getting most annoying."

She grinned. "Are you jealous? Of Joseph Decazes?"

"Of course I am jealous. The man was like a bee about a flower. I kept wanting to swat him."

Her smile faded a bit. "I feel sorry for him. Still, he must have known he'd get caught with so many masters."

Hugh recalled the men he'd known during Napoleon's reign who took foolish risks. "He's lucky he did not end up dead. And if Louis does not banish or kill him, he may yet face the wrath of the Prussians—not to mention the friends of Boney who are in league with them."

"What about Theresa?"

"Ah. Now there is a troubling person," Hugh admitted. "Her treachery was clear, which does not bode well for her. Her brother will intercede, of course, and the king may allow the Austrians to deal with her."

Mary took another bite of cheese and held his gaze as her foot rubbed his leg under the table. "And what has been your role in all of this?"

He considered pulling her into his lap, she was so adorable, but instead reached across the table, took her hand and smiled. "There are some things that are not mine to tell, my love. But what I can say is that I sometimes handle special matters for the Prince Regent. I was here to support your uncle, to provide him with useful information for his discussions and to check on some of our activities in Paris."

Mary shook her head. "For a duke's son, you've had some incredible adventures, yourself. Is your friend Lambeth a part of this?"

Adventures. There was that word again. Still, he would tell the woman who'd captured his heart as much as he could. "He is. Like me, he finds most things that occupy the peerage wearying. He has a gift for planning, and I was able to bring him into our work."

"I can see I have a lot to learn," she replied.

No. He wanted to keep his treasure safe. "I am trusting that when we return to London, it will be the end of this adventure of yours."

"Perhaps this one," she agreed with a mischievous smile. "I suspect being married to you will be the greatest adventure of all. I have loved being a part of my uncle's work, though. Perhaps in the future I might be a part of yours."

Hugh sighed. "I am hoping for some compromise as to your many freedoms, my love. I would not want to worry continually about your safety."

"Compromise is acceptable," she said, "but I will not be kept in a box, Hugh. That is one of the reasons marriage never appealed to me."

"Yes, I know," he said. "And I promise I will do my best to see you are not trapped in a dull life. But just now, my love, we need to be on the road. We are not yet home. Oh, by the way, I like the lacy chemise I pulled from you last night."

Mary gave him a coy smile. "I bought it with you in mind."

* * *

Hugh's words brought Mary back to the reality of their plight. Treacherous killers were searching for them. "Are you worried we could be discovered today?"

He shrugged. "By now your uncle has explained your departure, so many will know you left Paris. I assume the Prussians have searched for you and know you were not on the departing coaches. We must take the main road for a bit. Whether any of our enemies will be on it I cannot say."

As she dressed, Mary was careful to tuck her hair inside her cap and to make certain her feminine form was well hidden. Her back muscles ached and the cramping in her thighs reminded her that she was not used to being so long in the saddle. Nor was she used to spending her nights making love. Her cheeks heated at the memory of all she had shared with Hugh. He was hers now, and she was his.

She was glad when, after only a few hours of riding, Hugh reined to one side of the road.

"There's a clearing just through these trees where we can rest for a few minutes. How are you feeling?"

"Sore and very happy to be stopping." She smiled at him, then, and reached one hand to her lower back to rub out a cramp.

The two of them walked their horses through the woods until she saw a small meadow. On its other side was a dense copse of trees. Yellow and white wildflowers grew at one side of the clearing where the sun fell on a patch of grass. It was peaceful, with leaves rustling in the slight wind and birds chirping. The day was clear though cool. Mary was delighted they were not facing another storm.

Hugh gestured with a nod toward the grove. "If I remember correctly, there is a stream just beyond those trees. Stay here, sweetheart. I'm just going to get us some fresh water."

He swung onto his horse in one fluid movement and rode off. As the trees closed about him, Mary opened her saddlebags and took out the food Simeon had given them. The cold meat, bread, cheese and fruit would fill their hungry stomachs. She was absorbed in unwrapping the cheese and setting the food on a cloth when she suddenly realized the forest had grown silent; there were no birdcalls or noises of any other kind.

Then, a footfall on twigs behind her. She turned to welcome Hugh, but as she spun a hand came across her mouth and a man's gruff voice said in French, "Not a word!"

Fear seized her, and every nerve in her body came alive. She shouted a muffled protest, but the hand was firmly clamped over her mouth. In vain she tried to pull the man's arm away, but he was too strong. She was roughly wrenched to her feet and pushed into the brush where a horse waited. She struggled even harder.

Fighting for her life, she kicked the man's shins and bit the fingers pressed over her mouth. Her hat fell from her head as the man swore in German, then he dropped his hand from her mouth to slap her hard across her face, leaving her stunned and in pain. It was the second time a Prussian had hit her, and she'd had enough. Now more angry than afraid, she pushed him hard and darted toward the clearing.

She did not get far. He yanked her up to face him. Still fighting, she scratched his face with her nails and kicked his shins again. He swore an oath and grabbed her hands, holding her firm.

A second man rode up through the bushes. Both strangers were dirty, with long stubble on their faces and splashed mud on their boots and breeches. They must have ridden through the rain the day before. The one holding Mary called out, "I'll handle her. You take care of the one who was with her." Without responding, the second man wheeled his horse toward the stream.

The man holding Mary reached into his pocket and took out a length of cord to tie her hands. "Any more from you, and you will see nothing." Once her hands were bound, he lifted her still struggling against him, carried her to his waiting horse and flung her over the saddle. She was just trying to aright herself when she heard the voice.

"Let her go or you're dead!"

Mary's heart leapt as she recognized the deep, familiar sound, and she slipped from the saddle and turned to see an angry Hugh standing in the clearing with a pistol pointed at her captor. The man still stood near her and kept his back to Hugh. Slowly he reached for a pistol tucked at his waist.

Mary saw the movement. "He has a pistol!"

Before she could move, the man reached out and grabbed her, turning to face Hugh while pressing the pistol to her temple. "I'll not hesitate to use this. Lose your weapon."

Hugh dropped his pistol without hesitation.

"And the brace, too," said the man, motioning to Hugh's chest.

Hugh unfastened the brace still containing the other pistol dagger. Just as he began to lower it to the ground, though, Mary shoved her elbow hard into the ribs of the man holding her. The villain stepped backward with an oath, and in one swift movement Hugh had thrown one of his daggers across the small distance where it lodged in the man's chest. As the man began to collapse, Mary saw he still aimed his pistol at Hugh, preparing to fire. She kicked the pistol from his hand just as the gun went off. The bullet went into the trees instead of Hugh's chest. The man on the ground clutched at his chest and then collapsed.

Mary stood shaking from what had just transpired.

She watched as Hugh reached down and picked up his pistol, returning it to its brace. Then, unable to move, she stared at the man lying at her feet.

"Come to me, sweetheart."

Hugh's words sank in, and though still shaking badly, Mary found her feet and ran to him. He wrapped his arms around her, pressing her close. "It's all right, love. He won't hurt you now. My brave little minx. You saved me, you know."

"I couldn't let him shoot you!" Suddenly she had a thought. "There was another man—"

"Not anymore. He was a bit too loud in his steps. I heard him coming up behind me."

Leaning back, she eyed him and panicked when she saw blood on his white shirt. "You're wounded!"

"It's not my blood." A subtle smile crossed his face.

"Oh," she said. She gave a quick prayer of thanks.

Hugh untied Mary's hands. As he did, she began to speak in rapid bursts. "I didn't see them. Oh, Hugh! He came from behind me. I thought it was you!"

"It's all right," he repeated, his deep voice calming as he rubbed her back and kissed her forehead. "You're safe now."

He left her to retrieve their assailant's pistol and the dagger still lodged in his chest. He wiped the knife clean on the dead man's pants and replaced it in his brace alongside its mate.

Mary was shocked. She could hardly fathom how this reputed rake could be so calm in the face of danger. He had killed before, that much was obvious. With his dark breeches and boots and the brace of pistols, he seemed more the pirate than ever.

He handed her the fallen man's pistol. "Can you use this?"

"Yes," she admitted, "I have shot a pistol before. My uncle thought it might be good for me to know how to use them, though I've never had one of my own."

"Keep it with you." He looked grim. "Now come, my love. Our noon repast will have to be eaten while we ride. Others may soon know where we are."

Mary drew near to him and laid her head on his chest. She needed his comfort.

"Are you all right?" He put an arm around her.

"I'll be fine now. I'm just relieved it is over and you're unhurt. Oh, Hugh. You were magnificent."

He chuckled and kissed her gently. "You are easily impressed." But he did not seem displeased.

Chapter 26

Mary watched the harbor from where she stood on the cliff above Calais. Piers jutted out into the deep blue water. She was reminded how English the port city was in comparison to the rest of France; from her history lessons, she knew English kings had once reigned here, and the city had even been called "the brightest jewel in the English Crown" because of its importance to the tin, lead, cloth and wool trades. Now, with the Bourbons restored to power, Hugh told her the city was experiencing a burst of growth.

As she watched, ships and boats moved in and out and dockworkers loaded and unloaded goods. She reached her hand up to shelter her eyes. There was a glare despite the clouds overhead, but far off in the distance she could just make out the cliffs on England's shore, and her heart warmed at the thought of home. She would return as Lady Ormond, and that made her smile.

Hugh took her hand and pulled her toward the waiting horses. "You will find the accommodations here more to your liking, my love. Our safe house is larger, and there is even a cook."

She smiled sweetly. "I don't think I could love anyplace more than the cottage we shared last night." The memory of the intimacies they'd exchanged there caused heat to rise in her cheeks.

"My fondest memory as well, my love." Hugh kissed her, a warm promise of more, and lifted her back into the saddle.

They arrived late in the afternoon at a two-story dwelling, the last on a street of unremarkable Flemish houses.

"How long will we be here?" Mary asked as Hugh handed the reins of their horses to a skinny young man he introduced as John. Hearing her voice, John threw her a sharp glance, his eyes raking her body to take in the breeches and boots she still wore. Clearly he had never seen a woman wearing men's clothes. He walked the horses towards the stables while scratching his head.

"Just long enough to get married, my love, and to arrange for our crossing. But first a bath and some food, don't you think?"

The thought of a hot bath was suddenly all she could think about. They were both covered in dust from the ride, and Hugh's shirt bore dried blood from the altercation in the woods. She was glad she had managed to talk Hugh into bringing her blue gown so she would be able to change from her breeches. But another thought that slipped into her mind unbidden, entrancing, was of Hugh bathing with her.

"Yes, I'd like a bath very much. Is it a large tub, do you think?"

Hugh gave her a wry smile. "As I recall, it is."

Weary from all that had happened, Mary eagerly sank into the unusually large tub of steaming water and closed her eyes, her long golden locks freed of the plait and hanging over the edge of the tub. She had left Hugh downstairs talking to John and thought she'd have several minutes to herself when she heard the bedroom door open and close. She was no longer alone.

Her back to the door, she heard boots drop to the wood floor. Though her eyes remained closed, she recognized the sound of clothes being shed, and a shiver of anticipation coursed through her despite the heat of the bathwater. She felt movement in front of her then heard a splash as Hugh's legs slid down alongside hers. She opened her eyes.

He wore a lazy, self-assured grin—his pirate smile, she dubbed it. "It will be tight, but I think there is just enough room."

"Room for what?" she asked.

"You'll see." He reached for her, pulling her onto his lap. "Bend your knees, love, and spread your legs on either side of mine."

She found herself intimately resting on his groin, the warm flesh there hardening beneath her. The contact caused her nipples to tighten, and he pulled her in closer. The feeling of his warm chest against her breasts was so intoxicating that she involuntarily rocked her hips.

"Oh…."

It was a soft moan, but when he heard it Hugh bent his head to her breast and took one nipple into the warm wet suction of his mouth. "I have been looking forward to this all day," he said during a brief pause in which he stared up with loving eyes.

Mary melted into his caress, the warm water a blanket around them as she continued to move her hips back and forth over the hard ridge of his arousal. He moved his mouth to her throat and to the pulse raging there. His words filtered up to her.

"You keep moving like that, love, and this will soon be over."

Mary stilled. "Don't you like it?"

"Oh yes, I like it just fine. But I want this to go on longer."

She was growing wetter, and it was not from the bathwater. Placing her hands on his shoulders, she reached up to kiss him and her breasts made contact with the dark hair on his chest. He drew her closer, and his tongue stroked hers while his hands stroked her back. Suddenly, he lifted her.

"I want to be inside you."

Drawn to stare into his eyes, she saw his intent. Water cascaded off her slick body, then Hugh slowly lowered her atop his engorged flesh, thrusting up at the same time until she felt him deeply lodged within her. She shivered at the fullness.

His lips moved to her temple. "You feel so good. I can't get enough of you. I don't think I ever will."

The water sloshed out of the tub as Hugh lifted her hips and let her slide down onto his flesh once again. Then again. Mary moved in rhythm, her bent legs helping her to rise. Her hands cupped his face and she kissed him, wholly entranced by the pleasure of the act.

Her hair fell on either side of his face, and Hugh nuzzled her neck. "Your hair feels like soft rain."

The friction of his chest hair against her wet breasts was indescribable. Her body tensed, her muscles once more clenching around him. Mary could think of nothing but Hugh and being wrapped around him, being joined with him. It was more than a joining of two bodies. It was a joining of two souls. She held nothing back.

Their movements quickened, became a storm of pleasure. Water splashed over the lip of the tub in response. Mary was awed at his strength and the powerful muscles flexing in his arms. Suddenly new spasms swept over her, and she threw her head back as she floated on a riptide of pleasure. Hugh lifted her one last time, let out a groan and surged into her, finding his release.

He relaxed even as Mary was still floating in a feeling of deep contentment. Finally, she pressed her lips to his forehead and said, "I love you." Kissing him gently on his lips, she said, "Take me to bed, Hugh."

"My thought exactly." Hugh slowly lifted her and helped her to step out of the tub. He held her against his chest for a moment, their wet bodies still slick. "You make me crazy for you, Mary."

His words made her smile.

He dried them both off in quick movements then picked her up and carried her to the large bed in the center of the room. Turning back the cover with one hand, he gently laid her down. She reached for him as he slid in beside her. Burying her face in his neck, Mary pressed her body into his, warm from both their lovemaking and the bath. But that was not enough.

She wriggled one of her legs until it was wedged between his. "I can't get close enough."

He chuckled. "And with all that, I am still hungry for you, too. You have rendered me a lascivious man. Soon your lusty husband."

Mary smiled and let go a contented sigh. "It makes me happy to think you've developed an insatiable appetite for me, my lord."

It was some time before either of them thought of food.

Chapter 27

They dressed for dinner, Mary changing into her sapphire gown.

"I'm glad to see you have lost the breeches, my love. The Marchioness of Ormond should be wearing gowns."

"I won't mind returning to female frippery as long as I can ride Midnight in breeches," she replied.

"That is a sight I will never tire of. You can ride in men's breeches—at least for my viewing."

They strolled down the stairs hand in hand, but before they could sit down to the simple meal the cook had readied for them, the front door flew open. Turning, they saw Griffen Lambeth stride into the entry. He was dressed in a dark gray coat, black breeches and crimson waistcoat, every bit the gentleman. Lizzy would have loved it.

"Ormond! What are you doing here? I thought you were in Paris."

Hugh's brows drew together. "I would ask the same of you: why are you here?" He rose and went to his friend, concern on his face. "Is anything amiss?"

Lambeth glanced over Hugh's shoulder to see Mary. "I had some business with Martin that required my presence in Paris. I expected to find you with Lord Baynes."

"There is much to tell you," Hugh replied. "I was forced to adjust my plans. May I present Lady Mary Campbell, my betrothed." He stepped back and made the appropriate gestures.

Hurrying to bend over her hand, Lambeth grinned. "Lady Mary." He turned back to Hugh and said, "Congratulations!"

"Come into the study with me, Lambeth," Hugh commanded. "I'll give you the short version of the last several days." Turning to

Mary, he said, "Love, please go ahead with dinner. I'll only be a short while."

The two men stepped into a small parlor on the other side of the entryway. As they did, Lambeth raised an eyebrow.

"Love? Betrothed? If you don't mind my asking, Ormond, what has happened between you and the lovely Mary Campbell?"

"It is rather a long story, but to give you the short of it, Mary helped to uncover some treachery against King Louis. Those who are responsible—Prussians, in league with supporters of the former emperor—are hunting her. They are also hunting the Nighthawk. It seemed best to leave Paris, and Lord Baynes and I agreed I should bring her home using the safe houses." He paused. "Oh, yes, and along the way we became betrothed."

"Good Lord, Ormond. You've been a busy man." Lambeth slapped him on the back and laughed. Then his face grew serious. "I myself carry a message. I expected to deliver it to you in Paris, but since you are here you should see. I have a feeling it isn't good news, and perhaps most untimely." He took a sealed envelope from his pocket and handed it to Hugh. "It's from Amanda Hearnshaw. I don't know what it says, but I can imagine."

Hugh tore open the envelope and read the note. "My God. She's with child and claims it's mine. She's asking me to wed her. My *child*? I—"

A gasp sounded behind him, and he and Lambeth turned to find Mary in the doorway, frozen in shock.

"Mary." Hugh sighed the word.

She did not wait to hear the rest of his explanation, just turned and fled up the stairs.

Lambeth's eyes were full of sympathy. "I'm sorry, old man."

Hugh looked back at the note in his hands. "It is not my child. It can't be."

"But Lady Mary doesn't know that, does she?" Lambeth looked toward the stairs.

"No, she doesn't," said Hugh, shaking his head. "Hell and damnation."

He followed her up the stairs and into the bedroom where they had just made love. She was standing in front of the window, her back to him. He could feel the sadness in the air. He could hear her quiet sobs.

"Mary, let me explain."

She slowly turned, tears running down her cheeks. With the backs of her hands, she tried to wipe them away. "What explanation can there be, save the obvious? She was your mistress, was she not?"

"Yes," he admitted, "she was. I cannot believe it's my child, Mary." Not unless for once in his life he'd horribly miscalculated....

"You don't know that." Her voice sounded resolute, but he knew she must be dying inside.

"Mary, this doesn't change anything between us."

He dreaded he might be wrong. Then she confirmed it. Tears filled her green eyes. Her honey skin, now pale, reflected the agony she was feeling. "Not our love, perhaps, but she wants to marry you, to be a family. I cannot live with the thought of separating a family."

"But it is not my child!" He shouted the words, as if doing so would make them true. But he wondered if he hadn't made the mistake of his life with Amanda. Desperate to take Mary into his arms and assure her she was wrong, he crossed the room to where she stood and reached for her, but she stopped him with an outstretched hand.

"No, Hugh. I need time to think."

There was a way around this conundrum, if she would only accept it. *Perhaps...* "Even if you were right and this child were mine, I am certain Amanda would allow us to raise it."

"But she would be ruined. And what about the baby who will need both its parents? No, she needs a husband and her message said she wants to marry you! I would never hurt the child she carries. I would never deny that child a family." She turned back to face the window. "A family I never had."

Hugh could see argument was pointless. "All right. We will return to London and I'll sort out the facts there. But, Mary, do not give up on us."

She said nothing. As Hugh left, he heard quiet sobs.

Descending the stairs, he found Lambeth pouring himself a brandy. "I'll take one of those," he told his friend.

Lambeth reached for another glass. "How did she take it?"

"Not well. She has some notion in her mind that Amanda and I should be a family and raise the child together."

Lambeth poured a generous amount of brandy into a glass and handed it over. "Did you expect anything else?"

"No, I suppose not. Mary is not one of those who tolerate the loose moral climate England embraces. And she worries for the child. We were to be wed here in Calais. Amanda's timing could not have been worse." Hugh sipped his drink, deep in thought. "What is Amanda up to, do you think? Could it be she really wants to marry me? She never hinted at it before and she well knows I was never interested. I wonder if it's possible the child is mine."

"I don't know the answer to your questions. I suppose it is possible the child is yours and she wants a wedding to give it a name, but the results of my inquiries before I left London leave me wondering."

Hugh looked at his friend, one brow raised in question.

"It seems she has taken a lover."

Startled but relieved at this development and what it could mean, Hugh looked at his friend. "Well, that certainly changes the picture. Who?"

"James Harrison."

"The married Earl of Malmesby?"

"The very one. My sources tell me she has been with him for a while…perhaps even before you ended your affair with her. Malmesby cannot offer her marriage, even if she is large with his child."

"*Is* she large with child?"

"Not that I could tell, but you know women's clothing. Those gowns Josephine introduced to Europe do not exactly hug the form. When Lady Hearnshaw gave me the message I saw no difference in her shape, but the folds of her gown could have hidden much."

Hugh felt helpless. It was not a feeling he often experienced. "There is nothing I can do from here. I'll have to deal with this in London."

"I will finish my business in Paris and return as soon as I can. I'll not tarry. I have my own reasons for wanting to be back in England."

A knock sounded at the door, and John entered when admitted. His face bore an eager look. "I bought yer tickets, m'lord. Three of them, just like you asked."

Lambeth seemed surprised. "Three? Who is going with you?"

"I plan to take John. We may have escaped the Prussians this far, but I expect more of them will be waiting at the crossing. They will be looking for a woman—or possibly a man and a woman. They will not be looking for the three of us dressed as we will be."

Lambeth chuckled. "Like the old days, eh? Well, we did use that disguise with success. I suppose it could work again. I'm a little sorry I'll be on my way to Paris."

* * *

Mary slept alone that night. Hugh did not ask to share the bed, and she was somewhat relieved though she missed his arms around her. She found him brooding the next morning when she descended the stairs. Her own eyes were swollen and red from crying. She felt empty inside, too stunned to deal with all that Lady Hearnshaw's news could mean.

Hugh approached, very serious. From his appearance, he hadn't slept well either. Taking her hand he said, "Mary, it will come out all right. I promise."

She withdrew her hand as their eyes met. The words to respond would not come. She wanted to reach out for him, to hold him, but she resisted. He might never be hers again.

"We will cross the channel today in disguise," he said, clearly trying to distract her thoughts. "We've worn the garb of the church before to hide from Napoleon, and it may serve us well today, too. We will travel as monks. John will accompany us."

"Ah," she said. "I suppose it is a good thing the weather has turned cold. I can wear the hood over my face." Her voice sounded numb to her, without emotion. That seemed odd, since she was reeling with emotion she could not control. She had to get through this and get home, to a place where she could break down alone.

* * *

A cold fog hung over the channel. Hugh had arranged for passage on a new type of boat, a steamer named *The Majestic*. There would be two hundred aboard, and he hoped it would be enough of a crowd for them to get lost among the other passengers.

They stood off to one side, watching the busy harbor and the huge number of people gathering to board the boat or see it off; the afternoon was noisy with children scurrying here and there to catch a glimpse of the boat, peering around adults who were also hoping for a good view. Hugh had decided to wait until most of the passengers boarded. Already he had seen a small group of Prussian soldiers on a hill nearby the harbor. French soldiers stood close to the pier. For Mary's sake, he wanted to avoid a confrontation. She was in no condition to deal with more difficulties.

He studied her, comparing her size to John's. The habit she wore made her nearly the same. Padding helped disguise her, too, as long as no one noticed her face. They carried nothing save a few necessary items beneath their robes. Hugh wore his brace of pistol daggers. They were clean and loaded, but he prayed he would not need them.

* * *

The Prussian soldiers stood on the hill. In their dark blue jackets, they were a stark contrast to the French soldiers in light gray standing guard at the crossing. One of the Prussians raised his hand over his eyes to focus better on the scene below, and he called out to his commanding officer in German.

"Sir, we've been watching this crossing for days and have seen no sign of her. Why do you think she'll be on this boat?"

The senior officer considered the question. He didn't owe the younger man any explanation, but he decided to share his reasoning anyway. "Because she will have had enough time to get here from Paris, and because the steamer will carry enough passengers to make it the most attractive place to hide. Yes, I believe they will cross here and on this boat."

"And what exactly are we looking for again?"

"A tall young woman with blonde hair," the officer snapped. "I doubt she is traveling alone. She'll have protection. The last report suggested she might be traveling with one man, but two of our men have already been killed in an attempt to capture her."

Below, most of the passengers had already boarded, and the crew was in the final stages of readying the steamer for departure. The one young blonde they had stopped to question earlier was French and traveling with her husband and child. They had seen no other young woman matching the description.

The senior officer scanned the crowd, his eyes stopping on three figures that were just boarding. Three monks traveling to London? Two of them had hoods drawn over their heads. He turned to his junior officer.

"Major Yorck, take Dielhman and question those monks just now boarding. See what you can learn about them."

The young officer scanned the pier and saw his objective. "Yes, sir. Right away, sir."

Yorck and Dielhman descended the small hill to the dock. As they did, they were aware of being watched by the contingent guarding the crossing. It was clear from their faces the French soldiers deeply resented the presence of Prussian soldiers here. While they tolerated the allied soldiers posted in Paris, they had less tolerance outside that city. But there was little to be done about it.

"Where are you going, Father, and what is your business?" Yorck demanded in a brusque voice as he reached the three monks making their way slowly up the gangplank. The tall one turned, and Yorck had a brief moment of concern that he'd tangled with the wrong cleric.

* * *

Hugh paused, staring at the Prussian officer while contemplating what to say. Finally he answered in French. "We are about the business of the Church, and we have been summoned to England for special work with Father Christopher in London."

The young major carefully looked at him, and also his companions. John had peeled back his hood, so his face was visible, but Mary was focused on the wooden deck, her hood still up. All that could be seen was her nose, her jaw and her lips. There was no denying how fine were her features and lips, and the longer they stood there, the more certain Hugh became that the Prussian officer would notice.

The major appeared about to question him further when a French officer approached. "What is going on here?" he demanded in an agitated voice.

Hugh turned immediately and said in perfect French, "Good day to you, my son."

Major Yorck turned, too. "I was just asking the monks where they are going."

"Isn't it obvious? They are traveling to London. And why should that be your concern? These are French monks doing the work of the Church. How could that be your business, Prussian?"

Hugh breathed a sigh of relief, seeing the dynamic between the two. He also acted quickly when a loud bellow from the ship's horn signaled the imminent departure of the steamer. "We must be boarding, I fear." He spoke to the French soldier, exuding confidence but also conveying he was anxious to be on his way.

The Prussian did not respond but continued to study what he could see of Mary peeking out beneath her hood.

The French officer grew impatient. "*Eh alors*, I ask you again, Prussian, what concern is it of yours?"

The major turned to him. "We are looking for someone."

"A monk?"

"No."

"Well, you can look somewhere else and leave our men of the cloth alone, then. This steamer is about to depart. All must leave who do not have tickets."

"I'll purchase one," offered the Prussian major.

"Not for this sailing, you may not," the French officer said. "All tickets for this crossing have been sold. You will have to wait for the next one." Directing his voice to the waiting crowd he shouted, "The steamer is about to depart!" He then moved between the monks and the Prussians and motioned Hugh forward. "You may continue on, Father."

The Prussian major was displeased, but clearly there was nothing he could do; the French officer had jurisdiction. He gave one last look at the hooded trio and left, his young subordinate following.

Hugh relaxed only after the ship departed. Watching from the deck of the steamer as it left Calais, Hugh saw the Prussian return and report to his superior on the hill. The group of soldiers there all turned and watched until they could watch no longer, and neither could Hugh.

That had been close. God bless the French.

Chapter 28

Hugh had stopped at his town house first thing after the return to London, where he'd dropped John and changed clothes, and now he began the trip that would return Mary to Campbell Manor outside the city. Seeing the distance in her eyes, it felt to him like she was on the other side of the world, not the other side of his carriage. Silent for most of the journey, every so often she sighed deeply, as if the burden she carried was too heavy to keep inside. It was killing him. He was losing his golden girl; he could see it in her eyes. It was almost as if she had already said goodbye. She wasn't crying, but he thought it was only by sheer force of will.

As they neared Campbell Manor, he could stand it no longer. "Mary, look at me."

Sadly obedient green eyes rose to his. He wanted to pull her into his arms and comfort her, to tell her that all would be well, but he was certain she would resist. He reached out his hand and covered hers. "We will wed. You are mine now. I'll not give you up because some woman tells an untruth."

"Lady Hearnshaw is not 'some woman,' Hugh. She is your mistress. Or was." Her troubled gaze drifted out the window to the passing countryside, but he could tell she was not really seeing it. "And now she carries your child."

"There has been nothing between Amanda and I. It was over before you and I met. I don't believe she carries my child, not that it should make any difference to us. Have you considered the possibility that *you* might? I took no precautions with you. My plan was to be married by now. I would welcome our child."

Mary looked back at him with the eyes of a startled doe. It was plain on her face that she had not considered the possibility. But her expression did not seem to improve; in fact, her mood only soured.

"Mary, do not give up on us. I am not going anywhere. We *will* marry."

She did not reply, just turned back to stare out the window.

God, he was becoming the rake they said he was. His former mistress claimed to be carrying his child, and he had deflowered a virgin who now rejected him—the woman he loved, he reminded himself.

He could see her heart was breaking. The only thing that kept him from feeling a like despair was the hope that he could sort this out and win her back. He should be proud of her determination to do the noble thing, the selfless thing, but at the moment it was only causing them both pain. Mary Campbell probably didn't consider the fact that other women were devious creatures. Amanda Hearnshaw was not above trying to manipulate him; he was certain of that.

When the carriage stopped at Campbell Manor, Mary fled. Hugh followed, giving his hat to Hudson. Mary was still wearing the stable boy's clothes she had worn under the robe when they left Calais, but the butler did not give any indication he found his mistress's behavior or dress unusual. Hugh shook his head. The nobility played at such farce sometimes, and their servants were tolerant, and today he was glad for it.

He presented his card. "Is the countess at home, Hudson?"

"Yes, my lord. I will see if she is accepting visitors."

Hugh spent the next hour explaining to Mary's mother what had transpired in Paris, leaving out only his proposal, Mary's acceptance and then most of what followed in the past three days and nights. He made excuses for Mary's behavior upon her return, saying that they had suffered several incidents on the road from Paris and she was in desperate need of rest. That much was not a lie, and Mary's mother seemed to accept his explanations without pause. Perhaps she knew her daughter better than he realized. He finished by telling her, "Countess, I expect your brother, Lord Baynes will return shortly. He was just a day or two behind."

She smiled. "I will speak to him when he returns. Thank you, Lord Ormond, for bringing my daughter home. I know my brother would not have placed Mary in your charge unless he trusted you to keep her safe."

Hugh's thoughts were a tangle as he traveled back to his town house without Mary, most of them dark and depressing. Had he really assured her safety? No, he had not. Unless he wed her, she was ruined. And now that they were back in London there was the Prince Regent's interest to consider. *Hell.*

At home he made arrangements for John to return to Calais then had a bite to eat and fell into a chair exhausted. There was no one to turn to, no solace he could seek. Even Lambeth was unavailable to share his misery. Instead, he took a long drink of brandy, looked into the fire and considered what a mess his life had become.

Tomorrow, he supposed, there would be a reckoning.

* * *

As Hugh strode up the familiar steps of Lady Hearnshaw's Mayfair town house, the grand style of it reminded him she was a wealthy widow. That was one reason he'd allowed himself to get involved with her; she didn't need his money and she wouldn't want his title. Obviously she had made a mistake, the question was with whom. He hoped it was with the Earl of Malmesby. Hugh would not be the one coming to her rescue.

The door opened just as Hugh reached for the brass knocker. *Amanda.* She had been waiting for him. The gown she wore was sheer, and the low-cut bodice barely covered her full, rounded breasts. He peered over her shoulder. Not a servant in sight.

"What is your game, Amanda?"

"Hugh, darling, whatever do you mean?" She patted his lapel, purring into his ear.

Lifting her hand off his coat, he stepped back from the doorway. There was nowhere to run, though, so a moment later he stepped across the threshold. At the same time he said, "I am betrothed, madam—and it isn't to you."

She walked deeper into the house and laid her hand over her belly in a dramatic gesture. "But the child."

Hugh followed her inside, closing the door behind him. Moving close, he lifted her hand from her body and his gaze focused on her stomach. It was difficult to see if any roundedness had been added. "*If* there is a child, Amanda, it isn't mine and you well know it. We haven't been together for months, and I always took precautions."

"Darling," she cajoled, and he had to admit her voice had always been sensuous, "you know those measures cannot assure there will be no child."

"They do in my case," he snapped.

And yet, Hugh wondered. Could she really be carrying his child? He'd been very disciplined about the steps he took to avoid siring any bastards, but there was always a possibility. The Albany men had always been virile.

"Amanda, I am not ignorant of your doings. Are you expecting me to claim the Earl of Malmesby's child as mine? Because I won't."

The shock on her face was genuine, and it told him a great deal. Relief flooded him.

"You didn't think I was aware of your relationship with James Harrison."

"No." She began to stutter. "I-I…"

"Of course I know about your married lover, and so I know why you are in the market for a husband. But do not allow yourself to think it will be me." It was the bluff of a lifetime, but it seemed to be working.

She collapsed into a chair near the entry. "Hugh, you are being most disagreeable! What am I to do? You know James cannot marry me, and you and I cared about each other once, didn't we? You once said a marriage of convenience was what you expected, and what would be inconvenient about marrying me? I thought if you believed the child to be yours…"

Even if she was a friend, he found it hard to sympathize with a woman who would pin another's bastard on him, depriving him of the one he loved. Friendship could go only so far. "So you admit the child isn't mine."

Her face was downcast.

Hugh let out the breath he'd been holding, and a feeling of exhilaration swept over him. The child wasn't his! *Thank God.* His relief and his love for Mary made him more forgiving than he probably would have been otherwise. For the sake of what he and Amanda had once been to each other, he would help.

"I will see what I can do to assist you in this predicament—as a friend, Amanda. But that is all. And, my marriage will no longer be…convenient. It seems love rarely works that way."

* * *

From the window of her bedroom Mary watched the man she loved ride off. He had come again, and again she had refused to see him. Her emotions were too raw; she would not be able to endure his arguments. They would only be the same words he'd given her before, that the baby his mistress carried wasn't his, that

Lady Hearnshaw had another lover. Her bedroom had been her shelter for a week. Her tears would not stop. Inside she felt empty.

She had been persuaded for a moment as he talked that they could still marry, but as she'd thought about the solution, it just didn't feel right. Lady Hearnshaw would be alone and facing the entire ton and they would be quick to cut her and call her disgraced. Mary knew what it felt like to experience society's disdain for her rebellious ways. No, she would not bring that—and worse—on another woman, even a woman like Amanda Hearnshaw. And then there was the child. If it was Hugh's then it deserved the family God gave it. What a mistake it was to fall in love with a rake, and now she was suffering the consequences—just like Lady Hearnshaw. Hugh had left a message saying he was going to speak with his former mistress, but what could come of that?

He had said she would be his only woman: *"Not one of my women, my* only *woman. My wife."* Still, Mary did not see how he could distance himself from the mother of his child, and she would not respect him if he abandoned the babe. She did not know whether to believe him when he said the child wasn't his. How she hoped it was true, how she prayed she was being unfair. There seemed to be no true answer to this tangle, not when fate conspired against her.

After days of despair, anger had finally come; the spirit of the woman who would not be conquered rose once again within her. She was angry with herself for forgetting her commitment to be no man's prize, angry with Hugh for all his mistresses and for the fruit of his most recent liaison. She would not remain a victim! She would not.

Her uncle had come to Campbell Manor from Paris and stayed to hear her story of the trip back to London. She did not relate that she had agreed to marry Hugh, nor did she tell him of Lady

Hearnshaw's disclosure. Her uncle passed along several offers of marriage that he'd received for her. Surprisingly there were many, but none brought a smile to her face. Well, except perhaps for one.

The offer from Joseph Decazes was not wholly unexpected. She had grimaced at first, given his seeming treachery, but her uncle explained that the vicomte had become a much-favored subject of King Louis in the last few weeks, that he had been working for French interests all along, even while pretending to work for the other allies. He was now being celebrated in Paris. And he remembered her fondly. More than fondly, truth be told. With enthusiasm for a union stretching across the channel, he was summoning her back to Paris, should she agree to become his bride.

Though her heart was breaking, Mary knew she must consider the future. Would living in France be so bad? The vicomte was pleasant company. He had wanted her to stay in Paris, and he had told her she could have both her independence and love. It would not be love if she married him, she knew; her heart would always belong to Hugh. But if she could not have love, the love she'd always wanted, life could still be interesting. Like Germaine, she had suffered. Now perhaps she could live. She had a sense the vicomte would let her. He had sent a note with her uncle, a message for her: *Know this, Lady Mary, I am very sorry for my own test of your loyalty gone wrong at the cathedral that night, for I would not have hurt you for the world. You were so courageous, and as we parted I knew I must have you for my own. Please forgive me and be my wife, and I will spend my life making it up to you.*

He was taking the blame for the Prussians abducting them, but that wasn't really fair. They would have been seized anyway. They had known too much. Yes, she could forgive Decazes. He would want her love. And though she thought she could make a difference in France, she could not bring herself to marry another.

Then a new thought reared its head. What if, as Hugh had suggested, she was carrying his child? *Hugh's baby.* As much as the thought thrilled her, it horrified her as well. She would be in no better position than Amanda Hearnshaw. Until she knew for sure whether she was pregnant, she couldn't make a move. She didn't even want to consider what it would mean to be a ruined woman.

No, she didn't want to think about any of it. She wanted to ride.

Chapter 29

"I love her!" Hugh exclaimed, pacing in front of Lord Baynes, who sat observing from a large chair in his study. Two weeks had gone by since his return from France. Hugh had tried three times to see Mary, to explain and to persuade her to marry him. She had refused his card. She had refused to see him. He'd even run out of ideas to help Amanda. In desperation he had come to see Mary's uncle.

"Have you told her?"

"She refuses to see me. I have tried twice since learning the truth from Amanda."

Lord Baynes looked glum. "You should know, Hugh, that Mary has received many offers, including those from Arthur Bywood, Lord McGinnes and Joseph Decazes."

Hugh scoffed. "Bywood is a pup. He could never handle Mary. McGinnes is old enough to be her father, and after the disaster in Paris I can't believe Decazes has the temerity to pursue her."

"Those aren't her only offers," Lord Baynes reminded him. "She has a dozen others. It seems the 'young hellion' has won over at least half the ton, though the other half remains thoroughly unmoved. As for the vicomte, perhaps you haven't heard. Before I left Paris he became something of a hero in Louis's court. As I hoped, he was always France's man. Though he may have had more hair than wit in the way he went about it, he did entrap a number of entities disloyal to the king. The information he obtained, together with what Sir Martin and you learned, not to mention the warehouse finding, condemned an entire ring of treacherous scoundrels."

"It matters little," Hugh pronounced. "Mary agreed we would marry. I consider her engaged to me, whether anyone likes it or not."

"You were always my first choice."

Hugh was taken aback. He'd had no idea that Lord Baynes had wanted them to marry, but he wasn't about to complain. Not when it was what he wanted more than anything.

The older man sighed. "Alas, that bit about Amanda has set Mary off. Her mother informs me she is now entertaining the possibility of returning to France. She plans on living there, and I can't say I like the idea."

Hugh winced. Could Mary think she might be carrying his child and wanted to escape the eyes of the ton? The thought of that possibility stiffened his resolve to claim what was his. "She can't do that," he said. "I love her too much to ever let her go."

"I see." Lord Baynes pinched the bridge of his nose. "And what are your plans?"

"It is still my intention to marry her just as soon as it can be done. I've been carrying a special license since the day after I returned. The archbishop is a friend of my father's."

Lord Baynes wore a peculiar expression. "I expect I bear some responsibility for the situation you and Mary find yourselves in. I let you take her from Paris hoping you would get together. I just saw it working out a bit differently."

Hugh froze, startled.

"You need not look at me like that," said the older man. "You were taking too long to realize you cared for Mary, and she was too content to remain unmarried. It was like trying to coax two warring countries to the negotiating table. I merely took advantage of the circumstances. I was hoping that during the trip you would both realize you belong together."

"If it is any comfort, your plan worked. We couldn't stay away from each other. In fact, we have never been able to do that. It was my intention to marry her in Calais, but it was there that Mary learned about Amanda's condition and insisted I wed the woman."

"You are certain the child is not yours?"

"I am. Amanda admitted it to me."

"And you have told Mary?" Lord Baynes inquired.

"Not yet. She will not see me. Even if I can arrange that, I suspect she will want some solution for Amanda."

"I see. She has it in her mind to do the noble thing and let Amanda Hearnshaw have you." He sighed. "You'll recall I told you she could be quite determined, and right now she is set upon doing what she sees as the right thing even if it is the harder path. But fear not, she will soon know the truth. And there is a solution that will put Mary's mind at rest and at the same time remove all possibility the ton may think the child is your bastard."

"You have a plan?" Hugh asked, encouraged.

"I do, or at least the possibility of one." Lord Baynes sat rubbing his fingers over his mouth, his focus on the carpet as if working a puzzle in his mind. After a moment he raised his head. "As I recall, Lady Hearnshaw is a beautiful woman. Am I correct?"

"She is attractive."

Lord Baynes raised an eyebrow at Hugh, who had sunk into the chair next to him. "Is she also, by any stroke of luck, a horsewoman?"

"Yes. Though she cannot ride like your niece."

The diplomat dropped his hand and rose from his chair. "I think I may have a proposal I wish to explore. It will take some cleverness. Go now and wait for my message. If I am successful, and if you still have that magnificent chestnut, you will want to ride to Campbell Manor as fast as you can."

"Elizabeth!" Mary had never been so glad to see her dear friend, and she reached out her arms to give her a tight hug.

"I couldn't wait for an invitation, Mary. I had to come. So much has happened, I simply had to see you!" Lizzy's blue-gray eyes were sparkling, and her cheeks were flushed.

"Come, we'll have tea and you can tell me your news." Mary put her arm around Elizabeth and guided her into the parlor, asking Hudson to call for the appropriate comestibles. Taking position on the settee opposite her friend, Mary waited expectantly.

"While you have been in France, Mary, I have had a frequent caller. A very dashing and attentive suitor, actually."

"You have?" Mary would be happy for whichever young man had put such a glow on Elizabeth's face.

"Oh, Mary, he is so...so everything I knew he would be!"

Mary laughed. "Are you going to tell me who this god-like creature is, or will you continue to torture me?"

"Cannot you guess? Why, Griffen Lambeth, of course!"

Mary goggled. "Lizzy, I had no idea. You did not speak of him." She recalled the several letters she had received in Paris, but none spoke of Hugh's fair-haired chum.

"He came to call on me a week after you left, and he has been nearly a daily visitor to my home in London until just recently when he left for Paris. I didn't say anything because...well, because I wasn't sure what his intentions were."

"And now you are?"

"Well, now I *think* they are honorable—though he has not proposed marriage yet."

Mary wanted to be happy for her friend. She loved Elizabeth and wanted to see her with the husband of her dreams, but it was hard for Mary to rise above the fog of melancholy that seemed to follow her everywhere. Especially when her friend's joy seemed so similarly wrapped up in the dangers of loving a rake. Should she be afraid for her?

Lizzy seemed oblivious. "What of your news, Mary? In your letter, you said Lord Ormond appeared in Paris and was working with your uncle. Was there any more after that?"

Mary didn't want to go into it, especially not when her friend seemed so happy. No, Elizabeth didn't need to know of her broken betrothal. "No, there is no news as far as he goes, really."

Elizabeth sat back, looking somewhat disappointed. "What of the Frenchman you spoke of in your letter, Vicomte Decazes, who took you all over Paris?"

"Ah," Mary said. "Joseph Decazes. He is a very likeable man, Lizzy. I think you would find him handsome, too. He has blue eyes, but they are deeper in color than yours. He has already accomplished much for France with his brother the Comte Decazes. He will have a good future there, and…he has asked for my hand."

Elizabeth did not react. Instead. she looked at Mary with those probing blue eyes of hers. Suddenly serious she said, "Mary that would be wonderful news if you didn't look so downcast. Is he not appealing as a husband?"

Mary dropped her eyes to hide her pain. "He would make any woman a good husband," she admitted, "but I haven't decided whether to accept his offer. There are others. I'm really not sure yet what I will do. Perhaps I will not marry just now at all."

"Oh, Mary…if you married Vicomte Decazes, you would live in Paris, wouldn't you? I don't think I could bear to have you so far away!"

"Paris is an exciting place, Lizzy. It affords many opportunities for a woman. I was very taken with Germaine de Stael and the life she has there." Mary was not surprised to see her friend's worried look, and she said, "Don't worry, Lizzy. I'm not going anywhere soon. Come, let us have a spot of tea and take a walk in the gardens. You can tell me all about your new love, and I can tell you about my adventures in Paris, for there were many."

She forced a smile and went to pour the tea. For Elizabeth's sake, she would not be sad. She would trust her friend had done better than she, and for herself she would remember the adventures and not the man.

Chapter 30

It was two long, anxious days before Hugh received what he so desperately awaited. He was sitting in his study, trying to concentrate on dispatches with no success when it arrived. His valet placed the silver tray within his reach.

"My lord, a message has just been delivered by Lord Baynes's man."

Hugh lifted the envelope. "Does he await a reply?"

"No, my lord. He has already departed."

Hugh ripped the paper open and hurriedly read the note. "My God, the man is amazing. What a diplomat!" A grin slowly spread across his face.

His valet stared at him in wonder. "My lord?"

"We leave immediately for the country!" Hugh stood, stuffing the message in his pocket. He ran to the stairs and took them two at a time.

His valet followed. "What would you have me pack, my lord?"

Hugh shouted over his shoulder, never slowing his pace. "Riding clothes!"

* * *

Mary found the familiar rhythm of Midnight's hooves settled her. It didn't take away the pain, of course. It didn't take away the memory of the man who was always in her thoughts and in her heart, but riding fast did require her attention. The faster she rode, the easier it became to think of nothing but the horse, the wind in her face and the fierce sense of freedom she had when riding Midnight.

She was headed for a trail that led through a familiar grove of trees when she heard the pounding hooves of a horse coming up fast behind her. She turned in the saddle to see the last person she'd expect, Hugh, his jacket flying out behind him, his dark hair blowing across his forehead. He pulled up beside her and grabbed Midnight's reins, slowing both horses to a walk.

"What are you doing?" she shouted, realizing she must sound like a shrew but at that moment not caring.

"This is the only way I can see you. You've kept me away too long. We need to talk." He reined the horses toward the trees, dismounted and walked around to where Mary looked down on him from her horse.

"What is there to talk about?" She couldn't do this again. It was tempting to forget another woman's pain and take what she wanted, the man she wanted, even raise his bastard child, but she would not do it. She could not. Besides, did she even trust him now? She didn't think he'd lie to her, exactly, but in the face of another woman's child and—

He pulled her from her horse without answering. In his arms, she was held against his chest; her breasts pressed against him, reminding her of all they had shared when there were no clothes between them. "I'm not letting you go, Mary. You are mine. Do you hear me?"

"I've had an offer of marriage from Vicomte Decazes...," Mary replied, wanting to give him an out if he wanted it.

"Absolutely not. You will not marry him. You are betrothed to me and I'm not letting you go."

His face was so close she could barely think. She wanted to throw her arms around him, but instead she pushed away and walked into the grove of trees. When she'd put several yards between them, she turned. "We are done talking about this, Hugh. Have you forgotten about Lady Hearnshaw's child? *Your* child?"

"It's not mine. Amanda has admitted as much, which I always believed. She has stopped pursuing me—not that such pursuit would have mattered. Hell, Mary, I haven't even thought of another woman since I met you."

"Oh." Mary felt the air leave her chest. For a moment she just stared at him, but then her fears returned. "Why did she claim the child is yours?"

"The babe is the child of her married lover, James Harrison, the Earl of Malmesby. He cannot marry her. She had hoped to trap me into marriage to legitimize his by-blow, but your uncle has done a wonderful bit of diplomacy and she will now marry McGinnes. So the child will have a father—a family."

"Lord McGinnes?" Mary repeated, dazed. His words were beginning to sink in.

"Why not? He wants an heir, and a horsewoman for a wife. And, he isn't certain he can father his own heir. With Amanda, he can have both a wife who loves horses and, if the child is a boy, an heir. He is a generous and apparently very forgiving, since he knows the full details of the story. He's willing to claim the child as his. She should be grateful. It should be an interesting match."

Mary sagged, unable to believe her ears. Hugh stared intently into her eyes.

"So, you will marry me? Or, rather, *when* will you marry me?"

Her eyes fell. "You never said you loved—"

"You silly, beautiful girl," he interrupted. "Look at me." With one finger, he raised her chin. "You have only to look into my eyes to see how I feel about you."

Looking into his brandy-colored eyes, she could indeed see love. And a deep longing.

"I think I began to fall in love with you when I first saw you at that ball. I was enthralled when I observed you riding that stallion of yours. I was captivated at lunch as you sat there telling your uncle and me about the foolish rulers of Europe. The first time I kissed you I knew I could not stay away from you, and I have been jealous of every man who has ever wanted you since. I have not been able to think about another woman since the first time you argued with me. I even loved you when you so foolishly dressed up like a stable boy to break into that warehouse in Paris. Mary, I meant it when I said I want you for my wife. *I love you.*"

"Oh, Hugh." She threw her arms around his neck, and he kissed away her long held-back tears. He kissed her forehead, her temples, her lips. His passion raged across her like a storm, demanding all, and she melted against his heat just as she had done all the other times. Was it true? Was he really, finally hers?

As if he heard her thoughts, he broke the kiss and whispered at her temple, "Darling, there is no one but you. There never will be. Please don't ever doubt it again." Then he backed away a bit and considered her. "But while we are on this topic…we must discuss your foolishness. I cannot have you taking the risks you do."

Mary felt her world upended. "What are you talking about, Hugh? What risks?"

He looked incredulous. "You have to ask? I do not refer to your 'riding like the wind.' Or even to your independent decisions. Those I can accept. But I cannot live in fear of you getting involved in your uncle's work for the Crown—or mine—that would put you in danger."

Mary was not going to apologize for what she had done, but she could now see how her actions had brought the man she loved much anxiety. Adventure, even in the cause of one's country, was not so important that it should come before love. No, she could compromise. "Oh, Hugh, I do see that what I did caused you great disquiet. I will agree to be more…careful in what I get involved in, but only if you will do the same. I would hope you'd never again have a need to wear those pistol daggers you did in France. I need to be certain you will be coming home—at least if you're not going to take me with you."

He grinned. "A compromise." *Is that how one manages the difficult Mary Campbell?* "I like it. All right, minx, you have your deal."

They embraced, each holding on tightly to the other as if they feared what they had could be lost. Then as one they lowered themselves to the grass, desperately reaching to find skin through their clothing. Hugh took her hands in his and raised them over her head, entwining their fingers and pushing them into the soft grass as he rained kisses over her throat. He let go of her hands, and they cast aside clothes and boots. Finally they were skin upon skin. Mary relished all of him. He was hers.

Hugh's hand caressed the inside of her thigh, sending shivers down her spine in anticipation. She was wet and ready for him, her body remembering the joining she craved. How long it had been.

"Hugh."

It was fast and hard—a taking, a claiming. He demanded full surrender and she eagerly gave it. With one thrust he was buried deep inside her. His voice was rough and raw as he called her name.

Her body stretched to accommodate him, welcoming his hard thrusts. He was like a madman, feverish and crazed. "Never again will I leave you this long. I am starving for you," he gasped.

She matched his deep thrusts, lifting her hips to accept the full fury of his lovemaking. It was over in minutes as they reached the full measure of their passion together. Collapsing into each other's arms, they lay entwined beneath the trees for a long while, content just to hold each other.

Sometime later they returned to the manor. Mary changed her clothes before she and Hugh went to see her mother. Hugh seated her on the settee and bowed low. "Countess, I have asked Mary to become my wife and she has agreed. I am asking for your blessing."

Mary's mother's expression was one of pleasure. "What splendid news! I can think of no better man for my child than the son of the Duke and Duchess of Albany. Your parents were dear friends of the earl's. William would be happy, I think, to give his only daughter to you. Yes, Lord Ormond, you have my blessing."

Hugh smiled at both Mary and her mother. "We'd like to be married as soon as possible, by special license. If you are agreeable, there could be a reception later. My parents would be pleased to host it at our estate near here. This will come as very good news to them." He thought back on his parents' exhortations to wed. "Very good news indeed."

Hudson came into the room, interrupting them in his usual detached manner. "My lady, Lord Baynes has arrived for dinner."

Hugh had joined Mary on the settee where he held her hand, and the countess turned to them. "Apparently your uncle thought there might be some news for me, Mary, so I asked him to come round for dinner. Please stay, Lord Ormond. We can make it a celebration."

"Please call me Ormond, Countess. And, yes, I would love to stay. Actually, I don't think I could be persuaded to leave Mary's side just now. Or maybe ever again," he whispered. He squeezed her hand and they shared a warm glance.

Mary's uncle walked into the room, a grin on his face. "Ah, Ormond. I assume from your presence you received my message?"

Hugh smiled broadly—like a pirate who had just taken a galley full of treasure, Mary thought. "Yes, I did. Thank you, sir. Mary and I have just shared with the countess our own news. We are betrothed. She has given us her blessing. I would ask for yours as well."

Her uncle's face lit up. "You have it! I am delighted. I assume you related my news to Mary?" Without waiting for an answer, he walked over to where they were rising from the settee and kissed Mary on the cheek. She felt her eyes fill with tears of gratitude as he reached out to shake Hugh's hand. "Welcome to the family."

"Thank you, my lord. I hope you are comfortable with a small wedding. Mary and I want to be wed as soon as possible."

"Ah, yes," Lord Baynes agreed. "A small wedding would be just the thing—and a large reception."

Chapter 31

That evening after dinner Mary and Hugh visited his family estate where Hugh's parents expressed their joy at his finding a very suitable young lady to wed at long last. They had known the Campbells when the earl was alive and were glad to renew what would now become a much closer relationship.

"You can't imagine the happiness you have brought the duke and me, Lady Mary." The duchess's eyes were full of unshed tears. "I've never seen my son so happy. It has been much too long a time. Thank you."

Mary was grateful. With a reputation as a hoyden, she had been aware many mothers in the ton would not have wanted their sons to marry her. But all anxiety left her with the older woman's words.

Hugh's father, the Duke of Albany, also readily accepted the match. "I had almost given up hope Hugh would ever find the one for him. You are a rare woman, Lady Mary. And so lovely. I knew it would take a special lady to win his heart. Your father and I were friends, you know. I believe William would have been as pleased with this match as I am."

"Thank you, Your Grace." Mary immediately liked the handsome older man. Tall and broad shouldered, he had the same strong, masculine features and dark eyes and hair as his son, though the duke was graying at his temples. It made him look distinguished.

That is how Hugh will look many years from now. And she knew with certainty that she would love him no less then than she did this day.

"Come Mary," said the duchess, taking her arm. "I have something I want to show you."

As they strolled from the room, Mary looked over her shoulder to see Hugh and his father talking. She found herself smiling at the rake she loved. No, she corrected herself. He was no longer a rake. He was the man who loved her, who promised to be ever faithful. Even now, it was almost painful not to be touching him, this dark, mysterious, and yes, demanding man who had captured her heart.

As if Hugh felt her eyes on him, he lifted his head and smiled at her in return.

The duchess led Mary down a long hallway graced with large oil portraits on each side. "These are the men and women of Albany, my dear."

Mary pondered the handsome men and regal women in their golden frames. "All the men look alike." The similarity in each male portrait, no matter the age, was striking. That was so different from the blond and red-haired men of her family.

"Yes, they do. The imprint of the Albany line is quite dominant. Perhaps one day you and Hugh will have a son with those same dark looks."

Mary could not help but wonder if she already carried such a child. It caused her cheeks to warm.

The duchess stopped in front of a portrait of two boys, one several years older than the other. "Hugh and Henry?" Mary asked.

The duchess appeared surprised and turned back to the portrait. "Yes." She gazed wistfully at the boys with their dark locks and mischievous brown eyes. Mary noted they were dressed in formal riding clothes as if ready for a foxhunt, and Hugh's arm was draped around his brother's shoulders.

"Hugh loved Henry very much, and Henry idolized his older brother. When Henry…died, something in Hugh died. That is why he left, I think. For a while it was as if we lost both of them. Even when he returned to England, he wasn't really back. You could see it in his eyes. I don't believe he really returned to us until tonight." She faced Mary, tears in her eyes. "You have brought him home, Lady Mary. For that, we are so grateful."

* * *

Two days later, Mary and Hugh were married in the country church near the Albany estate that had once been part of an abbey. The congregation was few; only her uncle, her mother, the Duke and Duchess of Albany, and Elizabeth and Lambeth attended. Mary had only explained to Elizabeth last night all that had happened, and Lambeth had only returned from Paris the day before to stand up for Hugh.

Mary thought the church a fitting place for them to be wed. Though small, it had a stately tower. The sunlight filtered in through the stained glass windows, casting soft, colored light on the flowers in front of the altar. Everything was beautiful.

They knelt as they repeated their vows. Hugh held Mary's hands in his, his eyes never leaving hers. Mary's blue silk gown was a paler shade of the sapphire in Hugh's grandmother's ring that he had given her, which was mounted on a wide gold band and surrounded with diamonds. The ring seemed to belong on her long slim finger.

Mary was happy just to know he was hers.

* * *

Two weeks later, all of London, including the Prince Regent, was invited to the reception. In a flurry of preparations, the grand estate of the Duke and Duchess of Albany was turned into a paradise of lights, flowers and elegant decorations. The duke and duchess and Mary's mother had decided to celebrate Mary and Hugh's marriage in grand style.

Having denied everyone the wedding they might have desired, Mary decided to wear a gown befitting just such an event. It was made of ivory silk with lace sleeves that fell just off her shoulders, the fabric shimmering every time she moved. She felt like a princess, adorned as she was with gold embroidery on the skirt and a slim gold ribbon at the high waist embedded with gems. Hugh did not vary from his black formal attire except to add a gold brocade waistcoat.

He appeared very pleased with himself, did her husband, never leaving her side. Hands clasped together, Mary and Hugh walked among their guests in the large ballroom. Often the newlyweds leaned in to share their thoughts with each other. And when they danced, Hugh held Mary tight, gazing intently into her eyes.

"Judging from the looks we are getting, my love, I believe it is evident to all that ours is a love match," he said.

"You mean to say they realize the rake is truly retired?" Mary felt a flush of pleasure that doubled when he kissed her on the forehead.

"Truly."

Among those attending the reception were Lord and Lady Huntingdon, their house-party hosts. That seemed so long ago, the beginning of the season, and yet the pair seemed to Mary to be most delighted with their marriage.

"You make a handsome couple," said the earl with a winsome smile.

Lady Huntingdon gave Hugh a teasing look. "To think, it all began at our house party. That *was* your first kiss, was it not?"

Mary blushed, astonished. "How did you know?"

"Well, I didn't know it was your *first* kiss until this very moment, but I suspected it when I saw you returning from our gardens, only to be followed a moment later by Ormond. He was so preoccupied he didn't see me, though I stood right in front of him."

Mary's free hand covered her mouth. "Oh my."

Hugh chuckled. "We should have known we couldn't fool you, the observant Lady Huntingdon."

"Don't worry," the countess assured them. "Your secret is safe with us."

"Now you have them nervous, darling!" The earl laughed. Smiling at Hugh and Mary, he added, "We are most delighted for you both. Yours is an exceptional match, and it seems we thought so before either of you."

Mary and Hugh turned to each other, warmed by the realization that others who loved them were pleased by their connection.

"Darling," she said to Hugh, "did you see the message that came from Germaine?"

"Yes, your uncle showed it to me. Though I'm sorry she is too unwell to be with us, I am pleased she thought us the perfect match. She rather liked you from the beginning."

"I will miss her," Mary said wistfully.

In addition to their other friends, Mary had invited Elizabeth to the reception and was looking forward to seeing her. Though Lord Baynes confirmed she was in attendance, he didn't know where she was at the moment. Mary surveyed the crowded room, but the only red hair she could see belonged to Lizzy's mother and sisters, who had been invited along with their husbands. She saw Lady Harriet across the room and recalled fondly the warm greeting the girl had given her. Perhaps she'd been unfair to the vivacious brunette. Love had caused Mary to see many things differently.

The Prince Regent arrived shortly afterward, causing a great flurry of activity. The crowd made way then closed behind his entourage as they passed. Hugh bowed, and Mary curtsied before him.

"Good day, Lord and Lady Ormond," the Prince Regent said as his eyes raked Mary's ivory gown and the honeyed skin above her bodice. Uncomfortable, Mary squeezed Hugh's hand.

The Prince Regent smiled at her with a predatory gleam in his eye. "That was quick work, Ormond! You have stolen a great treasure from us." He leaned closer and whispered, "But perhaps that is appropriate, you being my best thief." Then the prince straightened but still in a whisper for only Mary and Hugh added, "And how fitting a match. The Nighthawk and the Swan, eh? Perhaps it was fate!"

Mary's uncle had told her of the Prince Regent's nickname for her, but the other... Could it be? She glanced at her husband and leaned close, speaking in a soft voice for his ears alone. "The Nighthawk? *You* are the Nighthawk?"

Hugh smiled, nodding.

"All this time..."

The Prince Regent raised an eyebrow at Hugh. "You did not tell her?"

"I have always considered that to be your secret, sire."

"Ah, yes, I suppose it is." The Prince Regent grinned, clearly amused, and inclined his head. "You have wed a most unusual man, Lady Ormond...and it appears from all Lord Baynes has told me, my favorite subject has wed a most unusual young woman. Perhaps it was fate indeed."

"I like to think so, sire." Hugh put a possessive arm around Mary's shoulders.

A look of resignation crossed the Prince Regent's face, and this time he spoke in a loud voice. "Indeed! Well, let us drink to your happiness!"

A tray of champagne appeared. As they drank, Hugh recounted for the Prince Regent in a few words what had transpired in Paris.

The Prince Regent chuckled. "It sounds as if Louis owes us a favor."

"It would seem that he does, Your Majesty."

Soon the Prince Regent's many followers distracted him, and Mary and Hugh took the opportunity to escape the crowded room. Mary put her arm in her husband's and cocked her head to one side as they strolled toward the doors to the terrace.

"So, I've married a legend, have I?"

"Apparently so." He gave her a boyish grin. "How would you like to be kissed by a legend?" But before she could answer, Hugh began to walk faster, urging her along. "Come, I have the perfect spot."

He guided her out the doors. She marveled at how the gardens formed a series of outdoor rooms enclosed by clipped boxwood hedges and tall yew plants. A wide stone path led down the center, and it was that path they took. They crossed under an arbor with white flowers cascading to the ground.

"It is so beautiful, Hugh." Mary had never seen gardens so lush, so well cared for or detailed. The English loved their manicured gardens, but these were exceptional.

"We are almost there," Hugh said, picking up the pace.

They strolled deeper into the gardens, passing a tall wall of colorful rhododendrons with a long bench in front. Mary considered resting for a moment but Hugh urged her on, holding her tightly to his side. They couldn't have been any closer.

"Where are we going?"

"I want to show you my favorite alcove where I played as a boy."

They walked a bit farther, but finally he slowed. His lips grazed her temple and he said, "Here we are, my love, my Mary of the Gardens."

She looked up into his smiling eyes, his pupils dilated so that his eyes seemed like black diamonds. She remembered fondly the nickname he'd given her in Paris, and the time they spent playing cat and mouse with each other. "It seems we are destined to be kissing among the flowers."

"Indeed," he said, "that was my purpose."

He led her toward a large rectangular garden with a stone floor enclosed by tall yew plants. As they stepped through the narrow opening, though, they nearly collided with a couple locked in an embrace.

"Oh…excuse us!" Hugh said as he stepped back. He began to pull Mary away but paused, looking more carefully at the couple.

Mary herself recognized that copper-colored hair. "Lizzy?"

Elizabeth St. Clair pulled free from her lover's embrace. "Mary! Oh, Mary…I'm so happy for you and Lord Ormond."

Hugh spoke just then. "Lambeth?"

The blond-haired man Elizabeth had been kissing turned to face Hugh. A sheepish grin settled on his face. "Hello, Ormond, Lady Ormond."

Hugh's mouth twisted in a smirk. "Apparently you two have been busy since our wedding."

His friend held Elizabeth close and looked into her eyes. "I was just thanking Miss St. Clair for agreeing to become my wife."

"Oh, Lizzy!" Mary rushed forward, and Lambeth released Elizabeth long enough for Mary to embrace her, while he reached out to shake Hugh's hand.

"Congratulations!" Hugh said.

"And to you as well," Lambeth offered, his blue eyes twinkling.

Mary was effusive. "It seems we all have something to be happy about."

"Aye, we do," said Lambeth. "Shall we return to the reception to share some champagne?"

Hugh sighed. "While that sounds delightful, perhaps we might meet you a bit later. I need a minute with my bride."

"No doubt," Lambeth said. He gave them a wink.

The blond man led Elizabeth back down the garden path toward the reception. Hugh took Mary's hand and walked deeper into the alcove. She let go of his hand to turn in a wide circle, her eyes taking in the beautiful flowered hedges, the tall willows behind them, the polished stones of the walkway and the marble fountain in one corner, gurgling water spilling from the top. It was so much more than an alcove. It reminded her of the grotto at the Luxembourg Palace, the island of peace he'd taken her to after the horrible scene at the gallery.

She stepped back to him and he took her in his arms. "It's magical, Hugh, like a room designed by a fairy."

"Ah, very well said. I spent many hours here pretending I was ruler of a mythical kingdom." He took both of her hands in his and kissed her fingers. "But I have learned since then that you are all I need. You are my kingdom. Today is for us—a day of celebration."

"Are you happy, Hugh?" Mary asked. For a moment she wondered if his words masked a longing for adventure that he believed married life would no longer afford him.

"Very happy, for I have the heart of the elusive Mary Campbell. You are finally mine. For a while, I did not think it could be done. Fortunately I do not easily take no for an answer."

"You had help, for my uncle has apparently been your secret ally."

Hugh grinned. "So it would seem, and I am most appreciative."

Mary reached up and swept a stray lock of hair from his forehead and looked into his brandy-colored eyes. "So it's forever, is it?"

He grinned broadly. "Indeed, my love," he promised as he drew her more tightly to him, "it is forever." Then he gave her the promised kiss.

Epilogue

Campbell Manor, not quite a year later

Elizabeth Lambeth stared lovingly into the face of the babe she held. "Oh, Griffen, Mary and Ormond's baby is adorable, isn't he?"

"Well, dear, I would never call a boy adorable, but I'll agree he is a bonny lad, as they say in the land of the Scots. Did you think he would be otherwise?"

"Of course not! He already looks like his father. Mary tells me all the Albany men have the same dark coloring. For that reason alone he would be a handsome child."

"I do think he has something of his mother in him as well. The perfectly shaped lips perhaps and the fine nose—"

"Yes, the lips, you're right. It all comes together quite nicely. He'll break hearts, this one will. Just like his father."

The morning was fair and far warmer than expected, as though spring had leapt into summer. Flowering vines framed the doors leading to the terrace, providing a wall of pink blossoms for the young couple to enjoy as they sat with the remains of their breakfast. Griffen read the *Times* and Elizabeth let her tea grow cold as she cooed at the baby who had just put his fist into his mouth.

At the sound of horses galloping across the lawn near the river, Griffen looked up and shielded his eyes against the sun to watch the approaching riders. A chestnut stallion carried a man with dark wavy hair leaning slightly forward in his saddle, his open jacket flying out behind him. The other rider sat astride a glistening black stallion with long mane and tail. As she threw back her head and laughed, her long golden hair reflected the sun.

"There they are, and about time!" Griffen said. "Still riding as if pursued by the hounds of hell, I see. You would think they'd had enough. They have been gone an hour or more."

"Don't be so impatient with them, darling. After all, it's the first time Ormond has allowed Mary to ride like that in a very long while. First he let her have her way, but once he discovered she carried his child he took away her many freedoms. I suppose it's a sign she has matured that she agreed it was probably for the best. But now that young Henry is well delivered, she couldn't wait another minute to be on that stallion of hers again. I think she has grown tired of watching her husband exercise her horse, though I suppose he's the only one who can."

The riders slowed their horses to a trot as they approached the terrace. Ormond reined in and dismounted, then helped Mary down before throwing the reins for both horses over a metal post. He put his arm around his wife's shoulders and kissed her temple as they greeted Elizabeth and Griffen.

"Are you two still lazing about this morning?" He gave them a mocking grin.

"You forget, my friend, we are consumed with the most important task of the day—guarding your young heir." Griffen attempted to look very official.

"How is my little prince?" Moving quickly to Elizabeth's side, Mary peered into the face of her child, who at the sound of her voice immediately turned and gurgled happily.

Elizabeth cradled the baby in two hands, lifting him to Mary. "He's been content and sweet since you fed him last. The lad is a pleasure to watch, I must say. But I can see he wants his mama."

"Come to me, little one." Mary's green eyes fixed on the dark-haired child's face, and she took the blanketed baby into her arms and kissed his rounded cheek. Mother and child gazed at each other as if there were no one else in the world, and it warmed Elizabeth's heart.

Ormond stepped forward to wrap his arms around them both, his eyes full of love. "You've given me a handsome son, sweetheart."

Mary laughed. "Careful, love, or people will think you conceited, since with that dark head of hair he favors you."

"Surely not, wife! His eyes are blue as the evening sky," Ormond replied.

"Ah, yes," Mary said. "That is my point. Those blue eyes, once the color of a *summer* sky, have grown dark in the last month. They will soon be as dark as your own. He is his father's son as you are your father's. He bears the Albany stamp, there is no denying it."

"Let me hold him." Ormond took the bundle from his wife, gently supporting the baby's small head. His face was full of pride. "I see what you mean now that I have a good look at him." Staring into the eyes of the baby, he instructed his son, "Now, Henry, we must discuss your first riding lesson…"

Mary rolled her eyes. "Don't you think it's a bit early for that, love?"

"Well, I've been thinking I might begin to teach him about the ways of the horse now. That way, by the time he's old enough to ride with us, he'll know what to expect. I'll be taking no chances with him." He kissed the dozing baby on his forehead and handed him back. "Seeing as his mother's a devil on a horse, I expect young Henry will pose a challenge as a student."

"I'm going to ignore that stab at my riding." Mary said. Smiling, she then turned to Elizabeth. "When are you two going to get serious about creating a playmate for our Henry?"

Elizabeth felt herself blush and turned to Griffen, who came to her rescue. "We are working toward that goal. Henry won't be so old he can't find a friendship with the young lad or lass." He took Elizabeth's hand and kissed it.

She smiled in response and spoke to Mary. "I was getting so attached to young Henry that it seems we simply must have one of our own."

As the four friends chatted away, making plans to travel together to Scotland to visit one of the Duke of Albany's estates, Lord Baynes came striding toward them across the terrace. "Greetings, all! How are you this fine morning?"

"We are well, Uncle," said Mary, "and even more so after a morning ride."

"So, you've returned to riding Midnight?"

Mary grinned. "Can't you tell? I'm certainly not dressed for the ton."

His eyes took in her riding clothes and boots. "Yes, I supposed that is rather plain to see. Ah well. I'm not surprised. And my grandnephew? Is all well with the lad?" He peered down at the sleeping baby.

"He's just off for a nod. Would you like some tea?" Mary inquired.

"Hudson is bringing some, I believe," Lord Baynes said.

As if summoned, Hudson stepped onto the terrace carrying a silver tray laden with tea and scones.

"What brings you to Campbell Manor today, Uncle?"

"I was hoping to talk to your husband." Pointedly he looked at Hugh, who had taken a seat between Mary and Griffen. Hudson began setting out food and drink as Lord Baynes sat down. "I was with the Prince Regent last evening. It seems he might have a new assignment for Sir Martin and is recalling him to London."

Ormond grew serious. "Martin is returning after all these years?"

"He is," Lord Baynes replied. "Prinny is calling him home. Something to do with that attack on his carriage early this year. Sir Martin has sent along a note for you." He took an envelope out of his jacket and handed it over.

Hugh read the message quickly; then looking at Mary he said, "Martin says he's not been told a word of what he's to do. He asks us to learn how we might assist, however. Apparently the Prince Regent has made Martin believe I'm still working for the Crown."

Mary gave him a mischievous grin. "Perhaps we are, my love."

AUTHOR'S NOTE

In *Racing with the Wind*, I included characters drawn from the pages of history, real people whose lives were very much a part of London and Paris in 1816. In doing so, I tried to be true to what we know of them, even using their words where possible. These include, of course, George, Prince Regent; but also Germaine de Stael—an amazing woman for her time—and her former lover Benjamin Constant, who really did look to Britain as a model; the Comte and Vicomte Decazes (the latter married Diane de Bancalis de Maurel d'Aragon later in 1816, so he wasn't too brokenhearted over losing the fictional Lady Mary Campbell); the Duke of Wellington, who commanded the allied troops in Paris, and other historical figures who make cameo appearances. I believe all that was said of Napoleon is accurate, both the good and the bad. He really did lose most of his six-hundred-thousand-man *Grande Armée* in Russia in 1812, though perhaps not owing to the Nighthawk's theft of the battle plans.

The rest of the characters were born of a fruitful imagination, but I trust reflect the people of the time. Though the agents of the Crown I describe are fictional, my own knowledge of governments and my understanding of the use of spies at the time tell me that many unofficial agents have been drafted to serve in special capacities at the whim of a ruler, so Hugh and Martin's roles could have existed. Certainly England had spies in France, including those working for Wellington. As to Mary Campbell, there were women who rode astride in those days and there have always been women who carved independent lives for themselves notwithstanding society's dictates, so young Lady Mary may not be as fictional as you might think. The buildings and architectural features I describe did exist and were open in 1816, with the exception of the gallery, which was fictional. My favorite restaurant in Paris is La Tour d'Argent, which today looks down on Notre Dame, and though it was open in 1816, it wasn't yet specializing in duck as it does today.

ABOUT THE AUTHOR

As a child, Regan Walker loved to write stories, particularly about adventure-loving girls, but by the time she got to college, more serious pursuits took priority. One of her professors thought her suited to the profession of law, and Regan realized it would be better to be a hammer than a nail. Years of serving clients in private practice and several stints in high levels of government gave her a love of international travel and a feel for the demands of the "Crown" on its subjects. Hence, her first romance novels involve a demanding Prince Regent who thinks of his subjects as his private talent pool. Her stories will always involve adventure as well as love.

Regan lives in San Diego with her golden retriever, Link, whom she says inspires her every day to relax and smell the roses.

THE NIGHTHAWK

Hugh Redgrave, Marquess of Ormond, had been warned. Prinny dubbed Lady Mary Campbell "the Swan," but no ordinary man could clip her wings. She was a bluestocking hellion, an ill-advised match by every account. Luckily, Hugh sought no bride. His work lay on the continent, where he'd become legend by stealing war secrets from Boney. And yet, his memories of Lady Mary riding her stallion were a thorn in his mind. He was the son of a duke and in the service of the Prince Regent…and he would not be whole until he had won her hand.

THE SWAN

It was unheard of for a Regency debutante to postpone her first season, yet Lady Mary had done just that. Far more interested in politics than a husband, she had no time for foolishness or frippery. Already she had assisted her statesman uncle in Paris, and she swore to return to the court of Louis XVIII no matter the danger. Like her black stallion, Midnight, she would always run free. Only the truest heart would race beside her.

Did you enjoy this book? Drop us a line and say so! We love to hear from readers, and so do our authors. To connect, visit www.boroughspublishinggroup.com online, send comments directly to info@boroughspublishinggroup.com, or friend us on Facebook and Twitter. And be sure to check back regularly for contests and new releases in your favorite subgenres of romance!

Are you an aspiring writer? Check out www.boroughspublishinggroup.com/submit and see if we can help you make your dreams come true.

14642266R00178

Printed in Poland
by Amazon Fulfillment
Poland Sp. z o.o., Wrocław